FIRE WARS

Drunk with the night's liberty and libations, drunk with exhilaration, fire reeled. More flames joined the capering, spinning circle as the last of the geysers died.

Faster and faster and faster!

Until they had drawn together as a single leaping pyre. The roots around them deflated, laying flat and dead upon the sand which no longer churned with battering rain, but curled under the broiling heat of flame. As the dance continued, the dry roots caught like kindling.

Pop, pop! POOF!

The branches gave up the last of their water, withered and scorched, and finally detonated with the technicolour splendour of a wizard's best fireworks display.

Also in the Point Fantasy series:

Doom Sword
Peter Beere

Brog the Stoop
Joe Boyle

The Renegades series:

Healer's Quest
Jessica Palmer

Wild Magic
Wolf-Speaker
Tamora Pierce

Foiling the Dragon
Susan Price

The Enchanted Forest Chronicles:

Dragonsbane
Patricia C. Wrede

Look out for:

The Enchanted Forest Chronicles:

Dragon Search
Patricia C. Wrede

Waterworld
Jenny Jones

Priests of Darkness
Peter Beere

The Emperor Mage
Tamora Pierce

The Renegades Series:

The Return of the Wizard
Jessica Palmer

Point Fantasy

FIRE WARS

Book Two in the Renegades Series

Jessica Palmer

Cover illustration by David Wyatt

SCHOLASTIC

Scholastic Children's Books,
Scholastic Publications Ltd,
7–9 Pratt Street, London NW1 0AE, UK

Scholastic Inc.,
555 Broadway, New York, NY 10012, USA

Scholastic Canada Ltd,
123 Newkirk Road, Richmond Hill,
Ontario, Canada L4C 3G5

Ashton Scholastic Pty Ltd,
P O Box 579, Gosford, New South Wales,
Australia

Ashton Scholastic Ltd,
Private Bag 92801, Penrose, Auckland,
New Zealand

First published by Scholastic Publications Ltd, 1994

ISBN 0 590 55491 3

Typeset by TW Typesetting, Midsomer Norton, Avon
Printed by Cox & Wyman Ltd, Reading, Berks

10 9 8 7 6 5 4 3 2 1

For my nephew Ian,
may you always remain
young at heart.

With special thanks to my "junior editors":
Lawrence Davies, Zoe and Jonathan Ironmonger.

– Oh, yes, and Julia Moffatt and Tony Chester, too –

Cast of Characters

The Mortals

Zelia Kazzam: cleric of Brigitta; heir to the Matriarch of Healers; Wizard Emeritus.
Ares the Adventurer: mercenary; affianced to Zelia; Wizard Emeritus.
Sheik Al Y Yabba Y Kazzam: minor Shamirian noble, leader of the Kazzams; and Zelia's father.
Lady Hadidge: chief wife and concubine to the Sheik.
Silenea Nivea: snow elf and Ares's mother.
Queb: evil necromancer and Satan's one-time vassal.
Philos the Benevolent: current Archmage of all Wizards.
Preston D. Igitor: the Grand Inquisitor of Wizards.
The Matriarch: head of all Healers and premier priestess of Brigitta.
Fidhl: the Matriarch's assistant.
Thesbos: Mayor of Thessalia, capital city of Pelopnos, the Isle of Learning.

The Elementals

Lady Astra: air's fair queen and Zelia's mother.
Fante Zephyr: second and aide to the Lady Astra.

Ignacious Roc: King of the earth elementals.
Vitreous Humour: Ignacious's son.
Aqua Prima: water's queen.
Pyro Teknix: acting leader and spokes-combustible for fire.

The Immortals

Satan (as himself).
Pun: Hades' court jester and imp of the fourth degree.
Sala: Goddess of Cycles.
Apsu the Devourer: her husband.

Other Players

Nepharious Hex: a jinn.
Joi Seraphim: Martyr's Bush and one of the guardians of time's gate.
Joi II: his son.
Ampitere: an aging wizard (retired).
Mad Thomas: a wizard (also retired).
Simon: a pig.

With divers others, including:
imps, fiends, archfiends and assorted demons,
and . . . various and sundry elementals
and mortals.

THE NINE PLANES

OUTER PLANE
THE DREAM FIELDS
NIGHT
WATER
EARTH
AIR
FIRE
HADES
HOME OF THE GODS

Prologue

A disconnected thought drifted across the desolate Wastes of Norvon.

". . . *I* . . ."

In truth, it was less than a thought, only a glimmer of a thought or a reflection. A fragment, it could not even be described as a partial ponder or an enthusiastic mull. Neither a full fancy nor a half-baked notion, it was the beginning of awareness. The first kernel of concept, the seed from which understanding would grow. Like the momentary recall when a long-forgotten scene surfaces from the amphibious pool of human unconsciousness only to vanish into the gaseous mists of mortal memory. That hazy *something* you swore you knew before someone had had the audacity to ask.

"Iyee . . ."

The sound echoed forlornly throughout the canting circle of stone. But no one was present to hear it, save the twisted vines of thorny star-flowers. The twined branches wove a magical sphere which held the fledgling notion a prisoner within the vast brown bowl of tundra, in the place that had once seen its birth.

Lost within this sorcerous shell, the hollow musing wandered aimlessly around, searching for others like itself and finding . . . nothing.

Sprinkled throughout the mortal planes floated other disassociated thoughts, or fragments of thoughts, much like the first. In a noxious swamp a continent away . . .

"A . . ."

In another stone circle further east . . .

"M . . ."

Hovering around the Wizard's College . . .

"Q . . ."

Beyond the gauzy veil of mortal time, buffeted about by elemental winds . . .

"U . . ."

Bubbling up in water's realm . . .

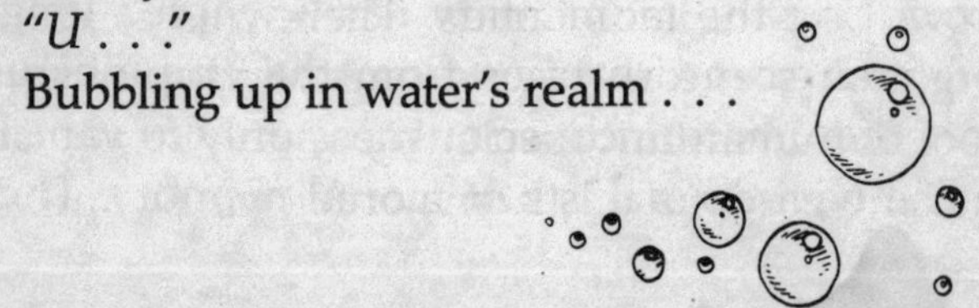

"EEEE"

"eee"

And bursting forth like crackling fire in Brimstone's realm . . .

"Buh, buh, buh . . . Bee . . ."

Beyond the first four elemental planes lies the Realm of Death. Sorcery is stronger there than it is in any of the previous planes. As if magic were a ball, slow and ponderous in the first plane. A ball that picked up speed and energy as it rolled forward through the elemental planes. Until it culminated in Death's realm in something larger than magic. Something super-supernatural. A power so potent that even the elementals shunned these planes.

The first plane in Death's realm is the Night plane, or Black Lands. This is the dark night of the soul so often discussed. All the nasty things that the human mind can conceive eventually gravitate to Night's dank realm.

For instance, all the spinach and brussel sprouts – hidden by disobedient children throughout the ages and secreted under dining-room tables or buried in potted plants – can be found in the Black Lands. There it is at home where it can grow creepy, long fronds of green, grey mould unhindered.

The Night plane is home of fell magic and all

manner of monsters and beasts who would rather avoid the light of day. Wampyr hang by their feet in Night's deep caverns. Werebeasts prowl in its shadows. The deadly werewolf howls at a black moon. While the somewhat comical, but equally lethal, were-hare strips its victims of flesh. Incubi and succubi fritter away the time, searching for weak mortals to entice. And the long-dead spirits of sinister sorcerers and evil enchantresses sigh, dreaming of days long gone when they summoned demons and imps with a wave of their hands.

Beyond Night's plane lies Hades, abode of sinners and heretics, and suchlike. All those mortals too wicked by human standards to find their way into the further Dream Fields dwell in Hades' halls. As planes go, it combines the worst features of both Brimstone and Night, with a few additional nasties thrown in on the side just to keep things interesting. It is the dominion of devils and demons, and the many-layered legions of imps, minor fiends, intermediate fiends and arch-fiends who serve them.

All this evil quite naturally leeches its environment of colour and light, and Hades and Night are dark indeed. To the mortal eye – assuming a human were able to survive the trip – those planes would appear as flat, matt-black, without benefit of stars. Blacker than the blackest pitch, blacker than the widow's reeds, blacker even than the deepest, darkest secret in a human soul.

Featureless. Dull. *Boring!*

And so it appears to its inhabitants. Despite its inherently profane nature, it is quite a dreary place. Without even someone to scare – heretics and sinners soon become immured to things that go bump in the night, and witches and warlocks are used to trafficking with demons.

Then Queb appeared – or parts of him did. For when the necromancer was destroyed, his spirit was dismantled and its particles scattered all across the known universes. Rightly or wrongly, the airy elementals decided to place like with like. So all that was once human remained in the mortal plane. While the wizard's thoughts ended up in air's domain, the realm of pure intellect. All his emotions, all that was green and capable of growth, went to water's fluid kingdom. And each idea that could burn with a touch was conveyed to Brimstone. The good – the part that had once loved a white-haired snowmaiden and had laughed like any other mortal man – was delivered to the Dream Fields, or should have been.

With similar logic, if less wisdom, the fairies distributed all that was wicked between Hades and Night. At least they tried, for flighty creatures that they are some of the pieces got mixed up. Bits of Queb, the good and the bad, floated throughout Death's realm. The evil appeared as pure black globules of human malice. Some so dark that they competed even with the darkness of the darkest night in Night's own plane. And so corrupt, that even Hades had nothing to rival its evil splendour. For having choice, the wickedness in the human heart is far worse than anything that can be unearthed within the heartless shell of the wampyr or under the furred scalp of the were-beast. Having free will, a human can elect to do good, to love rather than hate, to create rather than destroy.

Each drop of this once great mage contained the spark of human life. Each tiny sphere pulsated with a dull, burnished sheen. Like sombre jewels that throbbed and vibrated with a vitality all their own. And Queb's unadulterated mortal spite positively glowed. Glittering black diamonds that beckoned to the denizens of darkness who were drawn to them, in the same way the water elemental is drawn to fountains and the fire elemental to governmental scrolls. The wampyr sought out this essence of pure human malignity. The incubi and succubi trailed along behind, driving it before them. In Hades, the imp coveted the crystalline shards of rancour.

The demons were dazzled by them, thinking they had found a soul to sway, and the Devil plucked each and every one of them from the fluttering gloom. Then He summoned all His minions and commanded them to do His bidding: "Gather the pieces and put them back together again . . ."

The Martyr's Bush, Joi Seraphim, was only one of time's guardians on earth. As the spell was cast that opened the doors between the nine planes, Joi felt a faint tug deep within its roots. For the first time since his inception, the bush relaxed its death-grip on the earth and stretched its long branches in something like a herbal yawn.

This strange creature – neither animal nor vegetable, mortal nor immortal, elemental nor human – contained bits of each, although it had been elemental once. Long ago at time's beginning, Joi and his kind had formed the Grand Council of Earth's Elders – their more lithological relations being considered inferior – but they had given up their elemental existence in a pact between earth and the other immortals. This covenant had resulted in the locking of the portals between the planes.

Thus, the innocuous-looking tussock of spiny black and his brethren were the keepers of a great magic, beyond any known to puny mortals. The responsibility was awesome and the burden heavy. So, when the word came that, for this day and this day only, the doors would be propped open to allow traffic between the planes, Joi relinquished his hold gladly and welcomed the first holiday he had had in his aeons-long life.

Fante Zephyr, aide to the most regal Lady Astra, Queen of the air elementals, flitted nervously before the portal that led to Earth's plane. Never in his brief career as the queen's lieutenant had he been given such an important assignment, and he wanted no mistakes. It was his chance to prove himself to her. In truth, Fante had been waiting for something like this ever since he had taken his oath of fealty. He dusted his wings and puffed himself up as big as he could without losing himself.

As a zephyr, who seldom did anything more energetic than stir smoke, the queen's second had a better memory than most of air's denizens. So he had been assigned to introduce the wedding guests as they appeared at the door. Since he had heard that no court should be without one, Fante found a sceptre which he could tap self-importantly as he announced each guest in the queue that waited to arrive from the mortal plane.

The sceptre was unwieldy and tended to slip through his airy fingers and eventually he had to give it up, passing it on to an earth elemental. Discouraged, Fante deflated slightly. Another disappointment among many – for the Lady's court was nothing like he had imagined. He had expected grand castles floating in the air, with spindle-top minarets and windows made of shiny rainbows. What he had found was a simple stone circle with a single fountain. He had envisioned a retinue of hundreds, all clothed in star-silks, that precious stuff woven from motes of starlight, and each dripping jewels over flashy gowns. What he had discovered was a single lady dressed in a simple gossamer shift like any other elemental. Later he learned that castles in the air were unwarranted, since air hated all forms of confinement, and jewels tended to bore through air's flimsy flesh and necklaces became gnarled in fairy wings.

When the zephyr had first arrived, Lady Astra hadn't been able to understand why Fante, or any other elemental for that matter, would want – or need – to attend her. Still, after he had explained the concept – patiently, several times – she had accepted him. And Fante, a wind of his word, served her willingly (which usually included a lot of hanging about or trailing after Astra, who was always off chasing daydreams).

The airy queen's idea of ruling was at best passive, if not downright indolent. Astra wasn't much for responsibility or command, both of which she avoided at all costs. Generally, she left her subjects alone unless there was a grand bash somewhere which she would invariably crash. It was, after all, her right as queen. She never gave parties until this momentous marriage, between her daughter Zelia and the adventurer Ares. And, suddenly, the Lady found a responsibility she could not evade.

And Fante came into his own at last, for she was perfectly content to delegate all authority to him. Fante himself had sent out the wedding invitations since Astra couldn't be bothered. The zephyr made all the arrangements, and he hoped that the nuptials would go off without a hitch. Once he started the plans, he learned that Astra's method of ruling was not necessarily illogical. It didn't take too long for Fante to realize that it was almost impossible to get air to do anything in concert.

Fante blustered and fluttered about, until he had herded the wedding party into position next to the portal. The bride, Zelia, stood between her royal mother and her father, Al Y Yabba y Kazzam. The groom, Ares, was attended only by his mother Silenea Nivea. The celebration was about to begin when Astra went flitting away. Fante scowled and considered pursuing her, but gave up the thought as soon as it came.

With a cough that sounded like a hollow wind, the zephyr took his place next to a standing stone, glowered at his list and then in a voice magically augmented he boomed the first name: "The Matriarch of all Healers and her assistant, Fidhl."

A hawk-like woman wearing crystalline cloth materialized in a blaze of light. Before Fante could take a breath, he heard a commotion as a red-caped wizard elbowed his way through the door with a blinding flash.

"I tell you, I should be first. Precedent, precedent, I claim precedent!" The wizard said to another of his kind who clung to his gown, trying to prevent the mage's precipitous entrance.

"Ah, er," Fante stuttered, "Philos the Benevolent, Archmage of All Wizards and . . . ah . . . Preston D. Igitor, the Grand Inquisitor."

The two mages swooped down on the wedding party, greeting Zelia, Astra, the sheik, Ares and his mother in turn. Their conversation was lost as Fante returned to his list.

"The Lady Hadidge, chief wife and concubine to the Shiek of Kazzam, stepmother of the bride, and . . ." Fante squinted at the scroll in his hands as a number of black-cloaked figures stepped through the portal all at the same time. There were just too many to announce singly, so he winged it: ". . . numerous other wives and concubines."

Fante panted, trying to catch his breath, as another of the mortal contingent entered.

"Thesbos, Mayor of Thessalia, and his wife . . ."

Fire elementals danced atop flaming brands. Thesbos, Mayor of Thessalia, sidled anxiously away from the torches and closer to the wedding party. He had been afraid of fire ever since his pub, the Cock and Boar, had burnt down. The building was devastated in a brawl started by the blushing bride, when she, a healer by trade, had "killed" a slaver and exhibited a startling and unsettling propensity for magic. Not that Thesbos had done badly for himself since then.

He had been able to use his one-time acquaintance with the notorious Zelia to get elected to office. An astute businessman, the former innkeeper had saved the wanted poster, expecting the girl's status to change. Thesbos was always pleased to note to any who would listen that the adventure – where she had met her groom, the half-elfin Ares – had begun within his inn, and he capitalized on it. After Zelia's acceptance into the Wizards' Guild, a first for a woman, Thesbos had had his own likeness drawn beside that of the blue maid, an arm draped casually across her shoulder. This picture had become his campaign poster.

Thesbos embellished the story of her adventures until Zelia's, and vicariously his, participation grew to heroic proportions. He was in on it from the start – so he said – as one in a series of spies that kept her in touch with the Matriarch of Healers, and so forth. Thus, the besotted rout, which had destroyed his tavern, became a glorious victory and part of a master plan that led eventually to the vanquishing of the evil mage. He never knew quite how close to the truth this was.

There was a sputtering hiss next to him. A fire elemental beckoned, bending close so that Thesbos could hear. The former innkeeper blenched. He could almost make out features in the roiling face of orange-red flame. He found this disconcerting, so he concentrated on the fiery nimbus of a crown.

"Wood chips, plea-s-s-se," the elemental said as it swayed on its perch atop a torch.

Thesbos blanched. "Wood chips, of course, of course. Yes, sir, right away, sir," he muttered before hurrying off to do the creature's bidding. Unaccustomed to this aspect of fire – these tiny creatures with legs, arms and a mouth that could, if it chose, converse with man – Thesbos far preferred the earthy reflection of coal, its formless glow that stayed caged behind a grill. But ever a man to please and appease those in power, Thesbos did the errand willingly. Like the barkeeper of old.

Unlike water, air and earth, fire was and always would be harmful to man – such was the nature of the element. Unless it was kept contained within a hearth or a grate. Even in air's domain, the fiery elementals were required to stay within certain confines while condescending to illuminate the pre-nuptial festivities for the half-elemental bride whom they regarded as one of their own.

"Oi!" His wife waddled after Thesbos. The barman scooped sawdust, paper scraps and wood chips into a napkin. "Remember, you are Mayor of Thessalia now," she said, "not an innkeeper to wait on other peoples' pleasure."

"And would you anger such a one even here on the second elemental plane?" Thesbos pointed at the cavorting blaze. "Who's to say whether or not it can follow us back to earth . . ." He shuddered.

His eyes darted around the stone circle, seeking comfort in familiarity, but finding little. The constellations were unknown to him, different from those found on the first plane. Gone were Og's hammer and the rambling figure of the Cub, son of the bear god Urri. These had been replaced by the stars which were more sharp, more clear and brittle, as if in air's realm they found nothing to impede their light. Close to dawn, their outlines had softened only slightly as the sky of the second plane turned from amethyst to aquamarine.

His wife frowned at him. She too recalled the conflagration that had destroyed their home, for her arms still carried the scars.

"Here," she said, "I'll take it to him. It wouldn't do to have the Mayor of Thessalia behaving like some handmaiden."

Thesbos's gaze followed her to the torch and he flinched as the elemental seized the refreshment and consumed it, napkin and all, in one flaming gulp and then rocked drunkenly on its roost.

Again, Thesbos continued his guarded search of his surroundings. It was a party to dazzle the eye, boggle the mind and defy the senses; for Thesbos had found that each mortal participant bobbled in and out of what he would have once called "reality" often meeting former selves as they went. He, himself, had given up on dancing – or, at least, he thought he had – and Thessalia's mayor peered myopically at his double who grabbed his wife and pulled her to the dance floor. Suddenly, a younger, if no soberer, version of himself appeared beside himself, paling as a fire elemental leaned to request more sawdust and the entire conversation with his wife was replayed.

It was a situation which stretched human sanity to the limit of its endurance.

There was a soft chuckle next to his ear that sounded like the buffeting of dry branches in a breeze and a drink appeared in his hands. Thesbos slurped it thirstily, and it was immediately refilled. He felt a soft caress, like the kiss of wind on his temple, and the shadowy image of an airy elemental disappeared.

The denizens of air flew to and fro, as flighty as birds and about as substantial as gnats. Here and there they would stop, adding this jest to a flagging conversation, or prodding a mortal into discourse. As the intellectuals of the elements the discussions here always remained lively, if somewhat disconnected, for few elementals would complete a thought before they went onto the next. Elsewhere, the billowing visage of an air elemental would tickle the gloomy into laughter and tease the frightened into humour. For this was their home and they were the hosts of this momentous occasion.

Thesbos threw the burning liquid down his throat. He heard another dry chuckle, and the creature flew off. Thesbos peered forlornly into the bottom of his mug, afraid to look either left or right, afraid his eyes would meet another image of himself performing the same ritual.

Around him, circles of hoary earth elementals joined hands in what someone told him was a dance, although they didn't appear to move. Into the cavity made by the gnarled fingers of granite and quartz, their cousins, water, splashed and capered delightedly, creating a makeshift fountain. Others of the watery type sloshed freely throughout the throng of people, making little rivers and ponds at celebrants' feet. His wife bustled across the grassy vale, stepped in one, and a water nymph said, "ousch" in a voice somewhere between a bubble and a slur.

"So sorry," the good wife murmured as she clutched desperately at her husband's arm for support. He handed her a drink, understanding her dismay.

All mortals were aware of the nine planes in the same way they were of the sun or the five moons. But no one besides Zelia, her father, and the adventurer Ares had ever travelled beyond the first. The planes could be likened to the rings in a tree. The first four belonged to the elements. The Earth plane at its centre, the most dense, was man's home. But few mortal minds could truly comprehend the concept. Much in the same way an ant standing at a tree's roots can't understand the totality of the tree that towers above it.

To the human eye the elementals appeared flat, almost two-dimensional. Something about them lacked substance, and Thesbos was sure, if he wanted to, he could have reached through the figure of water that even now was hopping with one fluid foot clenched between two aqueous hands and glaring at his wife.

"Quite a do," his wife said nonchalantly.

Thesbos inclined his head in assent. Something of an understatement; for the celebration was a mingling of many cultures. All the guilds and gods were represented. The entry of Ares and Zelia into the Wizards' Guild as *Wizard Emeritus* ensured that the delegation of sorcerers was large. It seemed that the bowl was awash in waves of cloth embroidered with the golden symbols of magic. The bride herself was heir to the Matriarch of Healers, and the crystalline robes of that craft competed with the blinding gowns of the magicians.

The guests crossed all boundaries of country and class. They straddled the worlds and planes, mortal and immortal, human and not. The groom, Ares, hailed from the furthest reaches of the northern continent. Standing next to his mother, he was resplendent in his snow-white robes of the polar ice-cat. Half-human and half-elf, his silver hair matched his robes.

The half-elemental bride, Zelia, was the daughter of a sheik of Shamir, a country in the south-east corner of the desert continent of Daklha. So South and North met; half-elfin wed half-elemental, and Earth planes and Air planes joined for a time in this portal between the worlds.

The bride, dazzling in her gown of gauzy blue, moved from group to group greeting each and bidding them welcome.

Thesbos's wife sniffed her disdain as the maiden brushed past. "Disgusting."

The mayor eyed the indigo-haired, blue-skinned beauty. Unlike her affianced, she did not affect the restrictive clothing of her native land, preferring instead the light garb of her airy elemental mother. Her gown, woven using the ley as a loom, was a gift of her airy relations. Made of cobwebs and dreams after the fashion of air, it left little to the imagination, covering next to nothing in a veil-like cloud while jewels, gifts of the earth elementals, adorned her sapphire hair.

"She's very bluish," Mrs Thesbos said contemptuously.

Thesbos glanced from bride to groom, taking in the albino skin of the snow elf and noting the ice-blue eyes, with their distinctive cat-like pupil, and almost colourless hair.

"The groom doesn't look very healthy himself," the mayor added sagely.

The bride's mother, the Lady Astra, buzzed eagerly around Zelia's head. In rare quiet moments when Astra stilled, one could see the resemblance between mother and lovely maid, in the slight up-turned nose, delicate features and diminutive stature. The bride, air made flesh.

The voices of revellers echoed around the stone circle. The human laughter sounded alien, curiously empty as it competed with the crackle of fire, the whisper of air, the chuckle of water, and the occasional heavy thud of earth. In a time before time, the portals between planes had been closed to humans. Their entry forbidden and the stricture enforced by the most persuasive of all punishments, death.

It had taken powerful magic to permit mortals entry into Air's plane. Even to cast the spell required the permission of *all* the gods, and it was no easy feat to get the gods, goddesses and their many offspring, the godlings, to agree upon any subject. In the end, the fay queen of the air elementals, the Lady Astra had prevailed, for the gods were also relieved to be rid of the evil wizard Queb. Therefore, portals were opened, if only for the day, allowing all the couple's friends and relations to attend the wedding feast.

During a lull in the conversation, Zelia surveyed her guests. The stone circle had been transformed. Whether by spell or enchantment, or by some magic inherent in the portal itself which allowed the bowl within the circle to expand or contract at will, it had grown, stretching to accommodate all callers.

And Zelia worried lest some guest should feel slighted. The ceremony had been planned to heal old wounds and lessen the gulf that had grown between the races. She shouldn't have troubled herself. The air elementals had catered for every taste. There was wine, which in this environment didn't breath as much as it panted, and there was mead and beer for the northern palate, while *kumys* and *kvass* had been provided for those of the southern continent. Fire had their wood chips, and bits of delectable paper floated about like confetti. Zelia squinted; she couldn't see what had been provided for water. Someone had said salt, but it was difficult to distinguish the elemental from their refreshment. Still, she noted their slurping noises got louder as the night progressed. And they were able to maintain semi-human form – with aqueous arm, sinuous leg and glistening brow – less and less, getting sloppy and reverting to puddles and dribbling pools at the feet of the many participants.

The maid turned and smiled upon her tall and lithesome groom. Their courtship had been stormy, their bond forged in battle. He noticed her gaze and grinned, plucking at the snow-white fur and wiping imagined sweat from his brow. She nodded. The ceremony would begin at dawn, assuming, Zelia thought wryly, any of the guests remained upright by daybreak.

A roar of hatred and rage reverberated across the Hades plane, so loud that it caused all the demon armies to pause in their eternal march along Hades' sulphurous corridors. The members of the great court cringed as Satan stamped back and forth before the pool which was his looking glass to the other worlds.

"Leave me out, will they?" he bellowed. "Me! King of Kings, Prince of Darkness, Master of Imps and Overlord of Fiends. How dare they exclude me!"

Dressed in his finery of scarlet skin, burning crown, dark cloak of star-studded night and a very impressive set of horns, the devil had awaited the invitation, sure that as representative of his plane, he must be included on the wedding list. But no solicitations had been forthcoming.

'Twas another in a growing list of crimes committed by the fairy whelp, Zelia, and her companion, Ares, for it had been this couple who had thwarted his plans on earth and who destroyed the demonlord's minion. It had been *her* elemental relations who had scattered Queb's parts throughout the eight inner planes. And Satan was not one to forgive a slight.

Not about to be outdone by wispy air, the demonlord commanded that his court be decorated for celebration. The glittering bits of Queb were strung out in gala black, and all the lords and overlords invoked to attend the festivities. Pun, court jester and master of bad humour, had been called upon to entertain the guests. His brothers, Bon Mot and Beau Jeste, had fled, leaving Pun to face Satan's wrath alone.

An impromptu affair, it did not appease the Demon King's turbulent spirit, and the only laughter that sounded in Satan's high chamber came from the fiery Pit of Death, and Pun was starting to get worried. For now, though, the Fiend of Fiends ignored his harlequin, which was probably for the best, since every gag Pun had ever known currently escaped him.

"This is really too much," the Devil sputtered as he contemplated the pond. "They forget themselves, defying all rules of common decency, just as they defy the prohibition of marriage."

"But master," said Ignorance, a distant cousin to the imp Pun and overlord of fools, "don't—" But he said no more as a lightning bolt came down from the high-vaulted ceiling to turn him into a sizzling puddle in the middle of the central hall.

The other demons, imps and fiends skittered away from the mess.

"Have I not been patient?" Satan said. "Have I not been kind? Forgiving them for their sins. Overlooking the injury they have done to me and mine." He waved indiscriminately around the room and a few of Hades' denizens got caught in the backlash.

"Forgiving, master. Oh, yes, very forgiving," the remaining minions parroted, eager to agree.

"My poor friend over there, done to bits." The Devil indicated Queb, or what was left of him, with a meaningful stare.

"But this insult I do not pardon. This time they have gone too far!"

The King of Kings cupped his chin in his hand and tapped a long, curving talon – painted in a meticulous gold for the occasion – against the lip of the pool. Pun, shivering mutely upon the stage, watched the Devil as he glared at the wedding party.

His gaze lighted on one of the many wedding guests: the garish Archmage who stood glowering at the people around him. His thoughts echoed around the hushed Hades' cavern. "Precedent, they said. I should have come first, not that bandy-legged Matriarch."

"Ah, here we have an appropriate vessel," the demonlord continued as his court looked on. "Petty, demanding." His face twisted into a sneer. "Greedy. Yes, a most appropriate vessel indeed."

Within the pool, the Archmage grabbed a glass of wine from a passing tray. "Yes, drink up, little friend. Drink. Drink. And you too, little mother," Satan said as he reached out and touched first the wizard's and then the Matriarch's reflections in the laval pond. "You are much too stiff and formal."

Obligingly, the priestess drained her drink, seized another one and quaffed it.

"Perhaps, I can have a little fun yet." The Prince of Darkness propelled a rather bewildered-looking Matriarch into the arms of the Archmage and made them dance.

Not satisfied, he stormed round the circumference of the pit, his features moulting as he went. Gone was the bright scarlet skin and horned cap which was his party dress, replaced by the lashing body of a serpent. The archfiend was not pleased.

"And you," he said as he wrapped his body round the pit, his head arched on a delicate neck, hovering over the expectant bride and groom, "I don't know *what* I'm going to do with you yet."

There was a loud pop. The cavern filled with smoke, and the King of Demons reappeared in the semi-human aspect of master magician.

"Enough of this." He clapped his hands. "Let the festivities begin. Jester jest."

Pun's mouth dropped open. "Ah, ah, er, er!" he stammered.

The Prince of Darkness, meanwhile, continued to study the pool.

"Insult to injury," Satan muttered under his breath and then he spun.

"Hey, buffoon," he shouted and, pointing at Pun, the Devil blasted the quivering imp to smithereens.

"Get it? Insult to injury," the demonlord scanned the cowering crowd before him. "Buffoon, blast. Insult to injury!" He threw back his head and guffawed.

With a quick askance glance at their neighbours, the retinue began to twitter weakly at Satan's joke – whatever it was. Only Pun – relieved to have finally provided some merriment for his king – remained silent as he busily collected the pieces of himself from the far corners of the room.

Chapter 2

The bride's eyes came to rest upon the Matriarch of Healers where she sat huddled in a corner. The woman's discomfort was obvious. She kept swallowing and her gaze darted thither and yon. Zelia detached herself from the group of flapping air elementals and went to join her mistress.

Even before Zelia had seated herself, the Matriarch spoke. "I never thought I'd live to see the day. Entering a sacred circle and surviving. How did they do it?" she asked.

"Something about leaving the doors between the planes open. A bit of mortal time leaks through, along with earth's substance, which allows humans to survive, at least for a little while. The spell needs to be renewed periodically. See there." Zelia indicated an air elemental who brushed a filmy hand across the wizened cheek of the wizards' Grand Inquisitor, Preston D. Igitor. "It works better if the recipient is liberally dosed with mead or wine, or redcap, in the case of elves. I don't know much about it myself. I do know it took the combined power of all the elements to do it."

"To think that I have lived to see it. I will be able to tell my chil—" The Matriarch stopped herself when she realized what she had been about to say. "—my acolytes about it."

The maiden covered the high priestess's hand with her own and murmured softly so no other could hear. "The healers are your children, you know that. You have been more of a mother to me than any other."

The Matriarch gasped as her double drifted past. Zelia scowled. The opened doors let mortal time slip through haphazardly. It was fragmented by the nature of the place, and each mortal inhabitant was represented by several versions of themselves. Past, present and future. Thus, the priestess on the bench and Zelia may have had this conversation five minutes ago, and the Matriarch that had just gone flitting past may be the present one eavesdropping on a well-known dialogue. Or this could be the current Matriarch, and the one that now accepted an invitation to the dance floor, someone the Matriarch had yet to be.

Beside her, the Matriarch was drained of all colour. Her throat quivered and she gulped hard. Zelia turned. Across the room, another Matriarch dazzled the guests by doing a happy quadrille in a whirl of crystal-laden cloth and clanking of healers' bells. Her partner, all elbows, bony knees and flying limbs, was the head of the Wizard's College, Philos the Benevolent.

"By the heavens, I must have taken leave of my senses," the Matriarch sniffed, for there was little love between the leaders of the two crafts.

It was a ludicrous sight. Philos looked like a scarecrow despite his scarlet robes, encrusted with gems and embroidered in gold. He was bedecked with bits of magical paraphernalia. Wands clacked, amulets clattered and his conical cap had slipped to a rakish angle as he danced opposite the chinking cleric. Zelia realized with a shock that the two, wizard and priestess, looked alike. Like mirror images, as if the woes of office had become stamped upon their visages.

"Disorientating, isn't it?" Zelia indicated the dancing Matriarch with a quick duck of her head.

"Yes, why . . . how. . . ?" the Matriarch's voice dwindled.

Zelia, her second in command, gave a vague gesture around the circle. "The elements, of course, are timeless. Fire is as fire always has been and always will be; forever changing – leaping and cavorting – but forever unchanged in substance."

"Of course," the Matriarch said, "any school child knows that."

Zelia continued as though the priestess hadn't spoken. "So too, air, water and even earth, for each will be just what they are. For them there is no time, and it is right and proper that there should be no time on their planes. My mother, the Lady Astra existed then, as she exists now and as she exists at some unknown future time. For her it is not confusing that there might be an infinite number of herself doing an infinite number of things in an infinite number of places and times. That is the way of it; the way it was; the way it is; the way it always has been and will be."

"You said earth, but there's time on Earth's elemental plane, our plane," the Matriarch objected, but her voice quavered as if she longed for the solidity of earth right now, and who could blame the High Priestess as Philos planted a wet, sloppy kiss on the cheek of some image of herself – past, present or future.

"Yes, because earth is so compressed, so dense, time thrives. It is said that it can take years for an earth elemental to finish a sentence. I don't know, I've never talked to one. Although, surely, earth has a concept of a past. And to have some concept of past is to have some concept of time. Mayhap earth has been changed through its contact with man." A line formed on her forehead as Zelia tried to think of a way to explain. "But don't be fooled by that. The earthy elemental has the same eternal quality as their cousins. Earth *is* enduring, like a mountain is enduring – stolid, staid, stability itself. Therefore, earth can grasp the idea of a beginning, a middle, and even, an end while air, fire and water, forever moving, cannot.

"Notice how transparent the other elementals appear, as if lacking in some dimension. I think time is that dimension and that is found only on the Earth plane. An airy elemental would be weighed down by time, a lot like wading through thick treacle. My mother claims that is why the winds and rains create storms on earth, the like of which is never found in any of the other elemental planes, as the elements rebel against time's restraints," Zelia said.

"But why. . . ?" And the High Priestess of Healers blushed furiously as her double returned the Archmage of all Wizards' kiss with one of her own.

"The spell which permits you to be here allows time to seep through – enough for humans to survive. It is a difficult one, and it would appear it has been cast imperfectly. So what you see is time coming through, but not necessarily in a logical sequence. I sense past, present and future here, tumbling about in no particular order. And why should it, since no one here besides earth and the mortals understand it?" The maid stared at her gown. "Sorry. The spell *is* very complex."

"I can imagine," the Matriarch said. "You don't seem to be distressed."

"My elemental blood protects me." Zelia shrugged. "I am aware of these ghostly other-selves as things flickering out of the corner of my eye. I do not find it befuddling as you do. Who knows, maybe the same thing that permits earth elementals to understand mortal time, allows me to view time that doesn't follow a single straightforward line." She pointed at Ares and his mother. "Like the elves, descendants of the elementals on earth. When they became compressed, attaining density and mass, they became mortal, but it would appear that they too are protected from the worst of its effects."

The Matriarch surveyed the circle. To her left,

the snow elves' king was busy having a lively debate with himself over some policy of state. He hooked one of his advisers and, nodding to his double, said: "Too bad you can't be as sensible as this fellow." The king twittered, tickled by his wit, before tipping his mushroom cup at his chagrined minister.

Then the priestess's eye lit upon the copy of herself, who now leaned against the weaving Archmage. Her wimple was askew, and it seemed to be held in place only by the wizard's conical cap.

"You're not bad for a wishard," the vague double slurred, and the Matriarch on the bench winced.

The whole scene of tippling magician and clumsy cleric was too tempting for a youthful elemental who, diving from a height, tweaked the Archmage's beard. The magician jumped, and his cap slipped over one eye.

"A playful lot, aren't they?" the priestess commented.

"I suppose," Zelia agreed. "But they're not malicious. It's just that they can't comprehend the idea of cause and effect. When all times are one, beginnings and endings mingle and merge becoming fuzzy. The elemental doesn't understand that some deed of theirs might precipitate some event, that their actions can cause a reaction or a chain of reactions. They don't know if they tease Farmer Brown's cow, she will be affrighted, kick, hurting herself and souring her milk for a month. Because for them these things have happened, are happening and will happen – and not necessarily in that sequence. Maybe for them the milk was already sour when they pinched her flank causing her to kick and lame herself." Zelia added: "As you can see, it can be very confusing for an elemental on the Earth plane."

"Not so easy for mortals in this airy realm, either," the Matriarch said.

"No, and misunderstandings between elemental and man can escalate. I think that's why they closed the door in the first place."

The other Matriarch had disappeared, along with the Archmage, and the high priestess of Brigitta rose shakily. "Well, it looks like I've got a little catching up to do. I think my counterpart is having more fun than I am." The head of the Healers' College moved across the broad, green expanse towards the refreshments. An air elemental placed a crystal goblet in her hand, and she downed the amber liquid in a single swallow just as the Archmage asked her to dance.

Laughing, Zelia joined her father near the centre of the circle. The sheik was surrounded by all his favourite wives. The Lady Astra flitted around the fringe, much to the annoyance of his chief wife and concubine. The Lady Hadidge stood rigid, a black pillar of cloth without the softening of curves. So stiff was her pose that one could well imagine her expression beneath the heavy veil was disapproving. The Lady Astra chattered coyly about the sheik's head. Occasionally, she would nip in for a quick peck on the cheek or flirtatious kiss. The sheik, nonplussed by the Lady's attentions and such blatant advances in front of his wives, flushed despite his dark tan.

Propped against an upright stone, Ares examined his mother through eyes narrowed to slits. The snow elf Silenea Nivea lingered alone at the edge of the circle, avoiding the general festivities. Her movements seemed agitated, somehow bird-like, and when a Mage whisked past so that a hand skimmed her arm, she cried out as if in pain.

The groom didn't know what to think of her, and Ares studied this woman he had known but a few short weeks. She noticed his scrutiny and chided, "You are robbing the cradle with this marriage, my son."

He started at the jibe, for he had no idea how old he was. It seemed he aged as mortal men, but his childhood was shadowy at best, and who knew how long he had huddled within the stone circle, forsaken and lost, before he had been taken in by a mercenary and follower of the war god Og?

The human had seemed old – his face and body a crosshatch of scars – but then the adventurer had to admit that all adults seem old to the very young. The man himself *had* aged and died, but he had aged slowly. Or, as Ares now suspected, the old mercenary hadn't been all that old in the first place. Ares himself had never counted the turns. He had no "birthday" to celebrate, and his name day, the day his mentor had given him a name, went unremarked. His human mentor had no time for such frivolities. Since that obscure beginning, the half-breed warrior had seen innumerable battles, but Ares surmised that if he followed the convolutions of history – this war versus that one – he might discover himself turns older than the twenty he confessed.

"So how old am I?"

"In mortal turns, I do not know. You have been to our land now, and you should know that we mark time differently than humans do."

"How old?"

"Does it matter? Your magic protects you," she said.

"How do you know?"

"If it did not, you would—"

"How old would I be, mata," he said using the unfamiliar elvish address, "if my magic hadn't protected me?"

"You would be dust, my son."

Ares gasped. His eyes searched the crowd, seeking the blue maiden. Silenea followed his gaze.

"Oh, her?" she said. "Do not worry. Raised in mortal time, she aged as any mortal child would, but now that she is grown, she is much like you. She and you, protected by the magic in your blood, will live long. Should you remain in human lands, you will live long enough to cause jealousy among your peers. Take heed, son." Silenea Nivea shivered, despite what must have been oppressive heat after her icy abode in the far northern reaches of Szatmar.

At her throat she wore the white dove of Brigitta, in her manifestation as the goddess of fertility. Like his healer bride, Silenea Nivea was a priestess of Brigitta. The elfin people celebrated the gentle goddess differently than their human counterparts. Beyond the shadowy mists, disease was unknown, so what need had they for healers?

Separated from his kind almost since birth, Ares knew little about elfin culture, but, from what little he had gathered, the elves worshipped

Brigitta as the eternal mother. He knew that his mother had gained priestly status when she had taken a mortal lover. She had moved from neophyte to acolyte when she bore a child and sacrificed it for human rearing. For it was believed that only those strongest in sorcery – the most "elfin" – would return.

So, if the offspring's magic was strong enough, then he or she would find their way back through the sorcerous shroud to the ice palaces of the snow elves where they would be accepted as one of their own. Thus, elfin blood was strengthened from time to time, and only those who took a mortal lover, and conceived, acquired the title of Priestess. During his stay in the far-flung realm, Ares saw only a few children of pure elfin blood and those appeared sickly and weak. Not many survived to adulthood. His mother was such a one, for only those of pure blood were chosen to refresh the bloodline by taking a mortal lover, and it was discovered that few of them could conceive. His return to that ice-bound land had elevated his mother's status, and now she headed the temple that groomed women in the art of love.

Once Ares had hated her as much as he had loved her, hated her for abandoning him. Now that he had seen this ephemeral people he understood and accepted her actions, even if he had not yet completely forgiven her. Their lineage was dying and would die, if not for Brigitta's chosen who sacrificed love and offspring to strengthen the bloodline of her people, and he realized it was a slender thread upon which to base a race.

Her gown was of silver silk as loose and as light as the bride's. The faint sheen of perspiration moistened her snow-white brow and a tear traced a faint track along her cheek. His right hand clutched the hilt of his sword, awkward in the face of emotion. Instinctively, his left hand went to his great war-hammer, which was absent from his back, and again he wished he could have wed fully armed. It seemed fitting that a relationship forged in the conflict should be consummated wearing hammer, dagger and sword. Yet his bride eschewed her weapons, both the short scimitar of Shamir and the sacred sword of Brigitta, and he could do no less, relinquishing the hammer and many daggers to his hostess. Only the ceremonial blade, blunt and useless, remained.

His mother noticed the movement, the hand clenching empty space where war-hammer should be, and smiled. "Your mentor trained you well."

"You keep calling him that, why?"

"Did he not train you in the arts of war? Did

he not give you the secrets of his craft? Did he not teach you how to survive?"

"Of course, he was a follower of the god of war. What else would he do?"

"What else would you call him, then?" Silenea asked.

Ares settled back in a disgruntled silence.

"I chose him for those qualities," she said, "and I hoped you would prove yourself to be a worthy pupil."

The adventurer raised a single brow in question. "Chose him? I didn't know you chose him. This is the first I heard of it."

"Yes, I chose him," she hissed. "They could force me to give up my child, but they could not expect me to send him off to hostile lands defenceless."

Ares was taken aback by her vehemence. This was the first time his mother had talked about his abandonment.

"I knew I was sending you to a world that would not accept you, could not accept you. So I gave you protection such that humans have. Ensuring you would learn the arts of human war, so that you could fight and survive until you might find your magic and return to me." She turned sparkling eyes upon her son. "I always knew you would return. You have the magic of both elf and man running in your veins."

"My father was a wizard?" Ares held his breath, afraid to ask more.

Silenea shook her head. Her hair rippled in a sparkle of silver like moonlight skittering across ice. "Your father was a good man, but a bad sorcerer. Don't forget that."

The mercenary rocked back, considering this information. Perhaps his father lived still and was somewhere among the crowd. He examined the animated faces of the wizards, many leaning on wobbly legs against another of their craft. Others reclined against the solid mass of an earth elemental, some of which had been accommodating enough to take human form and so appeared a fixed and frozen statue.

"No," she said. "Not here. Not anywhere, anymore."

His mother turned her back to him, hiding her face, and Ares didn't know what to say to comfort her. He wasn't completely sure that he wanted to. Again, the adventurer was torn between his duties as groom and duties as a son. Out of the corner of his eye, he could see another version of himself greeting another guest and he relaxed slightly.

The adventurer opened his mouth to question her but she moved away, her expression grieved. The adventurer retreated further from the merrymakers. His mother had given him much to think about and Ares wondered if somewhere in the dusty old tomes of the Wizards' College they might have a record of alumni, a wizard who had forsaken the vows of the celibate or whose craft had taken him to the cold, frozen north.

"You must renounce me," Zelia said to her father.

With one eye on the dancing couple, the sheik shook his muddled head as the daughter next to him offered him more *kumys* and he wondered how he had survived his trip here. For Zelia had not been the first to tread the sacred circle. Long ago, he had been spirited away by the over-amorous Astra. His daughter remained as living proof of his visit to Air's elemental plane.

The Matriarch, now well soused, had converged upon her more inebriate counterpart, an older version of herself, and they swapped jokes about the Archmage's knobbly knees.

A hand flapped before his face and his daughter's face swam into focus. "Are you listening?"

The momentary discomfiture passed, the sheik glowered down upon his diminutive daughter. "You think I've grown simple, girl. I heard you. No, I will not change my mind."

"Well, I can always step down. It is risky to name me as heir. What tribe would be willingly led by a woman? Think of the shame."

"Shame? You have proven yourself in battle."

"Magical battle," she reminded him gently.

"What other kind of battle would you have with a necromancer? Any tribe should be proud to be led by the person who defeated the wizard Queb," he said. "Besides, you forget it is not for battle prowess that a man's family is elevated. It is for other skills. You cannot only find water, you can call it to your side."

"Nothing so grand, father," she said. "I might be able to bleat 'help' and if there just happens to be a passing water elemental in the neighbourhood who is looking for something to do, he or she may come to my aid."

He cut her off with an angry gesture. "Don't lecture me, child."

"But, father, they will rebel," Zelia said. "Already there is discontent."

"Never! You, my daughter, will reign after me. Your blood will be the blood of the rulers of Shamir, throughout the many rotations to follow. I have decreed this, and so it shall be."

Zelia sighed. Her father could be a stubborn man.

One imp, demon and fiend after another came

forward, bearing gifts. Some carried more of the shining pieces of the evil necromancer Queb. Others had offerings more in keeping with their nature. The twin demons of Pestilence and Plague gave to their overlord and master, wriggling bacteria and foul-smelling germs. Famine brought starvation, and War strife.

Besides the oozing globules of Queb – which the Devil had added to those bits already collected – there was nothing new here, and the Prince of Darkness soon became bored.

With a quick gesture, Satan signalled for his great throne to move closer to the deadly pit. Groaning, the many coiled salamanders got up on tiny little feet and scuttled closer to the pool. From his roost, the archfiend regarded the wedding celebration. It had grown rowdy, with many couples barely able to keep upright. Fire was drunk and flickering wildly. Air whirled like a Doivish, the dancing sect of the snake god Apsu. When the games began, the Devil saw his opportunity and took it. With another twitch of his hand, he whipped fire into a frenzy and then he sat back to watch, as the party really began to heat up.

A sleepy sun peeped cautiously through the portal between the planes. Snow-white man and sky-blue maid danced the wedding dance of the elemental, joined by their fay cousins. Air plucked teasingly at their garments and their hair. Water formed a fountainous circle, or a waterfall that cascaded around the couple, yet left them untouched, and even fire – well plied with wood chips and sawdust – had come down from the torch end and bonfire to enter the dance.

Frightened, air whipped in a whirlwind, forcing fire away from the participants who could easily be burned. It swirled in orange-red spirals and human observers backed away from the heat.

Ares shed his white fur and twirled, arms linked with Zelia, to the wild music of the wind. Off to one side, some members of the airy contingent had begun the rousing game of "Swat the Leaf". Not the sort of diversion to enchant more sober types, but something which kept air happy for hours. One team – if one could call a roiling mass of whispering images a team – blew at the leaves, batting them about and trying to get them over to the other side of the bowl, which, with as many leaves as there were blowing about, was visible only to them.

The crinkle of dry leaves drew the fire elementals, like bureaucrats to paper. Careless of their fay cousins, they dashed between the spiralling tinder, igniting it as they went. Burned, an airy elemental screamed and dived into a watery fountain. The water where the flaming air elemental grazed the surface boiled with a sizzle, and the surrounding water elementals seethed and steamed.

Angrily, they erupted from the safe haven of earth's slow dance to storm after their cousins, fire. The dance slowed further as scorched mortals stampeded like a herd of dumb beasts away from the conflagration.

The noise and commotion stirred the airy tribe into action, and they began whipping their fiery cousins into a frenzy. Pinching this bit, tempting that bit, teasing the flames from their human form until they broiled in a shapeless mass. Columns of flame leapt skyward, trying to catch the tantalizing wind and its airborne treasure, the few remaining golden leaves.

When the molten pool of magma that warmed the far reaches of the circle threatened to explode, the Lady Astra and those of her followers who still had their wits about them grabbed the humans and vanished, returning them to their homes. Even the earth elementals were moved from their lethargy, recoiling from the boiling waters and their more volatile cousins, lava, to clutch the remaining mortals whom they held so dear and to carry them back to their own realm.

Scattering like leaves upon the wind, the lady's loyal retainers left their fay brethren to sort the dispute out amongst themselves. It was more important to save the puny mortals from elemental wrath. Taking their precious burden with them, air and earth fled to the mortal planes.

In the centre of the portal, fire battled water, and water quenched fire. While the other elementals, who had yet to become involved with the squabble, strove without success to close the door behind the fleeing humans. But enraged fire slipped through the portal to escape onto mortal lands, unfettered and free.

As time slipped out of true, the doors must of necessity remain open – indefinitely.

CHAPTER 3

Rain swept across the plain in sheets. It battered the parched earth, turning the desert sands into a simmering yellow sea. The far north-western corner of Daklha bloomed with sickly yellow blossoms that resembled huge oozing sores more than flowers.

Into this annual deluge, the jinn, Nepharious Hex, plunged after popping back into mortal time to get his bearings straight. He immediately regretted it. The Miasmic Swamp of Abdha was one of the few places on the southern continent to receive rain. As a genie, he wasn't overly fond of the wet stuff that didn't so much fall as pummel the earth. Three-quarters of the year he would have considered the swamp a dandy place to visit, if a fellow wanted a change of scenery. But each spring, the land flooded, and it became a good place to avoid.

The red egstrich feather, pinned to his turban by a ruby brooch, gave up its fight against the elements and sagged. Nepharious stood in the centre of a stone circle, for the swamp was the unlikely setting that housed the second portal of Daklha. It was over this colossus of black stones that the jinn had tripped – or at least his rug had. The genie glowered at the rounded tops of the megaliths. Blunted and weathered by the yearly tempests and undermined by flood, they were positioned at odd angles, slanting listlessly this way and that, some leaning heavily upon their neighbours. The mud around their bases seethed. As he watched, a stone sank slightly into the mire with a sloppy burble and then settled with a weary groan.

The jinn brushed the feather from his face and hunched further down in his burnous. He hated rain. He glared owlishly at a piece of crumpled parchment, his thumb placed on the dripping map near his hoped-for destination. A portion of his turban unwound and curved sinuously before his eyes.

The jinn would have sworn the last signpost – where he'd turned left – had said: "Alba-Khur'ki", but he couldn't find it on the map. But then Nepharious couldn't find much on the map; the ink was starting to run.

The sky above was nearly as dark as the squatting stones, providing little illumination. He snarled at it, and it vomited forth more waters in response. Nepharious picked up his feet, now up to his ankles in mud, to examine the silk slippers with mild distaste. The toes uncurled as he watched.

Ruined, absolutely ruined!

He tried to remember what it said in the jinn manual about the history of the region, and his head throbbed with the effort. Something about the waters being contaminated by the soil itself.

"Yuck." He levitated slightly off the ground.

The rains were so thick that land, sky and water merged in one continuously nauseating yellow-greyish-green tableau. A lot like the map he held clenched in his fist.

His head ached so much he couldn't even recollect the spell to get himself out of here. Never mind where. Anywhere, away from here, and dry, would do. All he *could* remember was that there was some kind of strange plant that grew around here.

Apsu's Coat, that was it! Nepharious snapped his fingers and a small pocket of air dried around him. Much cheered, he struggled to recall more. The plant was named after the great lizard god of Abdha and thought to be his sloughing skin. It thrived here in the swamp as it did nowhere else in Daklha. He stared around him at the odd trees with their overlapping scales so thick and strong that they could easily have graced Brimstone's dragons. The plates were spread wide so that the tree looked like a series of opened parasols stacked neatly one on top of the other. The outstretched scales captured water from both above and below and, periodically, they would snap shut, after which followed swiftly a series of gulping noises.

The trees twisted and squirmed under the battering onslaught of rain. The long, snaking roots that normally criss-crossed the ground in search of moisture during the long, dry season had swelled until they were fat and glutted, looking like their serpentine lord, Apsu the Devourer. The misshapened limbs were covered with huge thorns, which had also become distended and gorged with water. Their branches bent low, as though under a crushing weight.

He didn't like this place. Nepharious murmured a slight warming spell, and his clothes began to dry. He whistled. The rug leapt up from the surging mud and shook itself like a dog, dousing him. Nepharious bawled his displeasure. "Garn!"

The rug trembled meekly and then slipped beneath the jinn's feet while he whisked the dirt from his body with a wave of a bejewelled hand.

"Away from here," he shouted into the tempest.

The rug rose slightly, hovered for a moment as though considering its options for a speedy get-away, and then, as if reaching a decision, it left. Simply that. Left – now you see it; now you don't – without flourish or fanfare, or even so much as a twitching of a tassel.

The rain rushed in to fill the empty space where the jinn used to be. Except for the monotonous thud of water and the slight whisper of the undulating plants, all was quiet until . . .

Inebriated fire exploded in the spot previously occupied, or unoccupied, by Nepharious Hex. The dark shades of slipping stones were bleached by the searing white heat. The fatted limbs whipped in frantic motion. The protective scales of bark along branch and trunk closed simultaneously with a thunderous clack. So intense was the heat that those that hadn't shut quickly enough ignited spontaneously with a soggy swoosh. The gulping noises that came from deep within the bloated belly of the tree turned to strangulated gasps. The once-glutted roots coiled, the water under the sleek surface of wood roiled, and the bark itself appeared to bubble and then burst, spewing forth great white geysers that hurtled towards heaven. The distended thorns also ruptured, disgorging water in a spray that quickly turned to vapour.

The air boiled. Rain turned to steam as still more fire elementals poured in from the open door, brought to this portal by the jinn's magic. So many that one creature was indistinguishable from the other. Occasionally, a sinewy arm of flame with a flicker of orange fingers, or a lithe leg complete with sparkling toes, appeared. The fiery hands joined and the elementals danced, ecstatic in their newfound freedom.

Of all the elementals, only fire was prohibited from the mortal realm. Humanity may have used its earthly likeness to cook his food, warm his hearth, and light his way; but this was only a feeble representation of the original element. For mortal man was too fragile to tolerate true fire's stunning brilliance.

Turns ago, before time's beginning, the angels had stolen away fire's secret reflection and given it to humanity. So its mirror image was held slave, summoned to do man's bidding. And fire felt, quite rightly, that they had been wronged, their secret exploited, while they were denied access to the earthen plane. The other elements were free to enter man's plane whither they will – although few did, most of the fairy folk finding mankind dull. Yet of all the planes, this forbidden realm with its offering of solid wood, grass and other combustibles, tempted fire most.

Drunk with the night's liberty and libations, drunk with exhilaration, they reeled. More flames joined the capering, spinning circle as the last of the geysers died.

Faster and faster and faster!

Until they had drawn together as a single leaping pyre. The roots around them deflated, laying flat and dead upon the sand which no longer churned with battering rain, but curled under the broiling heat of flame. As the dance continued, the dry roots caught like kindling.

Pop, pop! POOF!

The branches gave up the last of their water, withered and scorched, and finally detonated with the technicolour splendour of a wizard's best fireworks display.

The earth below the exploding roots dried, and the mud writhed. It baked slowly at first and then, as the heat increased, faster. Like a kiln, the earth was roasted until it had the consistency of fine pottery. Still the dance continued, and the pottery cracked and crumbled, melting. By then even the steam had dissipated. The clouds retreated from the heat. When the last wisp of the last wood had been burned and even the ash consumed, and the sand seared into fine glass, the fire elementals left the circle of stone looking for more fodder in man's fragile realm.

The fabled city of Alba-Khur'ki had no fixed location. Instead, it darted continuously around the southern continent. The city existed, or didn't quite exist, in a place no one knew where. Appearing, or at least appearing to appear, here and there. Its sole purpose to force the unwary traveller to turn aside from the known path.

Thus, the once-fixed spot upon the genie's bedraggled map was guided by the same spirit and intellect as the positioning of dragons beyond the landmasses, with the notation: "Here there be dragons" (which everyone knew resided in Brimstone's plane). And only the most bold of mapmakers drew it in.

Unlike most cities, which were crowded and filled with people, Alba-Khur'ki was empty, and its market-place reverberated with the sound of unsettled ghosts. It was said the city hated mankind, and some believed it had devoured its inhabitants. Those few who stumbled across it and survived swore that it echoed with unearthly laughter. And those foolish enough to go inside its walls never returned to gainsay them.

For whatever reason, Alba-Khur'ki avoided human contact, settling when and where it could far away from mankind. Usually, the Miasmic Swamp was a favoured spot to rest. During the rainy season, few came here. At least not voluntarily.

When Nepharious Hex arrived, the city contemplated the jinn with windows like lidless eyes. It considered leaping upon him and tearing him limb from limb for disturbing its repose. The great bulk shifted, ready to pounce, but before it could act on this impulse, the feckless jinn disappeared.

Alba-Khur'ki peeped out from its hiding-place and sank next to the swamp with a flap of curtains and the grinding of sandstone just as fire emerged from the second plane. With a shiver of timbers and a shuddering sigh, Alba-Khur'ki concluded that this place had become far too popular, and it vanished to hover aloof somewhere above the Daklhan plane.

The Martyr's Bush was one of the few species indigenous to Daklha. Earth's forebears, they were much more flexible versions of their rocky cousins, and an outgrowth of an ancient accord.

For when man appeared on the first plane, he was deemed too stupid to exist, and a meeting of the immortals was called. The gods, goddesses and godlings disliked humankind because they didn't believe humanity gave them the respect they deserved. Because man, busy crouching behind trees from predators larger and smarter than himself and scratching out a living from the stony soil, paid little heed to the gods in those dark days. The angels and daemons, who had given man fire's secret, were miffed because they had never received proper thanks, or even a note of acknowledgement, for their generosity. Fire, whose reflection had been stolen and given to these pretentious apes, also urged their extermination.

Earth, from whose breast mankind sprang, and the denizens of death and darkness voted for humanity's continuation. The latter cast a "yes" vote because humans were fair game.

Overall, air and water were apathetic. They not only abstained from voting, but didn't seem to think it an important enough issue to attend the council. Although it was rumoured that the airy elements just forgot. Thus, the quorum required for the destruction of a species was not present, and the meeting deadlocked.

Ever steady and patient, earth preached compromise. They suggested that the portals between planes be locked. This would permit time to accumulate upon earth while closing man off and thereby reducing the risk of confrontation between mortal and immortal – as much to shelter the latter from exposure to humans, who so annoyed them, as to protect the former from the wrath of the gods.

Forsooth man, whose future hung so precariously in the balance, wasn't overly bright. In a universe without time, he was forever tripping over various versions of himself.

Eventually an agreement was reached, but not without sacrifice. The gods always demanded payment for their aid, and somebody had to give up something. So, the elders who had fashioned the pact paid the price. They gave up their magic, their elemental existence, becoming something that was neither animal, vegetable nor mineral but a little bit of each. A sort of intelligent plant.

Their spirits remained immortal, but they could die, and no few ended up their earthly existence in the stomach of a roving dung-camel. While their essence lived on in their offspring.

Their sorcery was perpetually drained from them to keep the portals of power closed, but they were content because they remained tied to the element that begot them.

In return for their sacrifice, the angels gave them some small part of themselves, and they became seraphim – tiny, spiny seraphim. Man knew little of this accord, or the creatures that guarded them. Only the name remained: Martyr's Bush.

Joi was just one of many, and, through the turns, the bush had noted with cynical humour that man still tripped all over himself, but not because of the vagaries of time.

Now that the seraphim had relinquished its hold on the portals for the day, it marked time rather than guarded it, and Joi gazed across the arid lands with a prickly, bored expression. A ripple appeared in the desert haze, disturbing the normal heat waves that radiated across the parched soil, and the small tussock of black spikes rattled despite the breathlessness of the still desert air.

Joi did a kind of psychic-vegetable equivalent to a squint, trying to make out what was different about the orange-red sand and the sun-bleached sky. The area of disruption widened and, presently, what was left of its magical vision perceived shapes in the ruddy glow of sun reflected off the desert sands.

Fire!

Soon the mysterious intrusion filled the entire sky, and Joi could make out the serpentine body of a salamander, the great bulk of a dragon, or the more human form of pyre and blaze.

Not just fire, but fire elementals!

Silken creatures of flame, so like the burnished sand that they were difficult to differentiate from it. Here and there, the shrub saw a torso, a limb or two. They twined and intertwined like liquid gold. The figures dispersed and reformed in a new and intricate pattern, and the Martyr's Bush recognized fire's leaping dance of death.

The bush shook violently, but rooted to the earth it was held fast. They drew closer, and there were eyes, thousands of them, ancient and intelligent, filled with fire's elemental anger and leaping mischievousness. Their faces were beautiful, their expressions friendly, but they were destructive . . . oh . . . so destructive.

Impish grins surrounded Joi. Fingers like rivulets of colour and light reached for the straggly brush that housed the spirit of Joi Seraphim. Giggles, like a thousand crackles, encircled the spiny crown, and even their laughter was tinged red, orange and gold.

The seraphim began to scream. With a dying thought, the burning bush sent a warning spiralling down along a thread-like root, rocketing out across its many shoots through the soil to its brother shrubs: *Ware! Time's portal has been breached, and fire ranges free across mortal lands!*

The Lady Astra returned to the second plane.

The stone circle looked like a hurricane had hit it which, in fact, it had. Hysterical water mixed with agitated air to create a maelstrom tinged with fire's inferno.

The once-proud stones were blackened to onyx. Many had cracked, and the central fountain had shattered. Earth elementals wandered with their usual cumbersome gait, meaning that they were poised like statues, rocky arms extended to pick up the pieces of fallen comrades.

Water, connected as it was to its element on the Earth plane, wailed and wailed in profound agony. The Lady Astra put her fingers in her ears, shutting out their anguished caterwaul.

A few of the more-collected air elementals attempted to sweep together the debris of the abortive celebration, blowing it before them and raising a fierce cloud of dust and smoke.

The Lady Astra stared about her, placing ephemeral hands on fragile hips. *This would never do.*

Fante Zephyr, Lady Astra's minister, darted up to air's queen, blathering something about escape. Aqua Prima, water's sovereign, babbled incoherently, clutching wetly at her hand. Astra waved them to silence.

"Missstress," said Fante with a voice like wind flowing through long grasses. "The fire elementals have escaped to the Earth plane."

The soft, nearly transparent outlines of her shoulders drooped. Then the Lady Astra stiffened to the point that she almost appeared solid. Her wings fluttered in agitation which sent great clouds of smoke wafting through the circle.

She threw back her head and she shrieked: "This means war!"

A council was called, and those elementals who had not deigned to come to the wedding – or worse still, those who had not been invited – started arriving in droves. The fairy folk entered the circle from far and wide. Many came from their corresponding planes, while others travelled throughout the eight lower planes to swell the ranks. And even the magically expansive stone circle was jammed full to the bursting.

Fire elementals appeared from the Brimstone plane. Impassioned by the threat against their kind, they had difficulty maintaining human form. Blazing arms merged with blistering legs and feverish brows expanded redly with rage. While water wept over their losses at the Miasmic Swamp. Only slightly more stable and a lot wetter than either air or fire, they dissolved into an emotional puddle that was as black and sorrowful as any mortal mere.

Earth elementals piled on top of earth elementals. Strange, rock-like creatures, which on earth rarely moved, squatted stolidly on the landscape. When finally motivated into motion, suddenly a mountain would uproot itself, or a boulder uncurl arms and legs. By now, however, they had been incensed at ravages done to their plane so that their movements were almost perceptible. They rattled angrily, and the section of the circle in which they rested, resembled a glittering quarry of quivering stones.

Of all the elementals only Astra's troop maintained some semblance of order, and even they fluttered to and fro, trying to comfort here, console there, and calm fiery tempers elsewhere. Air represented pure thought usually without practical applications, but the circumstances had forced them to overcome their nature and direct their attention to the matter at hand.

Astra mounted the cracked column of the fountain. A wisp of vapour whose features hardened as she viewed the chaos around her.

"Order! Order!"

Water howled louder; fire flickered and flared while earth rumbled ominously.

"Order! I called this meeting to order so that we can deal with fire's violation of earth's space, as noted in the Elemental Code."

Fire roared, their bodies exploding up and out, in huge columns of flame. The air elementals flitted away, their vague features shredding in the resultant wind.

"Who says," shouted a flame which was slightly taller than the rest, "that fire has done this?"

His crackling voice was crushed in a flurry of pebbles and dissent: ". . . we have witnesses . . . gone right through the door they did, to our plane . . . the annual rain has been disrupted . . . even the rain clouds are consumed . . . good earth and sand burned to glass . . ."

Astra lifted a translucent arm that tattered as a single fire elemental separated from his fellows and strode forward on flaming legs.

"I claim mitigating circumstances; they were goaded. You," the pyre stabbed a finger of fire at the airy queen, "lured them here, plied them with sawdust and confetti, incited them to riot and now you cry foul just because they went off for a bit of fun!"

Again voices erupted from around the bowl: ". . . witnesses . . . the interruption of sacred cycles . . . earth turned to lava . . . boiling . . . broiling . . . baking . . ."

"Yes," Astra yelled, and oddly enough her breathy voice carried above the tumult. "And what of this interruption of sacred cycles? It wouldn't surprise me in the least if your brethren are in violation of some godly code or another."

"That is not within the jurisdiction of this tribunal!" blared a general conflagration and fire's elected leader, Pyro Teknix. Next to him a third-degree burn capered and jeered at the squadrons of the darting air.

"No, but there are plenty of violations that fall within our jurisdiction," Fante Zephyr interjected from his position that was somewhere slightly behind, and sheltered by, his mistress.

"Ah, excuse me," said Vitreous Humour, son of earth elemental's king, Ignacious Roq. An octahedron fluorite, he was quick-witted and spry for an earth elemental. "Aren't you forgetting something important? It doesn't really matter what laws have been broken. I mean, fire's destroying Earth's plane even as we speak."

Silence descended as each considered the practical import of the young prince's message. Trust earth to dig to the core of any issue.

Fire was forbidden from earth with good cause, but the appearance of any elemental besides earth upon the first plane was disorienting for a human. Their physical presence distorted the mortal time frame continuum of past, present and future. And *that* was the best thing that could happen. Mixing with elementals could be hazardous to human health, but mixing with fire elementals was downright fatal. Their fiery cousins must be captured, contained and persuaded to return to the Brimstone plane where they belonged.

Astra turned to Ignacious Roq – a big mountain of a creature and king of all earth elementals – and said: "What do you think?"

The group paused a breathless minute. Each leaned forward eagerly. A hush fell. No one moved. Water did not slosh. Air did not flutter. Even their earthy cousins grew more still, if a thing as unmoving and silent as earth can be more quiet than it already is.

Ignacious spoke: "WWWWWWW . . ."

The King of Kings, Prince of Darkness and Viscount of Evil had many names. Just as Satan had many faces, and not all of them were foul. His visage changed often along with his moods. At times, he chose to appear as human, or nearly so, for he was just a little too perfect. His teeth too straight, his flesh as unflawed and unblemished as porcelain, and his brow a bit too smooth. In that countenance, the demonlord had cream-coloured skin, hair the same warm brown as the finest Shamirian steed and eyes of liquid gold.

It was the eyes that gave him away. No mortal had eyes of fire.

The Prince of Darkness chose this comely face

when he meant to tempt, entice or cajole. The archfiend mainly wore that face for man, because man in his vanity wanted to believe that the immortals were formed in man's image and likeness – and it pleased the archfiend to pander to man's vanities, just as he pandered to man's fears. So Satan's daily face depended on what he wanted and from whom. The many visages varied, as fleeting as his moods. Sometimes he appeared as a Brimstone dragon. Other times he imitated one god or another, thumbing his nose – or noses, depending on the god – at the immortals, knowing they could not touch him here in his own realm. For the Devil was a great prankster and a mimic.

Today, though, Satan was in particularly nasty temper. The party was over. All those who could had fled the Demon King's court, except poor Pun who was putting the pieces of himself back together again. Around them, the implets, lowest of the low, scurried back and forth, picking up litter and rearranging it to suit their master's fancy.

And the King of Kings abandoned his party dress for another image equally fitting to his station as Guardian of Evil and Keeper of Hades' gates – an aspect much less appealing to the mortal eye. Reflecting his turbulent emotions, the Devil sloughed and changed continuously.

The demonlord sprouted eyes here, and mouths there that would ooze and run dripping down his face. But each part apparently functioned as desired, for the mouths spoke, spitting profanity and slime, and the eyes saw what went on around him. His skin – if it could be called that – was almost fluid, glistening and quivering at everything he observed in the flaming Pit of Death. In one of his many hands, he held the glass globe that contained the glowing darkness of Queb. Occasionally, the Demon King tapped it with rubbery fingers that made soft squooshing noises. *Schloop, schloop, schloop.*

The court jester quailed at his master's side, or parts of him did. Trying to make himself as small and insignificant as possible, he stuck the loose bits in a sack.

And Pun wished again that his father had been Plague's demon, or Pestilence's imp, instead of a member of the Droll family, for it wasn't easy being a Droll. He had inherited his position as court jester indirectly from his father, Double Entendre. Long ago, the demonlord's chief buffoon had split himself laughing, becoming nothing more than a couple of empty rejoinders and therefore, no longer worthy of his King's court. After his father, Pun's older brother Biting Sarcasm took over the position only to be fired – literally. His older brother was succeeded by his sister, Snappy Repartée, who had later been banished from court. (No one was allowed to be wittier than the King.) The twins, Beaux Jest and Bon Mot, the white sheep of the family, had escaped into the Dream Fields. Thus, the whole jocular bunch were on probation, and Pun was left to shoulder the responsibility alone.

Lulled by the schloop, schloop, schloop of viscous fingers against glass, Pun drifted and his needle slowed. Peering over a ragged seam, he began to daydream of a better life, a better job. A career with a future. Something civilized. Disease was a nice tidy business, unlike comedy which tended to depend upon the ear of the beholder. Something safe where there would be no days like today when Pun found himself blasted all over Hades after an ill-timed jibe.

With a pensive glance at his melting master, Pun tested the second leg by bending his knee and then wriggling his toes.

They worked!

Then he began a casual skulk towards the door that led to the lower levels.

"Jester!" the Prince of Darkness bellowed with a most princely roar.

Pun snapped to attention, executing a perfect nine-point pratt-fall. "Your deliriousness, sir," he saluted, rapping himself soundly on the head with the thigh bone which served the same purpose as the bladder-and-stick did for his mortal counterparts.

"This is most enlightening. You really should watch. It might improve your jokes to see fire rampage across the earthen plane."

The imp said nothing, only scarpered out of the way as a portion of the archfiend fell with a sickening plop to the floor, landing in the place Pun had just abandoned.

When the jester realized that his master was awaiting Pun's reply, he tripped all over himself to agree with the demonlord.

"Yes, sir, very good, sir, most satisfactory."

The Prince of Darkness was not amused by his tumbling antics.

"Satisfactory!" The sloughing fiend howled. "You call it satisfactory when I stay here, on this?" He slapped his throne of flaming salamanders, a gift from fire and Brimstone, who had an affinity for Hades.

The imp put his head on one side – which in this case meant that he literally lifted his head off his shoulders and placed it next to him – and waffled. "Well, now that you mention it, your hideousness, that doesn't seem very satisfactory at all."

The archfiend pinned poor Pun with a rapier stare. "Pun, have you ever wondered why I,

King of Kings, never walk on mortal lands?"

The jester contemplated the lovely striations in the ivory of his staff and then gnawed anxiously on the bone. *Was this a trick question?*

"Well, jester, have you?"

"Ah, er, ah, the question may have slithered across my mind, sire, but not for long." Pun brightened. "No, sir, nothing stays in my mind for long. Ideas are very slippery things, you know."

"And what did you decide?"

Head and shoulders reconnected, and the imp examined the great curving talons on his toes. He considered making a dive for it and digging himself into the next level, maybe, or at least scooping himself a nice grave before he answered. Having puns flying all over the place was so untidy.

"Well?" Satan asked.

And the jester knew by the Prince's melodious tone – the master's voice got positively syrupy when he was enraged – that Pun could not evade the query by pretending he hadn't heard it.

" 'Cos they won't let you," he mumbled around the thigh bone.

"Let me!" The demon erupted, spewing droplets of sludge all over the place. "Let me!"

"You don't want to, that's it. You don't really want to go to the mortal plane, do you, sir? Too cold, too clammy. All that grass and air and stuff."

Somewhat mollified, the demonlord sloshed back down into his throne.

"Something of that," he stated, and fell to brooding about a covenant even more ancient than that the Martyr's Bush had made with the Immortals. For the archfiend was bound here, just as assuredly as the spiny shrub was rooted to earth.

Pun eased his foot behind him and then began to inch his body over it. His slight movement caused the Prince of Darkness to notice him.

"Back when the universes were young and man a mere infant, I was given a choice. I could range free across the earthen plane and hunt man for sport as did the lowly werebeast and the wampyr, or I could promise not to interfere with material man on his material plane, unless called upon by man himself." Satan expounded in a smooth, persuasive voice. As he did, the demon began to transform, becoming more solid until the comely vision of the not-quite-human stood before the jester.

"I chose the latter. Do you know why?" He purred.

Pun mewled pathetically.

"Because if I eschewed the sport, I got the far greater prize – man's immortal soul. Needless to say the stakes were much higher and therefore the challenge greater. But my powers are greater still. Even from here, I can manipulate and turn men to my cause. I can send my messengers to the mortal plane. I can project my image. I can tantalize. I can tempt. I can, after a fashion, touch men in all things of the spirit. And, I may boast, I can touch them more profoundly than even death, for death touches man for only a moment, while I claim his soul for infinity.

"The decision, of course, was simple." The prince contemplated his nails. "I left the hunt of human flesh to the lesser creatures. They could have man's body; I would have man's eternal spirit."

The fiend expanded to a gargantuan height and the throne looked like a toy at his feet.

"When the time is ripe, then the man is mine. Humans have choice. If they choose unwisely, they find their way here. This is probably one of the finest examples of my work." The Fiend of Fiends spun the glass globe in his hands like a child's top.

"Now begone, fool, I need time to think."

Gratefully, the jester limped away, dragging the bag of body parts behind him.

Chapter 4

A very unhappy Archmage, who had only moments before been talking with one of the Matriarchs, found himself dangling precariously above the marble courtyard of the Wizards' College. From this height the sorcerer could see the white marble had yellowed – it needed a good cleaning – but he had more pressing matters that required his immediate attention.

The Archmage kicked and screamed, unsure how the nearly transparent air elementals could support his weight. It was the wrong thing to do, for they released their grip upon him. The pleasant warmth of mead in the pit of his stomach soured as he plummeted, clutching at anything he could to break his fall. What the Archmage seized was the hem of the Grand Inquisitor, who accommodatingly fell with him.

Philos landed with an undignified plop, hand in hand with the Inquisitor. Disproving once and for all the myth that sorcerers could fly. (Bounce, perchance, but not fly.) His breath rushed out of him with an unwizardly "ooph" and he lay stunned for a second.

Shaking his head to unrattle it, the Archmage started to disentangle himself from the Inquisitor. A procedure which was accomplished with great difficulty since his bits – amulets, charms, talismans and whatnot – had got snarled with the Inquisitor's bits. Finally after exchanging hats two or three times, they got themselves sorted, and the Archmage clambered to his feet, fuming.

"What in Hades happened?" he raged.

Preston D. Igitor, busy rearranging the folds of his rent robe, replied: "It would appear, sir, that elementals can get into rows and brawls just like young students do."

"And the creatures just dump us here like that?" the Archmage interrupted his assistant.

"Well, if I remember correctly, you did dislodge their grip somewhat, sir. I'm sure they would have set us down here nice and tidy if you hadn't ki—"

"Enough!" the Archmage roared, cutting off the Inquisitor's mild rebuke. "This is an insult! An outrage! We could have been killed. A row, indeed! Ruddy elementals fighting. I have a good mind to complain." He spun on his heel and headed for the college.

"To whom, sir?" the Inquisitor asked, but he discovered he was talking to air. Preston scurried after his superior.

The Chief Wizard, known generally as Philos the Benevolent, was not feeling particularly benevolent towards the newest guild members, Zelia and Ares, at this moment. His brow clouded and his mouth was working overtime as he hurled curses at receptive walls. One could see why the Matriarch in her less dignified moments referred to him as "the Malevolent". A hapless student wandered into his path and scuttled out of his way just in time to evade a lashing malediction.

"What's the matter with his eminence?" an apprentice queried his peer behind a cupped hand. The Inquisitor shot them a dirty look. The Archmage made a rude noise and the students giggled.

Preston hastened upon the first man's heels, wading through the aftermath of spells. It would cost a gold pentacle or two to replace the now twisted and scorched baubles which festooned their halls, and he had cause to recall that the masters at the college called the Archmage: "Ridiculous".

Abruptly, Philos the not-always Benevolent halted and whirled. The Inquisitor nearly tripped over his superior. "I know an insult when I see one," the Archmage bellowed.

The Inquisitor said nothing.

Philos would not let this humiliation pass uncontested. He believed in the absolute authority of sorcery, and he had more than sufficient cause already to despise the untrained talents of the two half-breeds whose powers exceeded the combined skills of all the students *and* the staff at the Wizards' College. The couple had defied every law and flouted every tradition known to wizardry and, together, they wielded truly awesome magic. During the fateful battle with Queb, they had held the entire college in thrall. Commanding a mind-link, they drew from the not-inconsiderable strength of the college, turning the great mages into mindless slaves within their own walls.

The Archmage had been persuaded against his better judgement to issue a stay of execution, to the excommunicate pair. Carried along by the current of popular opinion, he had even admitted the half-elf adventurer and the fay Zelia into their ranks.

Still, Philos had never received a satisfactory answer to his question: Why the renegade cleric, Zelia, had been fiddling about in magicians' business anyway? Queb was one of their own, and the wizards should have dealt with the matter. That the wizards had neither the capacity nor the ability nor the power to forge the link that enabled the couple to vanquish the necromancer, did not enter into the equation. Gratitude was a flighty thing and Philos had had little enough to begin with.

The Archmage could not forget that in the mortal plane, only Ares and Zelia could enter the sacred portals unaided, and survive. It rankled that they could do what he could not. Left unchecked, their unprecedented powers would threaten the authority of wizardry itself. And their talents were based upon elemental magic and not human sorcery. Now that Philos had seen elemental destruction at work, he shuddered to think what would happen if any of the half-breed Zelia's fairy relations got loose in the mortal plane.

Ares's and Zelia's landing inside the sheik's silken *yurti* was nearly as bumpy as the wizards'. The *terem* city spread outside the walls of the Shamirian capital, Al Khali.

The sheik turned to her, mouthing a question,

which was taken up by the wind. All Zelia could do was shrug – a difficult manoeuvre with her shoulders firmly clasped between fluttering elementals. *Something was wrong*. They had left the tribe far out in the desert, but something had brought them back to the seaport city.

The devastation became apparent as they glided closer to the *yurtis*. Zelia felt the icy cold and total blackness as they popped between planes to arrive within the tent itself. The delicate hands let go of her, and she plunged several handspans to the floor before rolling to her feet.

The murmured conversation inside the tent erupted to shouts of indignation as Ares, the sheik, the Lady Hadidge and the other favoured wives followed, tumbling like pebbles upon the sand.

There was an outraged cry, and someone pointed. Zelia swung to face the collected elders, warriors and husbandmen of the tribe.

"There, you see," one man whose name she could not recall said. "Not only does she refuse the veil, but she doesn't have the decency to cover her flesh."

The maid glanced down at her gauzy dress which was singed and completely burned through in places.

"What are you doing here in my tent?" Her father's bull roar drowned out the other screeches of protest.

"Your tent no more, but mine." His cousin, Gol Y Kazzam rose and elbowed his way through the elders to stand before the sheik, legs spread and hands planted on his hips.

The usurper began the ritual declaration. "What was once yours is now mine. Those wives of yours that you left behind have found protection in my *terem* and those that would not . . ." He made a swift slicing gesture at his throat. The women began to wail.

"My sons?" The sheik asked. His voice was choked, and his shoulders sagged as if he already knew the answer.

"You have no sons, Al Y Kazzam, no children except weak females and that half-breed witch," the usurper said, and the Lady Hadidge collapsed in a squall of black cloth.

Zelia scrutinized the many hostile faces, noticing gaps. "To replace my father requires a unanimous vote of the tribe. You don't have that vote; you can't have, for not everyone is here."

The usurper ignored her. "We come to Al Khali to seek the blessing of the Emir for my reign, but with your arrival, I see that won't be necessary. Accept my dominion, and I will let you live."

Hands were raised to fondle the hilts of sharp scimitars, and Zelia wished fervently that she had her sword. She had never felt so naked in her life, and it had nothing to do with her gossamer attire.

Behind her, Ares moved as silent as a werecat, unobserved by any other than herself. He wound his way through the weeping women until he stood by her side, hand hovering over his ceremonial blade.

"Never!" The sheik replied.

"Get them!" Gol brayed the command, and Ares's sword flickered from its sheath in the twinkling of an eye. It wove in a lightning-fast display, whittling the air before them, despite its blunted edge. One of the council fell, and Zelia pounced, relieving the man of his scimitar. Meanwhile, her father had not been idle. He cut a swath through the men, heading in the general direction of the open door. Seeing his need, the Lady Hadidge rose and herded the wives before her. They formed a straggling V-shape and created a wedge of bodies between the sheik and the opposing swordsmen. The women fell in pools of black and red, giving their lives for that of their lord and master. Isolated from the rest of her family, Zelia stood back to back with Ares, both their blades flashing. They pressed against each other, finding strength in the other's presence, and began a murderous crab-walk towards the door and freedom.

Intermittently, the maid saw her mother materialize in various parts of the *yurti*, looking confused. During her last appearance, she was covered head to toe in black dust, but Zelia had little time to consider this observation or its import. Instead, she and Ares pressed closer to the door, widening the path that her father followed.

The sheik shrieked a great battle-cry as he skewered Gol Y Kazzam. The usurper folded, eyes wide with surprise. His hands clenched the blade that protruded from his breast as the rest of the rebel council melted away. The sheik and his wives paused to regroup. Beyond the tent walls, there was a huge outcry, and those dissenters that could still move mounted their steeds to ride off into the desert, leaving the sheik to lick his wounds and bury his dead in the tattered remains of the tent city.

But this was only a brief respite, for by the rules of engagement and warfare of Shamir, the insurgents must return either to submit or subdue. Zelia had no reason to doubt that, once they elected a fresh leader, the rebels would not be ready to press their advantage against the bereaved man and his family.

Torn tents flapped forlornly around the

family. From within the walls of Al Khali came the sound of the town crier: ". . . o'clock and all's swell."

"Right," Zelia said with disgust as she rotated smartly, returning to the wounded women in the central pavilion. She ran practised hands over their bodies. Her head bent in prayer, she was enveloped in the blue-white glow. Perspiration broke out upon the blue maid's brow. Ares went to join her and placed his hands upon her shoulders, enhancing her powers with his own, and the woman over whom the healer toiled sat up, blinking.

Outside there was the soft swish of feet running across the sand. Ares dropped into a defensive crouch, divesting the nearest corpse of its weapon. Zelia half-rose, so that the snow-white half-elf was framed in blue. She retrieved her scimitar and the blade caught the Shamirian sun, cutting a golden smile above Ares's head.

The shredded flaps of one of the lesser tents parted, and women emerged. Or Ares assumed they were women because the only skin that was visible were the small, dark, sun-baked toes. The Lady Hadidge gave a sharp cry. Two hands appeared from the folds of cloth and clapped – whether in joy or command, Ares did not know. The sheik's chief wife and concubine rushed forward to embrace each in turn, and the sombre column that was Lady Hadidge chattered in incomprehensible Shami, patting each woman on the stomach and inclining what must have been her head in assent.

The surviving wives.

The adventurer relaxed his posture and pivoted to regard the sheik's reaction, for these were the women who had forsworn their master and been willing to accept the usurper to their bed.

Sheik Al Y Kazzam shouted in jubilation and then, throwing his hands towards the sky, said: "The nameless one be praised."

Amazed, Ares swung to Zelia. She was grinning from ear to ear.

"He will accept them back?" Ares asked.

"Of course, they are with child."

"They are?" Ares turned again to face the women. One lump of cloth looked pretty much like another lump of cloth. "How can you tell?"

"You can't, but the women know," she explained. "All his women who are with child have been instructed to accept another's protection. At least then the line will survive. If any of them had been visibly pregnant, I can imagine our dear cousin would have killed them."

"This is a harsh land," Ares said.

"Aye," said Zelia in the barest whisper.

Then, from beyond the bend of city wall and beyond the curve of a dune, there came a scratching noise. This time, Ares stood statue-still, waiting, sword held in readiness.

He gasped in amazement as women, clad only in sheer pyjamas, materialized. The escaped wives. Many supported large, meaty, if somewhat shapeless, men – the *terem* eunuchs and guards – their wounds bound in the black cloth of burnous and veil.

The Lady Hadidge raced forward, talking in the rough staccato of Shami. The sheik went to greet each wife as they bent their knees before him. He rested a hand on their foreheads in benediction. Zelia and Ares remained respectfully apart.

Only when this ceremony was complete were they released, to tend the wounds of the *terem* eunuchs who were absolved of all guilt for surviving. Their injuries were most grievous, and Zelia's energy was spent, even with Ares's power to strengthen her, and she was forced to use silken thread, unravelled from her wedding gown to sew the last of the wounds.

The sheik surveyed the wreakage, counting survivors, as Ares helped Zelia to her feet. She swayed and he grabbed her, muttered a quick "revive spell" that she had taught him, and Zelia thanked him with a kiss.

"So few," the sheik said. "The *terem* guard must be commended for their vigilance." He spun with a shimmer of white cloth. "The usurper shall die a thousand deaths for each wife he has felled and each son he has taken from me!"

Ares watched as the Lady Hadidge whipped the healthy wives into action. They moved without a sound. Some began to dismantle the ravaged *yurtis*. Others squatted like sand toads, pawing through shards of pottery and separating what could be used from what was irreparably damaged. Meanwhile, the lady bent to examine Zelia's stitchwork on the wounded eunuchs and snorted, as if to say she was surprised that the girl had done so well. The rest of the wives appeared, carrying large baskets and packing anything that could be repaired for later use.

The adventurer's attention was drawn away from the silent spectacle as Zelia called his name. He ducked back into the tent.

"What else could possibly happen," Zelia growled.

"Perhaps you should appeal to the Emir for protection." Ares suggested.

Al Y Yabba Y Kazzam snorted his scorn. "Go snivelling to that fat tub of lard! May a thousand dung-camels camp in my *yurti* before I do that."

Zelia looked from her father to Ares. "That, ah, doesn't sound like a viable alternative. Besides, it's unlikely that the Holiest of Holies would deign to get involved. He doesn't like to lower himself by taking sides in petty disputes, generally waiting until he can applaud the winning party with a hardy: 'I knew you would win. You see, you didn't need my help'."

"Sounds like a most regal resolution." Ares commented dryly.

Her father continued to swear, wishing a thousand tortures, a thousand demons, a thousand plagues, a thousand stings – everything in thousands – upon his opponent.

"Needless to say, he won't let this insult pass," Zelia said.

"Obviously," said Ares.

"We'll need some kind of plan," she continued, talking above the sheik's tirade.

"We? What's this we? I get nervous every time you use the word 'we'. I remember what happened the last time."

Zelia opened her mouth to retort and was halted by a wail as the *terem* women came upon the bodies of the dead children.

"I'm going to need your help," she said as she bolted through the door.

A woman in flimsy pyjamas rushed up to her, squawking in Shami. Ares flinched. The language sounded like a tenday turkey laying an egg to Ares's northern ears.

"The heir still breathes," Zelia said, seizing his hand and dragging him towards the burial pit.

"Heir? I thought you were the heir?"

"Not if I can help it, I'm not." She hunched next to the broken body of a young boy. Ares stared at her. "Don't you see?" Zelia said. "That's what all this is about, my father naming me as heir."

He nodded tersely and crouched down beside her. His skin tingled as the magical web she wove encased them and their small patient in a glimmering shell – and the three became one – Zelia pulling Ares with her as she descended into a healing trance. The next thing he knew his spirit was spiralling through red veins as she searched for the source of the young prince's bleeding. At each new injury she drew power, knitting vessel walls and restoring organs to operation. Until the child's heart beat strong and true.

Then they retreated from the boy's body to collapse in a heap upon the ground and the Lady Hadidge glided in, guiding the women to lift them and bear them back to the pavilion. When he looked wearily into the slit which exposed the lady's eyes, he realized she was crying. Of course, he thought, it had been her son that they had just saved.

He struggled into a sitting position. "You are right we need a plan, but shouldn't we wait until he calms down a bit first?" Ares indicated the sheik still spewing oaths at the empty air as if they alone could destroy his unseen adversary.

"Oh, that." She thumbed at her father as he swept the scimitar before him, exhorting he-who-cannot-be-named for strength. "That's the ritual required to declare war on a fellow tribe member."

"Does it take long?"

"A bit. You're just lucky it's a member of the same tribe. Another tribe, and we'd be here until next tenday."

Ares flopped down on a pillow. "Great."

The water elementals splashed anxiously about in makeshift bowls. They would pause intermittently to gaze dolefully at Ignacious Roq and then back at their weeping brethren. Fire danced nervously, again banished a' torch top. The Lady Astra looked bored. Her fingers rapped a rhythm that sounded like two twigs battered by a tempest.

Oblivious to their agitation, Ignacious continued his speech. "WWWWWWW . . ."

The Lady Astra got up and started to pace

round the broken fountain, expanding in her anger.

"WWWWWWWW . . ."

The fay folk around her were becoming more and more restless. The ceaseless, grinding "WWW" grated upon elemental nerves. Water began to pace with a soft squish, squish, squish. Fire, tired of prancing upon the fiery brands, picked a fight with water. Air, the self-proclaimed arbiters of the dispute, were buffeted about by the heat. Even the earth elementals were getting peevish and testy. Magma bubbled, and a few of their more solid and much slower brethren had blinked in dismay.

Would that idiot earth elemental ever get to the point, the Lady Astra wondered. With an impatient snap of her fingers, Air's queen vanished, Ignacious's booming "WWW" still resounding in her ears.

"I wish he'd get on with it," one watery elemental said with a voice like a brook over pebbly rocks, speaking for all of them, and fire, ready to pursue any flicker of contention, leapt on it.

"What? You would deny earth its voice?" a flaming spark crackled.

"You would and have," rumbled a striated sheet of slate. "In the Portals Accord, we lost some of our best then."

"'Twasn't only fire's doing," the incandescence sputtered, upsetting the air elemental that fluttered above him, muttering soothing imprecations to deaf ears.

The many conflagrations climbed down from their perches. Water spewed over the sides of the broken fountain. Air descended in a flurry of diaphanous wings, joining the fracas, and the circle became a boiling mass of steam.

Those of the fiery contingent who had not departed to the mortal lands were quickly quenched, and they fled from air's realm to flames' domain with a puff of indignation. Water and air thrashed boisterously.

Somewhere someone shouted: "To earth! To earth. United we shall trounce them and send them back to Brimstone bawling!"

And they exited with a swish and a slosh – both air and water, and those of earth small enough to fit in the palm of a watery hand or quick enough to grab onto airs' coat-tails.

Zelia's father had just got to the part which invited the Snake God Apsu the Devourer to sup upon the entrails of the usurper's descendants. He paused to catch his breath before starting upon the bit about one thousand stinging multipods, when suddenly the *yurti* was filled with winds of such force that the sides were lifted completely from their anchors. The air was recumbent with many flitting voices. Astra made a flirtatious loop round the sheik's head, but, preoccupied, he noticed her only as an insectile groan. He waved his hand in the air, and she went tumbling tip over tail. Her subjects giggled.

The lady alighted upon Zelia's shoulder and glared at her sniggering followers.

"Begone," she shouted in a voice like a tempest in a teacup, and her vassals disappeared with a dying bluster. The sides of the tent flagged.

The maid regarded her mother out of the corner of her eye.

"My daughter, I've come to warn you," the Lady Astra spoke in a rustling whisper. "The fire elementals have escaped to Earth's plane."

The sheik's voice faltered. The *yurti* went silent. Beyond the tent walls, the mute women were quieter still as if they hesitated in their chores.

"Where?" Zelia exclaimed.

The Lady Astra shrugged. She'd forgotten. The indigo hair on Zelia's opposite shoulder began to move as if it had developed a life of its own. A tiny hole was created, and the promise of a face almost appeared among the tangled locks.

"Pssssst!" it said, and Zelia jumped, dislodging her mother who flew away unharmed.

The other air elemental tumbled from its perch, clinging for dear life to the sapphire tresses.

The lady's second gave a clumsy bow only to get further ensnared in Zelia's hair.

"The Miasmic Swamp, your graciousness, that's where they went. The Miasmic Swamp," Fante said as he clambered up Zelia's chest to her shoulder.

Zelia moaned, and Ares's eyes rolled in their sockets to gaze upon the tent's ceiling. A chill ran up and down her spine despite the Shamirian heat. She was all too familiar with the Miasmic Swamp, for it had been the place where they had met Queb during the final contest which had seen his destruction. It was not a place that she had wanted to see again in this lifetime.

Yet fire's exodus required action. The sheik's problems seemed puny compared to the far greater threat of elemental fire running unchecked across the desert. On a continent this dry, Abdha would not be far enough away. While fuel was scant, the region arid, there would be more than enough fodder to sustain the elementals in the dry grasses and the mysterious Martyr's Bush that speckled the sands. Water was sparse, and those few watering holes that existed here and there across the desert – that belonged to a tribe and was the second measure of their wealth – would be boiled dry.

The sheik retired to a corner to complete a more subdued recital of his oath.

"How much longer does it go on?" Ares asked.

"I don't know, I've never heard it said before," Zelia said. "Although I have read the text. It depends on one's bloodline."

"Don't tell me. Let me guess," he said. "It goes back to the beginning of the tribe."

"You got it."

Chapter 5

Water and air plunged through the still-open door as earth began what was for them a rapid jump to their feet. This consisted of a crunching noise and, if you looked closely enough, a wrinkle in their thick legs as rocky knees bent and stony muscles bunched.

The hapless Fante returned to the circle at this same instant. But before he had a chance to assimilate what was happening around him, the zephyr was sucked through to the Earth's plane, drawn by the escaping elementals. The poor creature shouted his dismay as he was absorbed into the darkness of between. He tried to resist, but to no avail, for within less than a heartbeat, he was rolling head over heels above the desert.

The wily elements had timed their jump so they emerged within the portal of the Swamp before the soil had completely cooled. The once-fat Apsu's Coat was now only white ash that was quickly blown away. The ash of others had sunk into the molten sand, creating white whorls within the scarlet glow.

Water and air hit the sizzling sands. The ground spat in protest. Water and air linked hands. With a twinkling of transparent wing and the splish of watery leg, they began to whirl and twirl. The pace increased until they were spinning like tops. Each figure little more than a blue-green blur which expanded outwards in a billowing cloud. Muted by the angry, red sky, the cloud turned grey. The seasonal rains began again, and the earth responded with an indignant, boiling hiss.

Just outside the stone circle, in an area known as Miasma, in a swamp that was a swamp no more, there was a pip, a single pip. Small and hard, a solitary ebony stone that blended perfectly with charred and blackened soil, upon which it quaked.

Not just any seed, this was but one of thousands that the dying seraphim had scattered to the winds even as Joi transmitted the message of its impending demise. The only one to have escaped fire's notice and evaded its untender caress.

Already the seedling had knowledge; it had sentience. It thought, it lived, it breathed the harsh, hot air that flame had left behind. The grand plan, of which it was just a small part, was already implanted in its pea-sized brain. It understood its function, and it comprehended its purpose.

The first order of business was to grow, and to do that, the seedling needed moisture. But sitting in the aftermath of inferno, the prospect was remote. So Joi II – as it had come to think of itself – jigged, jumped, shimmied and shook, trying to keep as much of itself as possible off the baking earth. And it was losing strength rapidly.

Just when the tiny pip was about to give up, about to settle upon the broiling soil that would be its grave, it began to rain . . .

Ares cradled Zelia's head in his lap. Her body was limp and motionless, not even the gentle heaving of her chest indicated that she lived, and the adventurer had to repress the urge to shake her back into her earthly shell.

His cat-like pupils contracted as, with elfin

sight, he regarded the bright blue flame of her spirit. Freed from her body and ranging far and wide, she trod the magical grid that criss-crossed the world in search of her fay kinsmen, for if aught could persuade fire to return to the Brimstone, she could.

Ares would have accompanied her on this sorcerous journey, but Zelia had been adamant that he should linger here. Reluctantly he had remained behind, lest the traitorous tribesmen should again press their advantage against the sheik and his women. But nothing said that he couldn't take just a little peek at how her unearthly voyage progressed.

The elf-man placed slender white hands upon the maid's cool temples and inhaled deeply. And he was bound to Zelia, viewing the world through her eyes. Beneath her spectral feet, he could see the shadowy image of the ley-line grid. The many strands writhed and bucked, coiled and recoiled, as though blown about in a heavy gale. Warped by elemental presence, the line rippled askance and below him, Zelia's fists clenched, mirroring the action in the physical world that she performed in spirit, as ghostly hands gripped the twisting threads.

The ruddy glow of false dawn loomed, in a place where all the lines converged in turmoil. The adventurer blinked and his pupils retracted to a single slit, blotting out the worst effects of magic's blinding radiance. He felt a stomach-wrenching lurch as she descended into the tumult. The elfin eyes glazed and Ares gave a small cry, pulling back from her mind.

In the camp nestling at the feet of Al Khali, the women continued to move with the same crisp efficiency. The few remaining *yurtis* were stretched along the ground and, from this distance, it looked as if they had folded in upon themselves. Most of the debris of battle had disappeared.

The adventurer returned his gaze to Zelia and scowled as her brow grew feverish beneath his hands. *Where was she now,* he wondered. His light fingers touched her sweating forehead. The two minds merged and Ares was surrounded by liquid gold. Thousands of eyes, brilliant scarlet rimmed with molten yellow, peered at him/her, taunting. They frisked and capered, enclosing her in a spinning ring, and only the lines of ley wrapped about her in a tight cocoon prevented her spirit from shrivelling in the heat. Occasionally, a flaming finger would pierce the sorcerous chrysalis, and below him her flesh twitched and blistered.

Ares swore and gnashed his teeth. He heard her plaintive voice as though it were coming from a great distance. She pleaded with them to return to their home plane, but the burnished flames cackled and the cheery blazes scoffed, ignoring her entreaties. The burning orbs of their eyes were filled with contempt for Lady Astra's half-human offspring as they whirled around her.

Suddenly, he could make out words in the crackling madness. They chanted:

"Come too near and what you hold dear,
We will destroy with a touch.
With a nudge and a stare, a jab and a glare,
We'll consume you . . . and yours.
Ignite and flame, bother and blame.
Begone, whelp of air, warn others if you dare,
Here we are and here we'll stay,
Until mortals' debts have been well and truly paid!"

Something tickled his nose and he retreated back to earth, retracting his hand from Zelia's forehead, now flushed to a deep lavender. A strand of hair drifted above her head. It brushed his face as the Lady Astra lolled languidly in a couch of woven indigo that kept her moored to earth. The fairy queen dozed unconcerned. Ares prodded her away. Then his eyes dipped back to view Zelia as she stirred in his lap.

Her eyes popped open, and she sat up. "They won't see reason."

The adventurer extended his hand before him, palm up in a conciliatory gesture. "Did you expect them to?"

"No, I suppose not."

"You are burned," he said, pointing at the blistered skin.

She grunted.

"Can you heal it?"

"No, not now. I am exhausted."

"Perhaps I . . ." He let the sentence dangle unfinished.

For the first time, she smiled. "The wounds are minor and will heal themselves in a few days. Better to save your strength. We must get this group moving somehow. I fear it won't be long before the rival clan returns."

Rising with a single, fluid motion, she left him to examine her patients. She tarried longest over the young prince, checking her handiwork.

Her father's voice droned on in the background. The maid tilted her head and listened to her sire. "It won't be long now. He's going at a pretty fast pace. I think he's giving an abbreviated version of our ancestry. You have to be awfully angry to want to declare war in this country. I think that is why this country is more peaceful than any of our neighbours."

Ares nodded, knowing that she spoke the

truth. Of the four countries of Daklha, only the Shamir never bickered or quarrelled among themselves. The worse conflicts usually centred around horse thievery. While Hamadan, considered the Jewel of Daklha and the most cultured, was often racked by internal war and petty disputes. Both the goddess Sala and the one-whose-name-must-not-be-spoken claimed an equal number of followers. So when one tribe wasn't feuding with another over territory, there was a religious conflict going on somewhere.

They returned to the business at hand, talking in hushed tones. Probable plans were discussed and just as quickly discarded, for they, like any other mortal, were vulnerable and this was no earth-bound fire that could be smothered with a simple dousing. It could not be summoned with a flint or a spell. Neither could it be easily dismissed. This flame had a mind and would not compliantly do man's bidding. No human, or half-human, could hope to contain it.

"We know we can't face them unaided," Ares said. "If this one," he took a gentle poke at Astra, "would wake up, maybe we could solicit air's support."

"The problem is, we only know what we can't do. We don't even have a starting point." Zelia threw up her hands in exasperation.

Oath complete, her father stirred from his

corner. "If you don't know where to start, my dear, why don't you ask the gods?"

The central pavilion cascaded to the sand around them, and they were suddenly facing a group of solemn women who stooped as one to roll up the heavy cloth. The sheik turned to observe the women as they whisked the roll away and loaded it onto an already laden dung-camel. The knees on all six legs bent under the weight and then it righted itself, ruminating thoughtfully.

"Sala would be best, I think," the sheik mused aloud. "She's the goddess of cycles. It's spring and the rainy season in the swamps. If the fire elementals have gone there, then most likely they've halted the annual rains, and I think Sala might have a thing or two to say about that."

Zelia ducked her head in assent. "Her oracle is in Dali, the capital city of Abdha and not far from the swamps."

Since they had no better suggestions, it was agreed. By the time they had completed mapping their route, the great *yurti* had vanished. The women sat, swathed head to toe in black cloth, mute fixtures astride horses or sand snails, depending upon their rank within the *terem*.

Nepharious Hex sat on an outcrop of rock

somewhere in the southern continent. Of that he was sure, because it was desert – beyond that, where in Daklha was anybody's guess. Not that the jinn had been to the northern continent all that much. Just once when his father had taken him, his brother Heinous and the entire lamphold on holiday to Pelopnos, the Isle of Learning. They had bought passage on a north-bound vessel for the requisite three wishes – for the ship, of course. It was not fair throwing in a request for wealth or eternal life. No personal wishes were allowed, only those that ensured safe voyage.

It had been the worst holiday of his life. Nepharious hated the northern continent. It was damp and green, with grass and other such abominations. Worse, it had rain and Nepharious didn't like rain.

The genie sighed as the egstrich feather drooped dejectedly. The exhausted rug sprawled next to him, panting. Nepharious paused to examine his silk slippers. They were covered in muck, the once-lovely pointy toes flattened. The bells that adorned each slipper were caked, and their tiny clappers rumbled about inside with little, leaden thunks. Nepharious chanted a spell to rid himself of the dirt that crusted each foot and only succeeded in spreading it in a thin film across his body.

He cursed. The tiny ragged piece of carpet whimpered, and Nepharious shot it a hateful look. The rug sidled away from him. The genie gave it an ill-aimed kick, and the mud-weighted slipper flew wide.

It still irked that his father had given him this, this *thing*. Sure, he was a second son and he had flunked out of jinn school, but this scrap was an affront to his dignity. The rug, catching drift of his thoughts, quivered, and Nepharious contemplated blasting it into the next dimension but decided against it.

Then the jinn peered myopically at the letters on the map which were nothing more than a blue-black blur. No doubt about it, he was lost, hopelessly lost. He should have hitched a ride with his brother Heinous, on his fast, sleek Shamirian carpet instead of flying about on his own secondhand rag-rug. But it had been a point of pride that Nepharious would make it to his cousin Esmerelda's wedding feast on his own. He didn't need to tag along with his older, more competent brother. Heinous was head boy at jinn school and president of the skulling team. This was a much-favoured genie sport in which the participants shrank to the size of a lentil – so they could fit into a human skull. They would then row this odd conveyance across the desert sands. Nepharious had never mastered skulling, although it wasn't the rowing that bothered him – Nepharious had more than enough brawn – it was the shrinking that got him. Expansion, powered by anger, was easy. Nepharious blew up all the time. But shrinking required quiet concentration, and the genie never quite got the hang of it.

By taking this trip alone, Nepharious had hoped to impress his father so that he would exchange the rag-rug for something more grand, but now the much-maligned second son had proved just how inept he was. Not only was he not going to make it to the festivities, but even if he did manage to stumble across the wedding feast, all his best clothes were in tatters.

Grumbling angrily to himself, Nepharious dug a bit of dried mud from his ruby ring. Somewhere to the east, there came an earthly wail. The jinn shuddered as he realized that one of the Martyr's Bushes had perished, and time's hold on the world weakened perceptibly.

The Prince of Darkness and Archfiend of Archfiends examined the oozing spores of spite and malice that he had loosed from their glassy abode. The demonlord jabbed at the roiling mass. It clung to his clawed forefinger slimily. The seething globules could have been truly beautiful if it hadn't been for the disgusting little sparkles of light, bits of misplaced good that, like a magnet, had been attracted to its opposite pole.

One of his minions crept forward with a piece that had escaped the Demon King's notice. It opened knotted and twisted fingers. The black fleck hastened to join the others that adhered to the demonlord's flesh.

Satan snapped his fingers and a transparent ball floated before him. Grasping it with one hand, he thrust it through the glass. His lips moved in a whispered incantation, and he extracted it. The action caused all the sundry bits to be scraped from his fist. A loud sucking noise reverberated around his cavern.

So the demonlord kept the wizard Queb captive in a jar. Occasionally he would take the pieces out and play with them – flog them into a frenzy or stir them into a muddle. When the archfiend got particularly bored, he'd let the court jester juggle them.

The Devil sat upon his throne, his chin resting upon a cupped hand, and watched the floating ball.

This had once been one of his best creations. No other mortal had been so pliant, so receptive, so innovative! And now all that badness was in ruins. Destroyed by the mortal witch and her partner.

"What good are you to me now?" he snarled. "Useless, totally useless."

The pieces of good, which had escaped from the Dream Fields, gleamed like fireflies. They battered against the side of the glass trying to get free. And the King of Demons noted with a tremor of delight that the darker bits were getting blacker even still, as though they absorbed the evil that surrounded them.

The demonlord stood, red eyes glowing. He strode around his salamander throne.

"I gave you power beyond most mortal men, and what happens? This," the Prince of Darkness shook the globe. "You let a bunch of elementals take you to bits."

The Devil moved over to the pit and gazed at the molten-red surface with a sigh. "You can be replaced, you know," he paused, "with a gold fish." He glowered at the glass ball.

Under his scrutiny, the pond swirled and whirled with dizzying colours as it shifted through a continuous scan of the mortal environment. So many souls ripe for the plucking, but the archfiend must work his evil magic by proxy through his imps or his mortal representatives on earth. If he could only inveigle an invitation from some foolish human, for his primary agent on earth was trapped here inside the jar.

Somewhere on the mortal plane there must be someone who would be open to suggestion, someone who could be swayed . . .

Satan caught the glitter of gold embroidered cloth, the clank of magical talismans, and he touched the rocky protuberance, freezing the scene. Philos, the Archmage, scurried about his room, a black grimoire tucked underneath his arm. A slimy sneer spread across demonic lips as the Demon King bent forward to focus on the wizard's face.

The Grand Inquisitor slunk outside the Archmage's apartments. Philos shuffled about his room mumbling to himself. "Think they can make a fool out of me. Think they can wrest the power from me. Think they can . . ."

The Inquisitor winced. The master wizard's muttering maledictions had made the college no safe place to be. Preston, or Prez as his friends knew him, still walked with a crutch after running into one of the Archmage's more unruly spells. Indeed, so many of the students had been injured by the Archmage's misguided hexes that they had been dismissed and sent to their respective homes to wait until things might return to normal. While many of the master wizards had developed an irresistible urge to visit relatives they hadn't seen for turns. And the Grand Inquisitor noted that quite a few family rifts had been healed, and not a few feuds laid aside, in a remarkably short amount of time to facilitate this sudden upsurge of familial fidelity. The only wizards who remained were those unlucky enough to have no relatives – no matter how hated or how reviled – to visit.

The college itself was operating on skeleton staff – mainly the bones of former sorcerers resurrected from their dusty spellbound coffins and pressed into service to attend to the menial tasks normally assigned to the lesser students. The skeletons clattered around the empty halls, making the silence seem even more pronounced.

The Inquisitor nodded at the door. It opened with a mental nudge, and Prez scuttled into the shadows to listen unobserved.

Philos the Benevolent spun with an oath, and a vase shot from its place on the table and went crashing against the far wall. The Archmage gesticulated with his free hand, and a skeleton rattled forward and began to sweep up the broken shards.

In his corner, the Grand Inquisitor stuffed his hand in his mouth to stifle a gasp, for grasped in Philos's fist was the black grimoire, Queb's book of foul magic. Usually secreted in the Archmage's safe, the care and feeding of Queb's book was one of those responsibilities that the

Inquisitor did not envy, and one of the main reasons that Prez did not aspire to the position of Archmage. The Inquisitor had had to take care of it on those rare occasions when the Archmage left the college, and it – and the spells contained therein – frightened him.

Suddenly the air within the chamber began to shimmer in a bright yellow gold. A thousand tiny gilded dots, like twinkling dust caught in a mote of sunlight, swirled, rotating on a tight axis. Then the gleaming illumination began to take shape. First a grinning head appeared, then a torso and arms. Last of all came legs. Behind the leering visage Prez observed a throne of flaming salamanders, and he identified the fell face. The terrified Inquisitor pressed himself closer against the wall.

"Wizard." The voice was soft, seductive. Prez very nearly stepped forward, revealing himself, but not before the Archmage had answered.

"Wah . . . who?" Philos glared at the intruder. "Oh, it's you," he said as if he expected this grim visitation.

"You recognize me, I see," the image said, lowering itself to the jiggling throne.

"Of course," Philos gestured with the black grimoire. "Your mark is all over this book. Did I call you?"

"You hold the book," Satan said. "Which is, I

might add, definitely recommended reading for any sorcerer who does not want to be limited to mere mortal magic."

"What's wrong with mortal magic?" The Archmage advanced to the throne and thrust his hand through it. "Even I can do better than this. My creations have substance."

The Demon King rose to his full height and the wavering image towered above the Archmage. "You dare question me. I could destroy you where you stand, mortal, and then eat your soul as a tasty treat. And keep eating it for all eternity." He paused, letting his words sink in. "There are reasons why I don't come to you in person. You would die if you were to gaze upon my magnificence, unaided, and that would never do because I have other plans for you."

"You, uh, do?" Philos asked. "What, pray tell?"

"I would give you powers unrivalled by any other except, perhaps, the author of that book. I would give you an undefeatable army of the undead."

"And why would you do this for me?"

"Because we have common enemies, you and I."

"Who might that be?"

"That fairy whelp and her betrothed," Satan said.

"Ah," said Philos sagely.

"They have made you look the fool, have they not? Revealed your powers to be small and insignificant. Embarrassed you in front of your students and the Grand Inquisitor." The Devil motioned towards the corner of the room, and Prez cringed away.

"Your assistance would have a price, would it not?" the Archmage asked.

"A trifle, a mere trifle, comparatively speaking, and something easily within your powers."

Within his darkened corner, Prez saw revenge and greed war with caution and fear, and win.

"And what is it you desire?"

"Their souls on a stick." Satan's reflection marched around the room. The skeleton, which had remained quiet up until now, rattled back into the closet as the shade of the Demon King passed.

Prez could hear it clatter and clank as it trembled inside the wooden wardrobe.

"Right now, the whelp and her adventurer lover are protected by your guild. But, if they were declared heretic by excommunication, we could crush them – you and I – and they would be mine, forever . . ."

"Crush them? Just how do you propose to defeat them?" Philos asked.

"With an army that you shall create."

In his nook, Prez started, for in the book of

fell magic still clenched in Philos's hand, the Inquisitor had seen a recipe for homonuclei – soulless humans grown from bits of blood, flesh and bone. Prez shivered. Surely his master was not that far gone to dabble in the black arts.

"Queb was unable to raise this army, or so it says here," Philos brandished the book. "Why should I succeed where he failed?"

"Ah, but Queb didn't have my assistance. He angered me. The fool grew too proud, too confident of his own powers, forgetting from whence they came." The Devil raised a single talon. "But you are wiser than that."

His eyes narrowed as he watched the wizard's reaction to his flattery.

Unmoved, Philos said, "If I refuse?"

"I will place a thousand stinging scorpions inside your robes. But you will not, for you want them as badly as I do. It is such a simple request. Right, Inquisitor?" The Prince of Darkness spun to glower at the darkened corner. "I see you lurking behind the curtain."

Prez stepped from his hiding-place, eyes averted. A minor oath came creeping from between the Archmage's lips to drop listlessly to the floor.

"Don't cower in front of company," Philos growled uncharitably. "It is most unbecoming."

"But, sir, we have named the adventurer Ares

and the maid Zelia Wizards Emeritus. They are not liable to either the charge of witchcraft or heresy now that we have accepted them as a part of our guild."

"There has been precedent," Philos observed.

"Well, yes, there was Queb who interfered with the portals of power . . ." Prez's voice dwindled into a shuddering sigh, and the arch-fiend leered at him.

"You begin to understand," Satan said.

"Assemble the Masters, before I get very angry with you," Philos ordered imperiously.

"But, sir, almost everybody is gone. Three are required for the ceremony. Old Ampitere is completely bedridden and hasn't left his chambers for the last nine years. Mad Thomas, we dare not turn loose, and the apprentice Simon, I believe, is out in the sty with the sows. Surely you don't want me to bring him in?" The apprentice in question had been turned into a pig during the original fray, which had seen Zelia declared sorceress and heretic the first time. "Besides, we'll make ourselves into laughing-stocks if we rescind their status now," Prez finished weakly.

Philos glowered, anything but benevolent, and the oath which lay at his feet stirred to life and began to glare at Prez with eyes of pulsating green.

"And who do you think would be so foolhardy as to complain?" The oath took shape, stood upright and took a lumbering step towards the Inquisitor.

"No one," Prez mumbled. "No one at all."

"We are all agreed then." The glowing, hot image of the demon king began to fade.

The Archmage bowed to the dimming figure before swinging on the hapless Inquisitor. "Assemble the Masters for the convocation. Now!"

Prez glanced out of the window. The sun shone brightly across the waters that separated the Pelopnos from the mainland. He sighed. Caught between the devil and the deep blue sea, the Inquisitor had no choice but to obey. And the Inquisitor knew there was no place he could run. Even if he managed to escape the confines of the island, he could not evade Satan's all-powerful gaze forever.

An eldritch scream pierced the veil of the fairy's dream. Mortal time rippled around her, and the Lady Astra began to unravel herself from the soft cocoon she had made for herself in her daughter's hair. She floated lazily towards what she thought was the ceiling of the *yurti*, only to realize that the tent had been removed and she risked losing herself in the mortal sky.

A dark column curved below her, winding through the dunes and keeping to the leeside, away from both sun and slicing, hot wind. She concentrated her attention on the cavalcade below and the witless dung-camels suddenly thought about which of their six legs came first and got all gnarled up. Long limbs twisted in a tangle of knees. The caravan disintegrated into total chaos, as the camel-driver dismounted and tripped over versions of future selves already bent to unknot spindly leg from spindly leg.

The goatherd slipped and executed a perfect somersault. Even the women broke the normal ordered stillness to twitter tensely while the many animals spat like demons.

Bemused, the lady observed the human antics while thought teased at her consciousness. Something had awakened her. *Now what was it?*

Astra tapped a transparent temple with her forefinger, and she remembered the council of war. Now just *when* had she left her brethren? If she timed it right, Astra should be able to return before anybody noticed her missing.

The fairy zipped away, arriving somewhat later than she had expected, and the circle was empty of all save earth, who waited in stodgy impatience for their leader to finish his sentence.

She cocked her head.

"WWWWE . . ."

Spying her, Ignacious's son Vitreous bounced, end on pointy end, to the lady's side. He moved with amazing agility and speed, this one, and the Lady Astra realized he would – assuming he outlived his sire – be a leader to be reckoned with.

"As-s-stra," he sputtered, his words tumbling out like pebbles upon stones. "They're gone. All gone."

"Gone? Gone where?"

"To the Earth plane to find fire." The fluorite rattled like Fennec's cubes tossed upon his sacred altar.

The fay lady rocketed skyward in her distraction. The portals had been breached not just by fire, but by air and water as well. Astra vanished, hoping to reappear before the elementals' flight so perhaps she could dissuade them from this disastrous course.

There was a great hue and cry as dung-camels continued to totter on tangled limbs. The great stallions danced skittishly, moving sideways and bumping into their doubles. Side by side, Ares and Zelia watched the commotion unaffected. Zelia heard a buzz, scanned the chaos around them and then peered straight up at the sky. Her mother floated upon the breeze.

Zelia called to her and a bemused expression crossed the fairy's features. Capricious as the wind, the airy elemental vanished. With that, the scene righted itself as additional people, horses, camels and snails likewise disappeared.

"What was that?" Ares asked.

"I think, perhaps, my mother and her people carry some small part of the timelessness of their planes with them wherever they go."

"It didn't seem to bother us back in the camp when your mother and what's his name, her second, were both flitting about."

"Ah, but there were just the two of them, and they only came in contact with those who had attended the wedding and were still under the elemental spell," she said.

Ares inclined his head in acknowledgement. "And the spell has worn off?"

"It would appear so," she said.

"And later?"

"She was asleep."

The sheik did not move from his position at the head of the column – his back as rigid and taut as a bow string, his raven hair exposed to the wind. The chestnut stallion pranced spiritedly. At his brusque signal, the Lady Hadidge pulled her mare about and steered herself into the tumult, shouting orders in the strange, barking Shamirian tongue.

Without a sound, the many wives adjusted their mounts into positions appropriate to their station. In less than a minute, the dung-camels stood – heads drooping shamefacedly, hooves pointing ahead, one before the other, in correct order.

The snails circled slowly as the Lady Hadidge rode with due decorum back to her place behind the sheik. He warbled the signal to move on. The scimitar held loosely in his hand began to swoop and dip. Then it pointed in the chosen direction.

Ares regarded the undulating dunes. "How does he know which way to go? It all looks the same to me."

Zelia answered his question with one of her own. "Have you ever wondered how a tribe's leader gets elected?"

"A horse race?"

"You mean the Great Race of the Emir? No. No tribe who faces such a hostile land would be willing to chance so important a decision on a race. Would you gamble your life upon a single throw of Fennic's cubes?"

"It's, uh, been known to happen." Ares winced. "But you gamble the governance of a country upon a horse race."

"Ah, but the Emir is a figurehead. It is the bureaucracy that keeps the government running smoothly. A sheik is more important than that. The tribe's lives depend upon his skill, his weather sense. The sheik is selected because he can lead them unerringly to water and steer them to fresh grasses. Under normal circumstances, only if a man loses this sense is he replaced by unanimous vote of the clan's male members," she explained. "My father is such a man. I've watched him do it, and it's fantastic. Something akin to wizardry, it seems to run in families. Thus, one family within a tribe rises above the rest until that power deserts them. I think perhaps that's another reason why we have the race for the ruler of central government. To keep one tribe from becoming too strong, which indirectly nurtures this ability within each individual clan. For the Emir comes from the tribe whose stock is best, and the stock thrives only if the sheik has the ability to find water and feed for their steeds."

"Handy," Ares said.

Just then, the sheik reined his beast and spun round. The destrier curvetted nicely and then plunged forward. Wives and concubines parted like the sea before a rock. He pulled up next to Ares and Zelia.

"I sense water nearby. We should stop. The women are tired," he said. As one the wives slid from their mounts and began to unload the tents, sensing their lord's desire.

"Do you think we have lost them?" Ares inquired, thinking of the pretender who surely followed in their footsteps.

"Probably not," the sheik said, as if it were a matter of no concern.

"Garn! Does everyone in your family do that?" The adventurer threw her a murderous glance.

She returned it with an innocent gaze. "Do what?"

"Never mind," he grumbled.

Her father interrupted. Turning to his daughter, he said: "Do you think you can do something to conceal us?" The sheik waggled his fingers significantly.

"A spell, you mean?" she said, looking at the cavalcade. "I don't know. We're tired too. What do you think, Ares?"

He shook his head. A fade spell capable of hiding the entire camp would tax their strength considerably. The adventurer tugged at his lip. "Instead of trying to make all this blend into sand, why don't we do the reverse and make the sand blend into this?"

"I'm not sure I understand," Zelia said.

"Think mirrors."

"You mean, cast a spell that captures the desert's light and heat and reflect it back out again. Yes, I think it might work. It would be a lot easier than trying to make all this disappear."

The adventurer regarded the tents which ballooned before them. "What about the trail?" he asked.

"The goatherd follows behind. He erases our tracks," the sheik said.

Dark forms drifted around him, unrolling the ragged *yurtis*.

Ares surveyed the diminished household. Only a tenth of the once thriving *terem* survived. Their ranks had been decimated, and yet the women worked without complaint. That they were able to keep up this quickened pace and stoic silence after their ordeal surprised him as did their fortitude and endurance.

Ares commented on the women's stamina, and Zelia laughed at his awe. "They are nomads, after all."

The jinn stretched out across the sand, caught in a light doze. Nepharious had wrapped himself up in the tatty rug to protect his already florid skin from the glaring sun. He held on to the cloth like a security blanket. A much beringed thumb tucked in his mouth muffled his thunderous snores.

Had he or his companion carpet been awake they might have noticed the roiling cloud bank that had materialized to the north. They might have remarked how it raced across sky with supernatural speed. Nepharious might have dodged for cover or have the carpet beat a hasty retreat to the lamp he called home. With its coordinates magically woven into the woof of the rug, all the jinn had to do was imagine the shining brass walls and the curved spout of home, and he would be transported immediately away. Instead, the genie slumbered, having decided he didn't want to go where he might have to explain his absence.

Nepharious snorted and blew through lips loose and slack with sleep, as the cloud of infinitesimal figures burst over head. Rain whipped horizontally across the ground, and his already broken feather was battered about even more. The slippers which he had sculpted into a curved point were dragged down by the weight of the bells.

He rose with a sharp cry, arrowing into the heavens, the trembling rug still clutched in his hands. The jinn darted this way and that, wrestling with the rug which had plastered itself across his person, until Nepharious wrested it from his flank and held it over his head.

His fury was such that he expanded to a great height until his head protruded from the clouds. Nepharious searched his sleep-drugged brain for a spell to dynamite this squall to kingdom come, and the rug dodged from its place above his head to tie itself round his fingers. The spell died on his lips as he noticed for the first time that this strange cloud formation seemed to be made up of teeny, tiny people.

Elementals!

The jinn recoiled and the carpet, wiser than its master, hauled him swiftly away from danger. The laughing fairies trailed in his wake as he trudged, disheartened, through the desert – his scrap of carpet slung over his shoulders. His feet went squelch, squelch, squelch across the wet sand.

The genie was soaked clear through to the skin, and no enchantment would remove this water, for not even the most skilled jinn could overpower elemental wrath. Neither could the finest carpet fly through an elemental maelstrom.

Out of the corner of his eye, he could see the flickering forms of water and air. As wet as he was, Nepharious could no longer think of the words of the spell that would spirit him away from his position, and none of his incantations would deflect their magical assault.

The twittering fay folk teased at his turban until it tipped jauntily upon his proud bald head. They unravelled it several times before he tired of rewinding it and it now slithered behind him like a blood-red snake.

Wind tickled his side and water splashed at his cheek. The jinn swatted ineffectually at them. The rug quivered and quaked, afraid for itself and its master. Jinns were not known for their charitable temper, and Nepharious's choler had been tried to the limit already today. Sooner or later, the jinn might cut loose with a curse which was bound to bounce off the elementals and back on him. So the rug clung to the genie and prayed to whatever gods rag-rugs normally petition for protection.

It need not have bothered, for Nepharious's mind was engaged in more practical pursuits – his brain busy trying to recollect the name of the weird device he had once seen in the far north. An odd accoutrement with a central column and cloth attached to wires that radiated outwards from the support, like spokes on a wheel. When opened, the cloth was pulled taut and the pale northerners looked like pixies carrying mushrooms on their heads. But it would hold off the rain.

He rifled through memories. *Bumber . . . umber . . . umbrella! That was it.*

The jinn halted. His brow wrinkled as he tried to imagine an umbrella, right down to the smallest detail. His fists and jaw clenched with the effort. The muscles on both sides of his neck bulged and his brows dipped down, almost meeting the tip of his nose. The outline of a huge brolly shimmered within the spinning elemental cloud.

Nepharious Hex concentrated harder, and the brolly became more solid. The fairy rain retreated a bit as if making room for its mass. When he could no longer view the faint phantoms of water and air through the device, the genie grunted, and the umbrella fell, dropping on his toes with a heavy thud.

"Ouch!" Nepharious grabbed one foot between his hands and considered drawing a thunderbolt from the cloud to destroy the umbrella. Then he slipped in a puddle mid-hop and landed with a splash on his bottom, nearly biting off his tongue in the process. He counted to ten, reminding himself that the implement was too useful to destroy. It could at least keep him dry.

With that thought, the jinn crept on all fours towards the umbrella and examined his treasure. Nepharious frowned when he realized that the umbrella was closed and he had absolutely no idea how to open it. Keeping a cautious jinn-length from it, he hunkered down on his elbows to study it. After a few soggy moments – when it had neither opened of its own accord nor exploded – Nepharious got brave and stuck his nose between the folds, only to impale a nostril on a wire rod.

It bit!

His head emerged from the cloth, and he swore roundly.

Now why hadn't he pictured one already unfurled, the jinn wondered. There had to be a way to open the thing. He had seen it done. The mechanism was somewhere near here. Gingerly, the jinn clutched the parrot handle and held it away from his body, as though it might nip at him again. Nepharious felt for a hook or a catch, and the parrot-shaped handle did precisely that. It bit him. He dropped it, cradling his injured hand to his chest.

His already ruddy complexion grew even redder with rage, so that the genie's face resembled a parboiled sand-lobster on a plate. He sprang upon the umbrella, seized the parrot handle by the throat and lifted it aloft, brandishing it like a sword. His bejewelled hand shoved at the metal rods and they rose, carrying the cloth with it.

"Aha!" he bellowed triumphantly. "Success!"

Nepharious placed the umbrella strategically over his head. The rug slithered from his shoulders and began inching along the ground away from him.

"Hey, wait!" Nepharious shouted after the rug. "It's just an umbrella, and it works."

He shook it jubilantly.

And the brolly snapped shut, encasing the jinn in an oil-slick shroud, from the tip of his uncoiled, blood-red turban to his now-deflated toes. Air rushed in to pluck at the umbrella.

Water bashed at it. But the best the fay folk could do was ripple the many folds. They swirled round and round their victim. But sealed inside the umbrella, Nepharious was sheltered from their capering taunts and their pinching fingers.

The only problem was . . . he couldn't move!

In his fair face, the Demon King leaned over the deadly magma pit, brooding. As he did, his features began to sag and melt until he was again an amorphous blob whose expressions flittered quickly across a weeping visage. Several eyebrows rose above eyes which were evenly distributed across face, stomach and chest.

His mood had been foul ever since fire had escaped to Earth's plane. Here was the opportunity of a long, bleak eternity. The elements rampaged the length and breadth of Daklha, while *he,* King of Kings, was immured here, forced to work through minions and those human representatives the Devil had on earth, puling and weak mortals whom he had swayed to his cause. He longed to enter the fray directly, but, bound by magic more powerful than that which banned fire from earth's elemental plane, he couldn't.

The demonlord had tried, really *tried,* to slip through time's gates with fire's first incursion, but the spell had held. No mere weakening of the portals would let him through. It would take their total destruction.

His eyes drifted to the burbling pool of lava, detaching themselves from his body, and hovered over the surface so he could get a closer look at the scene within. Fire rode their salamander steeds in a swirling curtain of amber and topaz, carnelian and gold. Hungry flames gobbled greedily at precious wood and fuel. Sand blistered and scorched as the elder Martyr's Bush turned to dust.

The demonlord reached a proud talon into the glowing pool and gave a quick twirl. And water arrived, steamy hot on fire's flickering heels. Not as the soft mists of spring to caress and heal, nor as the season's cyclical showers. It did not fall as Eubonia's gentle rain to freshen and cleanse. Instead it battered the earth, a deluge that split the sky like an angry god. The desert was drenched, and the charred sands transformed into a churning sea.

The Prince's dripping sneer turned to a slithering scowl as seedlings sprouted from the ghostly, sodden remains, releasing their first green shoots and tender roots.

This would never do.

The huge claw moved in ever smaller circles within the bubbling pond, and Satan observed air as it sliced across the land with winds as sharp as a knife. Its usual caress, a blow, like the ungentle kiss of a blade or sting of the whip. The blast dried the sands too soon and those seeds whose roots were ill-formed or whose grip upon the earth was incomplete, were carried away in the gale.

That was more like it!

He reached more hands into the pool and lashed the ruddy liquid into a froth.

The three elements careened into each other, and where fire met water and air, a maelstrom shook the land. Green watery elementals glinted and rippled against the hard brilliance of fire's light. They clashed, and unnatural thunder echoed distantly across the desert. The shrieks of the wounded elementals joined the death cry of the Martyr's Bush. And Daklha became a sweltering steam-bath.

The demonlord's throaty chuckle turned into a guffaw that sounded like claws being drawn across glass. Unwittingly, the elements worked for him, creating Hades on earth. When things got bad enough, the mortals would be easily persuaded; for the great trickster could promise them anything – even the peace they desired – and give them nothing.

The Prince fiddled with a rocky protuberance on the pit's lip, and his perspective changed. The sloughing fiend focused on the quivering infant seraphim and shivered with a mixture of disgust and delight.

Opened by the searing heat of flame, nurtured by rains and then bent by winds, the tree's life cycle usually turns long, was completed in less than a day. If he worked it right, the remaining seedlings would be burned, doused, or drowned, and then fanned none-too-gently dry, so the cycle began anew. That ought to get old Sala's attention, the Demon King thought, and he spun, thumbing his noses in the general direction of the eighth plane.

Here was the ultimate opportunity. If the portals fell, all mortals would eventually perish, and he could harvest those souls without waiting on time's orderly progression. Better still, with the seraphim gone, he, the King of Kings, would be released from the ties that bound him. He could walk abroad upon mortal lands, scything through men and reaping their souls at his leisure.

The demon glowered and his brows oozed down to the tip of his nose in consternation. He could do naught more than what he had done. Not yet. Not now. Even as he watched, another seedling take root as the dim-witted elementals ranged elsewhere across the plane.

Joi Seraphim was no more, but its knowledge,

its purpose, did not die with it. All its learning, wisdom and experience were embraced in the tiny seeds it had hurled to the wind with its passing.

Even as the Demon King watched, a kernel stirred upon the earthen plane. Its belly, bloated from the elemental rain, burst and Joi's son sent its first experimental roots into the blackened soil. It was a slow, arduous process, for the ground had been seared almost to glass. But, like the rest of its kind, the little creature was patient, and at this point in its life cycle, optimistic.

Oblivious to the hateful eye of Satan that glared at its reflection in a far plane, it dug and jabbed, delved and bored, exploring the parched earth, trying to find purchase. With a single serpentine tendril it drilled relentlessly. Slowly, the thin sheet of obdurate obsidian gave way. Breaking to bits. Until at long last the root cracked the crystalline crust beyond the Miasmic circle and found the nourishment it needed to blossom and grow.

Chapter 7

The constant splatter of water and the whisper of air ceased. They had departed, leaving the irate jinn to simmer within the suffocating folds of the brolly. Nepharious repeated the names of a thousand plagues, a thousand demons, a thousand banes, a thousand blights and a thousand curses, and was down to reciting the list of a thousand "nasty, but not really fatal" hexes, when fire approached. The rug, with remarkable instinct for self-preservation, buried itself in the wet sand as the elementals devoured the cloth. Then starting at the melancholy toes of his slippers and going up to the tip of his crimson turban, flame consumed every scrap of material on the jinn's body, blistering no small amount of flesh.

By the time they withdrew, Nepharious was stark naked and so tightly encased in the hot metal cage that he could neither waggle his fingers nor wiggle his ears, a necessary part of jinn sorcery, in order to magick up a pair of trousers or even a discreet fig-nut leaf. He would have liked to turn himself into a cloud of smoke and blow away, but Nepharious had slept through that particular lesson in jinn school. Like shrinking, he'd never quite mastered it. Thus, the genie was destined to pop in and out of places, with an occasional announcing thunderclap, which any babe could do, rather than arriving in a theatrical cloud of smoke.

Trapped, Nepharious rattled his cage furiously as the parrot-beak handle chuckled at his discomfort, and the irate genie swore on his grandfather's south-sea lamphold and old ancestral home that if he could do nothing else, at least he could kill the next elemental he met.

The sun hovered indecisively in the sky as the first moon peered hesitantly over the horizon. The shimmering magical mirror blended perfectly with the twinkle of tentative starlight upon the still radiant sands. Zelia nodded her approval. Their encampment was guarded from prying mortal eyes.

The maid glanced askance at Ares, and then at the camp's perimeter which reflected the sands beyond. She pivoted, facing each point of the compass in turn.

Ares looped his arms loosely across his chest, watching her. "Something bothering you?"

She blew through puffed cheeks. "Surely, there is something we could *do*." She indicated with a quick dip of her head some unseen place, far beyond the warded circle. "I can't stand this, cooling our heels here while fire, air and water run loose upon the land."

Ares dug at the sand with a booted foot. "I wouldn't exactly call this cool."

"You know what I mean."

"What would you suggest? You tried to coax them back to their home planes. They will not listen. Now that it's begun, they are intent on their fairy rade. Their war is more important than any potential harm they can do to us."

"My *shadow*," she emphasized the word, "walked the ley to talk to them. Perhaps if we approached them directly . . ."

"You mean to go there? What about all this?" He motioned towards the camp where the women worked with typical speed and efficiency. *Yurtis* sprouted from the ground like deformed toadstools – the many tents having been repaired as well as time would permit. Some were oddly misshapen as two disparate tents were joined, so that a boxy square jutted from the onion-shaped cone.

"We can only go so fast. We have the others to think of," he reminded her gently.

"*We* have other ways, you know that."

"You mean . . ."

She nodded.

"And if we misjudge? We could find ourselves in the midst of flame, roasting like a sausage?"

"Or we could find ourselves lashed by wind and rain. What of it?" Zelia swung with a clanking of healer's bells. "We've got to try."

"You won't give me a moment's peace until we do, will you?" he said. "Oh, very well, give me your hand."

"Wait a second." Zelia closed her eyes and let her mind drift, flitting free and seeking that of her mother's. A gentle breeze stirred her psyche as she encountered another mind doing the same. She reached out to Ares. He took her hand, and the world whirled around them. The hesitant sun was doused, everything went black, and the next thing they knew, they stood hand in hand next to burgeoning madness.

The Lady's second swooped down from his station above the elemental storm.

"Zelia?" Fante zoomed in upon Ares's shoulder

and sat. "I was looking for your mother."

"So was I. She is not here?"

"No." The zephyr drooped, dismayed. "I saw her, just as I was pulled from the portal, but she's gone now."

"We came to see if there was anything we could do." Ares's voice, booming next to the fairy's ear, unsettled it. Fante bolted away, pivoted upon flapping wings to face the adventurer.

"Do? There is naught any can do." He glared at the cyclone of lashing wind, caterwauling water and frantic flame. "I wouldn't tarry if I were you. You could be harmed."

"Perhaps, if we could talk to some representative, in person. Someone in authority."

"Authority!" Fante wheezed laughter. "Do you see any authority or discipline in that?"

Ares continued smoothly. "To cajole or persuade?"

"Persuade," he wailed. "Don't you think I have tried to persuade? No one heeds. Nay, lord and lady, there is nothing for you to do alone, but if you see your mother, would you send her to me? I could use her help. So far I, and those few of air I could petition, have been able to steer them away from human settlements. But the battle frenzy is upon them, and I'm not sure how much longer we can continue."

"Perhaps we can help?" Zelia asked without

real conviction, her eyes went to her hands which were covered with blisters.

"Can you blow like the winds or bluster like a gale? No, my lady, it is not within your power."

She lifted her shoulders in a shrug, just as one of the many squalling elementals noticed her presence. With a crackling war-cry, fire descended upon them as air and water gathered to form a buffer between mortal and flame.

Ares tugged at her hand. "Satisfied?"

"No, not satisfied, but I am convinced. We must follow the course we've set and hope that the goddess Sala can present us with a solution."

And they stepped into nothingness. The warded air around the camp rippled as they materialized again in the desert twilight.

The Lady Hadidge stood as a brooding presence over the women, and who could tell if under the dark burnous she moved. Only the tapping of the lady's sun-darkened toes revealed her impatience, and when that happened, the women around them redoubled their efforts.

The chief wife didn't even blink when the two appeared in the sultry air before her. The woman's eyes narrowed as she regarded Zelia who had replaced her bridal gown with Tocinian leathers rather than the more accepted billowing black robes, but the woman said nothing. Her hand reached out and pulled the princeling to her side. Then the lady ducked her head to her stepdaughter and turned away.

Ares crouched down next to the sheik and started to carve images in the sand. *Sand, sand everywhere,* the adventurer thought. By Og's great hammer he was sick of it.

Zelia walked over to the pile of gathered wood. With a whispered spell, she lighted it, and her father, busy with tinder and flint, leapt back shouting.

Just then the first moon sighted the meandering sun as it slid closer to earth, and the lady moon shot across the sky in hot pursuit. The sun, having reached a sudden decision, dipped towards the horizon.

The sheik nodded at the diminished orb. "The sun loiters on day's edge as Apsu approaches."

The half-elf looked up from the crude stick-figures he had scratched into the earth's breast with his dagger and swept the drawings away.

"Apsu? The devourer?" Ares turned his questioning gaze to Zelia.

"Here on the southern continent, it is believed that Apsu swallows the sun every night, and Sala, the Goddess of Cycles, squeezes her consort until he releases it the following morning. Thus day is restored to man," she said. "Why else do you think Apsu is called the Devourer?"

"I don't know, because he has a hardy appetite?" He stood, brushing grit from his hands. "Come now, Zelia. That's a bunch of superstitious nonsense. Everyone *knows* that the sun hides from the questing sister moons."

The sheik raised a single brow in enquiry.

"The five moons, daughters of Brigitta," Zelia explained, "and wives to the sun."

"Pah," he said. "Is not man ruler in his *terem*? Why would the sun wish to desert his wives? If he needs to run, why marry then? Much easier to banish them. No, Apsu the Devourer causes night to fall, and Sala delivers day. If you do not believe, look." He waved vaguely at the skyline, where orange-red sand mingled with the rays of the fleeing sun. The elf squinted and shrugged.

"Look from above." The sheik pointed at a nearby dune. "Come, I will show you."

The men set off with Zelia bringing up the rear. The hill sloped into a crest, like a wave frozen in time and space. At its peak, the two men halted, and Ares examined the scene with a sharp intake of breath. From this perspective at the summit, Ares could see what he had failed to notice in the trough. There was a pattern to the dunes, the same snaking S-curve he had seen cut into the sand in the wake of a slithering sand serpent.

Zelia stopped beside him. "You see it? It is always like this. Many believe the winds shape the dunes, but the desert dweller knows otherwise."

"But how?" Ares faltered as he studied the twisting trail that seemed to lead straight to the sun, and then, in an instant, all went dark as if the luminary's flame had been snuffed out.

"Wha . . . what happened?"

"Apsu has eaten his fill," the sheik said knowingly. They swung towards the light of the fire and headed back to camp.

"If Apsu swallows the sun each day," Ares said, "then what of the five sisters? Is all that we have learned in northern lands a myth?"

The young maid extended her arm before her, palm upwards. "Who's to say that one is right and the other is wrong?" She placed the other arm before her, hand cupped, and then let them drop and rise, as if she were balancing a scale. "Why must one overrule the other? Don't you think that there is room for more than one explanation on the Earth's plane?"

"But how could both be right?" Ares wondered, musing aloud as the whisper of black silk announced the arrival of dinner.

Bong!

Somewhere on the eighth plane, Apsu's head

recoiled from the strength of his wife's blow.

Bang! Crash!

The frying-pan fell from Sala's mouth.

The serpent god groaned. He spun woozily. He should have known better than to hand her a skillet and suggest a fry-up. She was always a bit touchy when she had a clutch.

"That's all right," Apsu said, backing rapidly away and getting tangled in his own coils. "I've got a touch of heartburn, anyway. I don't think I'm hungry after all."

The great worm belched, rotated and attempted to creep quietly from the room, but Sala, Goddess of Cycles, would have none of it. She eyed the round bulge in his serpentine midriff. Then her head snaked round to count the eggs. While she was so occupied, Apsu lowered his great hooded head to the ground and prepared to make a run for it.

But his wife was not easily duped. Sala leapt, skimming through air, and wrapped great loops round her distraught spouse.

"What . . . *grunt* . . . have . . . *grunt* . . . you . . . *grunt* . . . been eating?" And she began to compress the twined tail round his rotund form. "It's an egg, isn't it? You've been at the clutch again, haven't you?"

"No!" he protested as another coil wrapped itself round him, like swaddling round a babe, until the snake god's entire body below the bulge was encased. Sala squeezed, driving the round ball relentlessly up his gullet towards his mouth.

"I should have listened to my mother," Sala said as she applied a bit more pressure. "My mother told me not to marry any god named Devourer. She said no good would come of it. But I didn't listen. Ooph!" She brought more weight to bear on his protruding stomach.

Apsu swallowed, unwilling to relinquish his hold on the sun. He didn't bother to rebut this oft-repeated complaint, for Apsu knew why the goddess Sala had wed him. Because he was the only other snake god in the entire pantheon of gods who still held sway over mortal imagination. And she, the Mother of Cycles, had wanted it all. A powerful consort and a fellow serpent with whom she could breed.

But Sala hadn't figured on his appetite. None of their young had survived Apsu's nightly raids. It wasn't that he was mean or anything. He couldn't help it; he was just hungry all the time. He wasn't called the Devourer for nothing.

"Come on, come on, cough it up!" Sala's deadly embrace tightened another notch. Breath went out of him with a whoosh.

"It was just a light snack," Apsu shouted, but that was a mistake, for the sun popped from his gaping jaws. For a second, the luminary glowered at the snake, a look of incredulity and betrayal on its blazing face. Sala breathed a sigh of relief, realizing that her eggs were safe. Then she went to wrap herself round her clutch, as the sun scurried off to find another more amenable place to hide.

With the dawning of a new day, Philos shambled across his room to collect the black grimoire from its hidden niche. The Archmage's hand fluttered hesitantly over the book. Did he really want to dabble in black sorcery? Did he really want to bind his power to the Dark Lord?

Then Philos recalled the indignity of the elementals' treatment, and the far deeper injury done to him and the college by the couple whose untrained powers more than rivalled his own, and the magician's resolution hardened. Determined, the Archmage picked up the spellbook, unsheathed it from its protective cloth and began to leaf through the pages. He stopped at a particular page and skimmed it, grunting in satisfaction.

Homonucleus, a recipe . . . His lips moved as he read the ingredients. He could do it if he must, although he wasn't so sure that he would find a wizard willing to act as a sacrifice. Still, there was Mad Thomas or Ampitere, and who would notice them missing? The Archmage snapped the book shut and replaced it upon its pedestal. Then he spun and paced to his wardrobe to rummage about the mythballs, looking for his sombre black robes of excommunication. A splotch of mustard covered the gold-embroidered hammer, symbol of the war god Og. He rang for a servant and a skeleton clattered out of the open closet door and set to work.

A few minutes later, clean and pressed, Philos the Benevolent padded down the empty corridors towards the Grand Hall. The skeleton rattled in his wake. He swept into the room, making a grand entrance, only to discover that the chamber was empty. He'd forgotten that the students had gone on some sort of holiday, and he tried to remember what had happened to cause the college to close so untimely. He paused, relishing the silence and shrugged. Perhaps it was better this way.

With a critical eye, Philos turned to examine the great hall. The huge rafters were festooned, not only with their normal complement of cobwebs, but also with the requisite black cloth of excommunication. Twin effigies, dressed in sorcerer's robes – one painted blue, the other white – hung in the middle of the room. Torches adorned every sconce and tallows burned smokily in the corners. The room was thick with the smell of incense. The shutters were closed against the sun, for according to tradition, heretics live in darkness without ever seeing the light of truth, symbolized by the sun. And likewise, once convicted, they were burned in darkness. Assuming, of course, the accused were present. If not the dummies stood – or in this case, hung – in their stead.

A high-pitched squeal resounded off the walls followed by a series of terrified snorts. The Archmage twirled with a rustle of heavy black cloth, just in time to observe the Grand Inquisitor wrestling a pig through the doorway.

The Archmage's gaze lighted on the swine, draped in apprentice's garb. "What is *that*?"

"That's young Simon. Surely you remember him? The young man who was transmorphed during the brawl at the Cock and Boar."

The Archmage scrutinized the pig. "Looks like he's grown?"

"Yes, he's . . . ah, er . . . fattened up quite nicely," the Inquisitor said, and the porker fixed Prez with a distrustful stare.

"Well, what's he doing here?" the Archmage asked.

"Uh, remember, it takes a minimum of three, sir, to perform the rite," the Grand Inquisitor reminded him gently.

"What about Ampitere?"

"He died last night." The Inquisitor shook his head sadly.

"Oh, yes, I forgot," the Archmage said.

"I didn't realize that you knew."

"Of course, I knew," Philos snapped. "I am Archmage, after all. It is my business to know what goes on within these walls."

The Archmage opened his mouth to ask that Mad Thomas be brought in to make up the quorum and decided against it. The man was too violent and unpredictable. From his place beside the podium, the Inquisitor peered anxiously at Philos, awaiting some sign of approval.

"All right. This will have to do," the Archmage said.

With a sigh, Prez lifted his hands above his head and began to chant the interdict. "Let no law-biding man receive them, feed them, or give them shelter from the night. Let no one, noble or peasant, give them succour."

The Inquisitor swayed in the guttering torchlight while the Archmage blinked away the smoke.

"We name them damned. Damned by all the gods. Damned and heretic." The Inquisitor's arms flailed in the ceremonial gesture of anathema. The blue-black sleeves decorated with gilt fell back to reveal wraith-thin arms, for

Prez was by nature a nervous man.

"Let them find no rest under the seven planets and the five moons. Curse the food they drink, the ground upon which they walk, and any home where they lay their heads."

The effigies rocked with a shrill *skriegh* and Philos snickered humourlessly.

With a worried glance at the Archmage, the Inquisitor continued with the sentence. "For their heresies, they are branded heretic and will be burned in absentia, until such time when sorcery's righteous wrath may find them." His eyes rested upon the sacks of straw that hung from the ceiling. His normally full-rich baritone faltered as he spoke the final words. "May the fire consume the candle flame of their spirits even as their effigies are consumed upon the pyre."

The Archmage and the Inquisitor thrust their torches at the images, and the straw ignited with a roar.

"And once consumed," the Inquisitor continued, "may the light of their spirit be extinguished." With a whisper of heavy cloth, Prez's arms dropped and every flame in the room, save the two burning images, was doused.

Fidhl's expression was grim. The eunuch regarded the Matriarch as she marched, agitated, across the room. The crystalline cloth clattered and the cacophonous chatter of bells rang shrilly.

"Of all the foolish, stupid, idiotic," she paused unable to find the words. "This is twice now. Twice!"

Fidhl nodded. He could count.

"What does Philos hope to prove?" she asked. "His own absurdity? First they're named heretic. Then they're heroes. Now they're heretics again. The wizards make themselves appear ridiculous."

Fidhl tried to calm her. "They reason, quite correctly, that Ares and Zelia are the cause of the current problems that plague Daklha. If there had been no wedding . . ." The assistant left the sentence unfinished.

"There wasn't a wedding! Besides, I think all mortals – and that includes Ares and Zelia – were whisked away before any of this happened. How can they be blamed?" The Matriarch rotated on the ball of her foot ready to make another circuit of the room. "Sweet Brigitta, don't they know that only Zelia with her elemental blood can possibly hope to handle her fay cousins?"

"Reverend Mother, you really shouldn't excite yourself." He tapped his chest meaningfully.

"Not excite myself! My second and heir is convicted of heresy and sentenced to the stake for the second time in less than a year, and you say I shouldn't excite myself? Fire rages across the southern continent, with water and air following quickly upon its heels, and I shouldn't excite myself?"

The high priestess of Brigitta spun. Her crystal cloak swirled about her catching the light of the sun and it bounced around the room in laughing prisms of colour. The irritated Matriarch swung to begin another revolution when a faint breeze blew down the chimney. It caught the ash upon the cold grate and sent it outwards in a billowing cloud.

The wind intensified, although Fidhl noted that not so much as a breath stirred the trees outside the walls of the crystal chamber. The cloud rotated, reeling around the chamber like a drunken dust devil. Fidhl stepped back and frantically tried to brush the soot from his robes. The Matriarch stood still and stared expectantly at the hearth.

There was a soft plop. Fidhl looked up from his soot-streaked chest, and another puff of ash swelled from which a delicate sneeze emanated. A small figure rose from amongst the ashes, its features made solid by a dark coat of grime.

The airy elemental coughed and smaller clouds of black joined the first, to parade around the room.

"My lady." The Matriarch curtsied, and the figure shot up to flit around the room surrounded by a dusty nimbus of soot.

Fidhl felt a tickle in his nose, and someone beside him sneezed. The stunned assistant turned to behold himself holding a handkerchief to his nose. The Matriarch grimaced and looked decidedly green.

Something droned beside his ear, and Fidhl's head pivoted on his neck so that he stared eye to eye with a faintly human image of the airy queen.

The Matriarch moved up closer to the lady. The soot-blackened features brightened for a second as the fay creature recognized Brigitta's priestess.

"Zelia?" Lady Astra asked in a voice like the wind whispering through the cracks of an old house on a winter's day. Then her face fell as she realized her daughter was not there. The fairy fluttered to and fro distractedly.

"No, Zelia's not here. She is in Daklha," the Matriarch said.

The lady bobbed slightly and vanished.

Flying through time's portals, a bedraggled Lady Astra zipped past the broken fountain of her home. The audience of earth elementals had thinned. Those that remained were frozen in the various postures of rising – some in a semi-squat, others with a cumbersome leg half-lifted.

Ignacious's voice still resounded in the background, but his speech had advanced smartly. "WEEEEEE."

And she zoomed on.

The column moved swiftly through a deep clough. None of the normal mutters and murmurs was apparent. Even Ares's and Zelia's rough banter was hushed, for the goatherd's son had arrived today. The enemy had been spotted and was coming up fast from the south. So they hurried along, eager to pass the border into Abdha where they hoped the rebels wouldn't follow.

The sheik nodded at the couple. Ares and Zelia approached from their assigned position two steps behind him.

"Round that dune, I believe, is Abdha."

Ares glanced about him at the sand and grimaced. "How can you tell?"

"See that outcrop of rock." The sheik pointed, and Ares had to squint to distinguish between one bit of orange-red matter from another, but now that he was concentrating, he saw it and his elfin eyes discerned something else standing close by.

"And what's that next to it?" he asked.

"Next to it? The rock?" The sheik shook his head. "It's hard enough for me to see the boulder itself, even though I have travelled this route before and know what I am looking for."

Ares's pupils contracted as his eyes widened in shock, for his sensitive vision perceived radiant magic. "I don't know what it is, but I think we should approach it cautiously."

So saying, the adventurer extracted his war-hammer from his belt and glided silently away as Zelia pulled the firemaker's wand from her pocket and followed. When they rounded the curve of the dune they found themselves facing the flat salt plain of Abdha. It was graced here and there with huge outcrops of granite and shale.

Leading the way, Ares slunk with typical stealth from one shallow shadow to another. Zelia flitted after him. They paused, side by side, to draw breath, and then as if on cue, both plunged into the harsh light, weapons ready. Zelia nearly dropped the wand as they were confronted with the image of a spitting, sputtering and fuming jinn neatly caged in the skeletal frame of an umbrella.

Clinging tenaciously to its tiny hole in the hard-crust that had once been a swamp, Joi II went about the business of growing. An ambitious enterprise in such a hostile environment. A single tap root dug deep, keeping it anchored firmly to earth, and the seraphim produced its first experimental shoot as two teensy leaves unfurled coyly just a hairbreadth above the ground.

Like any other plant at this stage of its evolution, the seraphim was green. It had yet to develop the hard spiky shell that would later shelter it from the sun. Eventually it would be encased in a coat of spines that would protect it from most grazing animals – except the dung-camel which, it was said, could eat almost anything, even glass – and provide it with just enough of the sun's warmth for it to thrive.

A mere sprout, its leaves were meant to reap the full benefit of the sun's rays while all its energies were bent upon strengthening its roots' grip upon the soil. For it was through this rocky instrument that Joi conversed with its fellows. Through it, the seraphim sensed the acceleration of time's cycles, even though the surrounding land was at rest. Elsewhere in Daklha, the seasons advanced at dizzying speeds. The seraphim sensed their passage in the terror that was communicated back to Joi from its brethren as they expired.

Goaded by urgency, life's force surged through it, and Joi shivered and stretched as two more leaves unfolded, reaching for the desert sky.

Sala reeled around her diminished clutch, tail clenched between her lips. As the cycles hastened across the mortal plane, the goddess was caught up by the relentless whirl.

Apsu coiled next to the door – a legless mess. Any moment now, he'd be asking for breakfast, and despite the dance thrust upon her by earth's accelerated cycles, she struggled valiantly to keep the eggs within the protective circle.

Sala rotated one more time and stopped. The goddess lifted a giddy head above her clutch to peer cross-eyed at the nest.

"Thisss iss ridiculousssss," she sputtered, swayed and passed out.

Confronted with the furiously jiggling jinn and his quaking rug, Zelia had to bury her face in Ares's shoulder to stifle the giggle that tickled at the back of her throat and threatened to erupt out loud. The jinn were renowned for their peevish temper, and it would not do to irritate him any more than he was already. The genie spat vile oaths in her direction which fell impotently to earth, for jinn magic was propelled with waggling fingers and wiggling ears; not easily accomplished when immobilized by a wire frame.

Ares raised a quizzical brow and began to question her, but she shook her head no.

"May your blood boil in your veins, and your body turn to powder and dust," the genie ranted. "May a thousand dung-camels sit in your soup!"

Zelia rolled her eyes towards the heavens.

"May all your children be blue!" The jinn fumed.

"Hey, let's not get personal," Ares said, fingering his war-hammer.

"Personal! Personal! I've been soaked by elemental rains, buffeted by elemental winds and singed by elemental fire. My finest clothes have been ruined by water and mud, and, as if that wasn't enough, then they are consumed by fire and turned to ash. Elementals everywhere. More elementals than you can shake a stick at. And now you!" He glared at Zelia. "You can't fool me. I recognize a fairy whelp when I see one. If I were free, I'd, I'd . . ."

"But you're not free, are you." Zelia pointed out. "And you're not likely to get free as long as you're hurling threats in all directions."

This gave the genie a moment's pause, and his voice when he next spoke was a little more civil. "So, what do you want, changeling? To come back and gloat?"

"As a matter of fact, no. You merely lie in our path between here and where we want to go," Zelia said.

Ares, who stood back to assess the jinn, spoke, "And seeing how you are sufficiently preoccupied, we'll just leave you to it and get along our way." He pulled at Zelia's sleeve and began to herd her back the way they came.

"You can't leave me like this." The jinn's voice took on a whining quality.

"Why don't you just turn yourself into smoke?" Zelia suggested.

The genie blushed and would have hung his head in shame if he had not been so constrained.

"And why should we free you?" Ares added. "You've already revealed yourself as hostile to myself and my lady."

"But, but," the genie stuttered. His voice broke.

"I think we should lead the *terem* women around this spot. They would find your attire, or lack of it, quite shocking," Ares said. "You really should dress yourself, master jinn. You might get nasty sunburn."

Zelia winced as the jinn began a ritual curse even nastier than the ones that had preceded it. She dodged behind the outcrop of rock, dragging her lover with her, sure that the genie would find a way to make his hexes stick. When nothing happened, the blue maid peeked out from behind the boulder and tilted her head to one side speculatively. Ares, who knew the half-elemental well, groaned inwardly. That look spelled trouble. She crawled out from behind their shelter and knelt at the genie's feet.

"We have been unkind. I can see you have been pushed beyond endurance by my fay cousins, and I apologize. I am sure my partner and I can find something for you to wear within our stores. It may not be as grand as the clothing you are used to, but it would fulfil modesty's needs." The girl considered the jinn. "I'm not sure, though, how such apparel would stand up against sudden expansion, so you would have to keep your temper in check. Do you think you can do that?"

The jinn stopped mid-jinx, his tirade arrested, and he blinked at her. He sniffed disdainfully. "I can magick up my own clothes. Once," his face took on a crafty expression, "you have bent back a wire or two."

"I'm afraid, we cannot do that, oh esteemed jinn," Zelia purred softly.

"And why not?" The genie deigned to look affronted.

"For then I would loose a finger and you would have magic at your disposal. As my partner here has already pointed out, you have very eloquently described what you would do to me and my kith and kin if I freed you." Zelia lifted her hand in a conciliatory manner. "What guarantee do I have you would not harm us? Better that I dress you myself to save the maidenly eyes of the *terem* women."

"No! Don't leave me!" the jinn pleaded. He hesitated a moment and then said, "Three wishes! What if I grant you three wishes? I can't very well kill you until you've used them, now can I?"

"Four," countered Ares, always one to drive a hard bargain.

"Sorry, only three per customer. Guild regulations, you see," the jinn explained.

Ares nodded, familiar with the rigidity of guild rules. "All right, three. What do you think, Zelia? Fair enough?"

Zelia marched around the strange cage with its wicked parrot-beak handle. "It doesn't look like it will be easy. How about three wishes each?"

"Sorry, guild rules cover your entire group," the genie stated unequivocally.

Zelia recoiled. "One condition then," she said.

"Condition? You would put conditions on me!" The jinn tried to expand in wrath, but only succeeded in digging the metal frame deeper into his flesh.

Ares hauled her aside to parley. "Hey, don't blow it now by putting on conditions. This could be quite useful."

"Agreed, but you don't know the jinn like I do. They are noted for their trickery. If this covers all of us, all it's going to take is one of the women wishing her rump didn't hurt so much, a goatherd wanting water changed into wine, or whatever, and the wishes are gone."

"I see what you mean. OK, go for it." He

inclined his head in a nod of approval. They sidled back to the jinn.

"The conditions I speak of would not be placed on you, but on me. Or us rather," Zelia said. "The only wishes granted must come from our lips. Either Ares, here." She pointed at Ares to make sure there was no misunderstanding. "Or mine."

The genie glared at her.

"Oh yes, and your name," she added, knowing that a genie could be controlled by his name.

"My name! Why should I give my name to some half-breed peasant?" he spat.

"Because how are we to call you without it, and we won't free you unless you do." She folded her arms across her chest and pondered the jinn for a moment. "Come to think of it, I don't believe any of the clothes we have would fit you. Perhaps you were right, Ares, we should get on our way. Sorry we couldn't come to some agreement."

Both turned their back on him and Zelia hoped fervently that the genie didn't have a stray enchantment or two that could be flung without benefit of fingers.

"No wait! Wait!" the jinn shouted. "All right. All right! You win. It's Nepharious, Nepharious Hex."

Zelia spun. "Not Hex. Not one of *the* Hexes."

"You've heard of us?" the genie preened.

And next to her, Ares hissed. "You've heard of them?"

She waved both questions away with a dismissive gesture. Touching forehead, lips and chest, Zelia bowed deeply.

"Pleased to make your acquaintance," she said.

"I'm sure," said Nepharious.

"If we are going to free you from such a," Zelia repressed a snigger, "demon, my affianced and I must confer."

The adventurer followed her as she skirted around the stone and stared at her. "What was all that about? You know him?"

"Not really, but genies are rare, and all of them are proud of their heritage, thinking their lineage the finest. With the jinn, flattery doesn't hurt. It can keep them in line. Now he'll think that I'm a friend of the family."

"So how should we get him out of there?" Ares asked.

"I don't know. I don't like the look of that beak. It's a thing of magic and I wouldn't be at all surprised if it took a leg off if we got too close."

Ares strode back to the umbrella frame until he stood within two arms' length of the cruel, curved parrot beak. He studied the wood. She followed at a safe distance.

"Heartwood, don't you think?" he asked.

"Well, yes, most likely," she mumbled. "But I don't see what that has to do with it . . ."

"And," Ares said, "if it is heartwood it still lives, even though severed from the bush, so perhaps if we can find its wooden heart . . ." With a quick flick of his wrist, the dagger concealed in his sleeve appeared in his hand.

The parrot handle squawked, released its hold on the unfortunate genie and flew away, with a great flapping of metal ribs and a steely rattle.

"Well, genie," Ares began, but Nepharious disappeared in a barrage of invectives. "Hey, wait! What about our three wishes?" the adventurer shouted after him, but Zelia silenced him.

"Let him go! He's in a bit of a temper. We'll get our three wishes. It's union rules. But I think it would be better for all of us if he vents his spleen somewhere else."

Her gaze drifted to the cloud of dust that rose in the south. The new pretender drew near.

Thumbing in that general direction, Ares said, "Don't you think we'd better get a move on."

She glanced up. "Well, we should at least get the rest of the group over the border. They won't follow here."

"Why not?"

"Rules of warfare. If a sheik flees his land

rather than fight, he has, in essence, abdicated. There's no need to follow him here."

"Does your father know?"

"Of course, he knows," she said. "It's a matter of priorities. Which is the greater threat, the loss of the portals or the loss of his tribe which is, in fact, already lost?"

Ares shrugged. "Strange people the Shamir."

"Not strange, practical." Zelia swung to survey the terrain, frowning. "Funny, I don't remember all those rocks being here before."

"You've been here?" Ares asked.

"Only once when I was very young. My father brought me when he came as ambassador of the Emir to negotiate the Treaty of Girth with the Supreme Sultan of Abdha. The boundary between the two nations was set, and the boulder brought in from the fjords of Firth to mark it. Up until that time the only way to tell where the border lay was by counting the number of dunes, which were forever shifting."

"You mean you imported a rock?"

"Do you see many rocks around you?" She glowered at the many boulders that had seemingly appeared from nowhere. "Until now, I mean."

"I can't say that I have seen any before this," he conceded her point.

"That's because there aren't any besides the

standing stones." She examined the rocky plain. "Notice how they are all leaning in the direction of the Miasmic Swamp, as if they're hurrying to get there."

The adventurer's pupils narrowed to a thin line. Zelia touched him and his eyes came back into focus. "I notice something else, too." Ares paused. "Ripples of magic radiating from each stone."

Her lips formed a small "o".

"We'd, uh, better make sure no one takes it into their mind to carve anything on any of the native—"

"Or not so native," Zelia corrected.

"—rocks," he completed his sentence as if she hadn't spoken.

"Yes, I'd hate to have one of those bearing down on me in a fit of pique."

On the far northern continent of Eubonia, with its three major portals, the fabric of magic that normally came in manageable seepages from the other planes had been torn asunder. The sorcery students – reluctantly brought back from their extended holiday – suddenly discovered that their powers were enhanced. A simple spell of illusion became the real thing. A major enchantment ran uncontrolled and the monsters they had created raged on the streets of Thessalia.

Its mayor, Thesbos, reacted true to kind. He hid under his bed, until someone dragged him to his offices. Then he hid under his desk. The city offices were in a state of seige as angry citizens clamoured for relief, only to be crowded out by enchantments run rampant. City Hall was running on a skeletal staff, kindly lent by the college after the students returned. The skeletons were no longer needed on campus, but the Archmage had found, much to his dismay, that the former magicians were reluctant to return to the graves after this brief taste of "afterdeath".

They intended to stay, even if they had to stay in servitude.

To further confuse the issue, the dreams of normal citizens came to life, and strange fairy-like creatures of magic gambolled with beasts no *conscious* mind would ever conjure. This effect undulated outwards in an ever-widening band, radiating from the circles until the port city of Abruzzi was influenced and beyond it, the lands of Ticino and Uri. Reports filtered in from Norvon and Szatmar that the north was similarly affected.

News from Hamadan, Quattara and Shamir was bleak, and bulletins few. Philos gave Prez a knowing smile when a skittering student announced a visitor from the Hamadan court of

Nuf'sed. The Archmage's lunatic leer widened as if he were pleased to have his predications confirmed.

"It's insanity," the herald, Hamadan's court mage, panted. "We have been lucky. Except for a stray one or two, the elementals have left us pretty much alone, but our spies in Shamir say they're turning north. And that seems to be confirmed because more and more have been sighted in our territory. Right now they come in dribs and drabs, but soon they will arrive in a great tidal wave that will destroy the farmlands, and then Daklha – all of Daklha – will be lost, for it is the irrigated fields of Hamadan that feed the continent."

The magician, clad in strange southron robes, wheezed, "Furthermore, everywhere an elemental tarries, seen or unseen, time leaks out and the planes dribble through, a trickle at first and then a torrent. Hence a man may stride down the street only to find out it's yesterday, or meet himself hurrying away from an appointment he has yet to keep. Commerce is in chaos. The law courts have ground to a halt, not sure whether it is appropriate to prosecute a man who was, by some bizarre quirk of time, convicted yesterday for a crime that will not be committed until tomorrow. It's hopeless."

Prez and Philos nodded in unison. They too

had witnessed similar effects here in Thessalia.

"I do not know if the sea will contain it. There are other portals, other doors. Who's to say that when the food and fuel of Daklha are consumed they won't slip through . . ." the mage let the thought dangle. "You think you have it bad now with dreams coming to life and minor illusions turning real. Wait until you bend to a task only to find it already done, or still worse find yourself doing it now! I tell you, you don't know whether you are coming or going. My master is up to his navel in dancing girls because I unwittingly cast the same spell three times. Mind you, I don't say he's complaining, but the expenditure of power has exhausted me, and I won't be able to conjure up so much as a wraith for the next month.

"So I thought I'd leave the court at Nuf'sed and come here to warn you before the sultan took it into his head to replace me," the mage concluded, mumbling at his feet.

Philos opened his mouth to speak, but was interrupted by the rambling wizard. "I'm a nervous wreck, and feel lucky that I escaped with my head still firmly clamped to my shoulders." With those words, his hands darted to his temples and felt about to make sure that this statement was indeed correct. "Look at me." He held out a hand which quivered like a dying bird. Then the mage dropped to his knees and seized the Archmage's gnarled fist between his own. "You've got to help us. Surely somewhere there is a spell that will send the elements back where they belong."

"Ah, well, yes, I can see you are overwrought. Perhaps you should retire so that the Grand Inquisitor and I can discuss this. Simon," Philos turned and spoke to the pig who now wore specially made robes of apprentice blue. The Archmage had got rather fond of his former pupil in the past few rotations. The pig didn't talk back the way the other apprentices did.

The swine grunted.

"Why don't you take our esteemed colleague to the guest wing so that he can rest?"

Simon gave a quick duck of his warty head.

As the pig waddled past the Grand Inquisitor, Prez bent over and whispered in a porcine ear. "I think you ought to try to keep him as far away from the student wing as possible. No point in subjecting him to their experiments."

The swine snorted his contempt before shambling from the room, the trembling wizard trailing behind.

Philos spun on the Grand Inquisitor. "See! See! I told you! I told you that those two were no good. Now look what has happened."

And he swept from the room to storm through

the halls, righteous in his wrath. With a sigh, the Inquisitor darted after his superior, to keep a close eye on the raving Archmage, who, in this state of mind, was as bad as all the escaped spells combined.

The Archmage rubbed his hands together and cackled. If this worked, he could raise armies of undead who would answer to none other but him. Philos circled the body of old Ampitere. A gaping hole had been opened in the desiccated corpse.

And there were intestines everywhere.

Bushy brows met across a scowling face as the wizard looked from the recipe to the corpse. There had to be some kind of mistake. No matter how many ways he rearranged them. They just wouldn't fit.

"Intestines!" he said, vexed. They were really overrated as far as Philos was concerned. Some priests said they could see the future in them, read them like a book. It was an untidy business. Personally, the Archmage doubted the assertion. They looked like just so much junk to the Archmage, and no map to the future.

Undaunted, the wizard rolled up his sleeve. He would try one last time.

The Prince of Darkness rubbed his hands. They stuck together.

Within the mirror, the tiny specks of insignificant life fled before the storm. A tiny zephyr preceded the roiling mass of elementals, pleading unsuccessfully with them to turn aside from the puling mortals in their path. Satan chuffed.

On command the scenes shifted and changed as the Quattarean took to the sea on their great slave ships. Many of the free tribes happily gave themselves into servitude for a place aboard a boat, any boat, that would carry them away from Daklha. The great horses of Shamir stampeded across the land, their herdsmen barely able to keep abreast of their beasts, and many a fine steed was lost. The pool slipped into a scanning mode and the King of Kings viewed stripped, fire-blackened bones, a silent testament to elemental destruction.

Yet fire's rage seemed to be burning out.

Certainly, Daklha's scarce vegetation wouldn't feed them for long, and the fiery creatures' attention was already starting to wane. The demonlord could not, would not, let this happen. Fire must remain on the mortal plane long enough for one more jaunt through the Martyr's Brush. Until that time . . .

The Prince of Darkness glowered at the cowering seraphim, and then fell light gleamed in his eyes. Another quick twiddle of the protruding rock; the scene changed and fire appeared, dazzling hot and streaked with scarlet. Satan stooped so that his head was submerged in the pit of boiling lava, and he began to whisper to far-flung fire.

He spoke of the cities, bastions of bureaucracy. Of vast tomes and weighty records that kept the governments running. Papers on top of papers on top of papers. He murmured soft seductive phrases. Libraries. Wood. Books!

In Hades' dark region, all that could be heard was a soft, *glug, glug, glug,* as bubbles surfaced in the deadly pond, but on earth, the pyramid of fire paused mid-cavort. Within the surging mass, tiny ears pricked and listened. Then the myriad of flickering flames turned *en masse,* heading in the direction of the nearest city.

The Prince of Darkness withdrew not one but several heads, like Brimstone's Dragons. Each mouth opened and roared with laughter. One small part of his plans had been implemented. He had bought time. Now, how to ensure they turned back to the desert once glutted and replete with the vast paperwork of bureaucracy's red tape?

Viscous fingers drummed against the glass, and Satan was aware of the ball that he clasped in his hand for the first time. Repugnant light battered at the glass. As a pet, Satan thought, the former sorcerer left a lot to be desired. Even that foolish jester was more entertaining, but maybe the wizard would prove useful after all. With that idea in mind, the Demon King gave the ball a mighty heave, tossing it through Hades' Gate to Fire's elemental plane. The Prince of Darkness twittered as it shattered on an outcrop of yellow brimstone. The dark slime of Queb's evil sizzled, evaporated into a darkening cloud and slunk away in a thin black stream.

The demonlord grimaced his farewell, aware that it was not enough. What happened if the thing was too witless to make its way back to the mortal plane, or still worse, if it – like himself – was exiled for all eternity?

And he knew better than to trust the idiot Philos; he could prove to be as weak and insipid as his forebear, Queb. The demonlord recognized that he needed a little insurance.

"Oh, Pun. Come here, Pun," Satan crooned with a gooey, sweet voice.

The imp was bent nearly double, testing the last appendages to be replaced to make sure they worked properly. At the sound of Satan's call, he jumped out of his skin. The demonlord glared at him.

"Pull yourself together," he snapped at the imp.

Compliantly, Pun slipped back into his epidermis the way a mortal would don a cloak or a coat.

"I have a little job for you," the archfiend said.

The Archmage scuttled sideways, hugging the walls. He'd been trying to lose that nosy Inquisitor ever since he'd left his secret laboratory that morning. Philos had noted the jet-black robes of Inquisition in the classroom as the Archmage lectured on the Ethics of Wizardry. The same dark shadow fluttered in the background as Philos ate his noon meal in the dining hall, and he'd even noticed the flick of black cloth in the gardrobe. Of all places!

There was a faint rustle of movement, like the scraping of stone against stone. The Archmage gasped and whirled, ready to reprimand the Inquisitor, when an imp – wearing a ridiculous hat of bells and an even more ludicrous expression which the Archmage presumed was supposed to be menacing – lurched forward. The creature held a human thigh bone, almost as large as himself. Tucked under his arm was a scroll. The Hades' shade unrolled it with a flourish.

"I understand you are trying to do foul magic," the imp said, businesslike despite its absurd attire.

Walking crab-wise, Philos moved from the tenebrous shadows to stand next to the imp. The Archmage examined the parchment, which appeared to be made of human skin.

"According to the Demonic Code, no evil sorcery can take place without the proper contractual agreement." A huge hat-pin materialized in the air before them. The imp seized it and jabbed the wizard before Philos had a chance to react.

"Ow!" he yelled.

"Sign here." The imp proffered the dripping pin as a pen.

The Archmage's eyes glittered, two brittle points of madness in the gloomy corridor. He scratched his name on the dotted line without even glancing at the text. He was a busy mage; he didn't have time to quibble about fine print.

The creature saluted, thunking himself roundly on the head with the scroll, gave the magician an impish grin and vanished.

Philos shuffled on, intent on continuing his experiments.

All these disturbances! The wizard halted, turned back to where the imp had disappeared and frowned. It was difficult – not to mention distasteful – enough to gather the bits he needed for the homonucleus, without that idiot Inquisitor tagging along everywhere or demons popping out at you after each turn.

Already, Philos had had to brave the students' shower to get the essential nail parings, hair and flakes of sorcerous flesh. The recipe called for such. And the Archmage fervently hoped that the spell would allow a loose definition of the term sorcerer, because no master worth an amulet would leave anything so precious behind.

Some of the items were too disgusting to think about. For these he used the swine Simon, whom he had conscripted as assistant. The pig had proved himself an efficient subordinate.

The remaining ingredients promised to be even more onerous. A cadaver, for instance. Ampitere had had the consideration to expire, but the first experiment was a failure. Now he needed another body, and few wizards were willing to lay down and die before their time, no matter how worthy the cause.

Mad Thomas would not be missed, but Philos gathered, rightly, that Mad Thomas was a little too healthy to pass over naturally and too robust to allow himself to be helped along the way. Fortunately, the recipe didn't seem to require a wizard's corpse – any old cadaver would do – but even these were in short supply. Magicians didn't have much cause to keep bodies around.

The Archmage paused next to a door to stare at the purple face of the fourth moon.

Entrails were another problem. Although intestines were stock in trade for certain visceral enchantments, usually chicken or goat were sufficient to fill the college's meagre needs. As with bodies, most wizards – and most humans, too – were reluctant to give up bits of themselves that they could still use.

The Archmage paced. The stinking swine, still wallowing in the glory of being chosen as Philos's assistant, tangled in his robes. Philos kicked at it. Simon's curly tail straightened and he rushed headlong into the night, squealing. The Archmage followed his flight as the pig made a bee-line for the . . . Healers' College.

"Aha!" Of course, why hadn't he thought of it before? Now he knew how to solve his dilemma. All of them. Body, parts and all.

"Oh, Simon," he crooned in an oily voice,

"Simon, here piggy, piggy, piggy, piggy." And the wizard hastened across the courtyard in pursuit of the swine.

There was a metallic clatter and a muffled bang. A dustbin was upset beyond the carved crystal walls that formed the herbarium of the Healers' College. The Matriarch gazed in the sacred fountain of Brigitta where she was confronted by the rippling face of the Archmage as he rummaged through rubbish.

"What the—" The Matriarch raised her head with a muted tinkle of her ornate head-dress. She crept to the door. Exquisitely-wrought chains adorned the woman's wrists and ankles, and, hanging from the golden links, were tiny chimes which pealed tremulously with each motion.

The figure silhouetted against the crystal wall froze. The Matriarch sprung, flinging herself through the door. "Caught you!"

The Archmage cringed, throwing his hands up to conceal his face. Then he collected himself, stuffed his hands in his pockets and began to whistle nonchalantly. Finally, as if noticing her for the first time, he looked up.

"Lovely night, isn't it," he said.

"Just what do you think you are doing out here, rooting about in temple rubbish?" she asked archly.

"I was just looking for my pig."

"Your what?"

"Pig. Swine. You know, *sus scrofum*."

"I haven't the vaguest idea what you are talking about."

"Oh, you know, you *must* remember him, the apprentice that got turned into a pig during the ruckus at the Old Cock and Boar." His eyes hardened as he waited for her reaction.

The Matriarch clenched her jaw and said nothing. Of course, she recalled the brawl that had started Zelia's adventure long ago.

"He's run off and he, uh, er, likes places like this. I needed him to help me with an experiment." The Archmage leaned forward conspiratorially. "He's been elevated to acting assistant."

"A pig, the assistant to chief of all wizards? Absurd!"

"I suppose it sounds that way, doesn't it?" The wizard looked bashfully at his toes. "But the other young apprentices are always so eager that I find they are more trouble than they are worth. By adopting the pig I am fulfilling the charter to train one apprentice personally without the bother of having some fresh-faced kid always underfoot."

The woman snorted. The retort she was about to form faltered on her lips and she listened with a certain amount of sympathy. Hadn't she had more than her share of over-enthusiastic novices, all thumbs and good intentions? She ducked her head in assent. "Surely, you don't plan to train a pig to take over the task of Arch-mage?"

With this comment, Philos raised himself up to full height and stared her straight in the chin. "You expect me to expire sometime in the near future, Madame?" He blustered, insulted by the mere mention of his own mortality and quite forgetting why he was here.

It was the Matriarch's turn to be nervous. "Of course not," she mumbled.

"Good, good," he said, changing the topic. "I should come here more often."

And the priestess glanced about the rubbish tip, baffled.

"It's quite gratifying to see how tidy you keep the place. Even your dustbins," the mage said, indicating the row of still upright cans. "Neat, neat, very neat."

"Uh, uh," she stammered. "Thank you."

"Tell me, this can't be all of it." His hand dipped into a can and pulled out a wilted stalk of many-legged cilliary. "I mean this is a hospital. I see no bandages, no, uh . . ." he groped for words. "Nothing to imply that this is a hospital. It cannot be that the Healers' have no patients. Because if that's true then we'll have to look into your accounts."

The Matriarch blanched, for the Archmage was referring to the fact that all monies, supplies and stipends that came to the Healers' College was filtered through the Wizards' College. It was believed that healers, mainly women, were too frivolous to manage their own accounts.

"Of course not, I'll gladly take you on a tour of the facility. We have a particularly engrossing case of bloody flux, or there's a case of pox that might interest you."

The Archmage reeled, backing away from her as though she carried the diseases on her person. "Ah, no," he said. "That's all right if you'll just direct me to the other bins so I can look for my pig I'll be on my way."

"Other bins?"

"Yes, surely, you must have some place where you keep used bandages, ah, bits and pieces that you, er, throw away. You know, hospital stuff."

"Well, most 'hospital stuff', as you so quaintly put it, we burn. We can't take the chance that they might be contaminated."

The wizard looked crestfallen, even his conical cap drooped.

The priestess took pity on him. "But if you're looking for your pig you might try the root cellar."

The Archmage didn't appear to be listening. His tongue probed his cheek. It poked and prodded the inside of his mouth, moving about like a worm. "Tell me, where do you keep the bodies?"

"Bodies? What bodies?"

"Come now, you can't say that no one ever dies here?"

"No, you're right, some people's souls do pass onto the Dream Fields, despite our care. The bodies, though, are kept until the relatives can arrange services appropriate to the individual's religion and rank."

"What about the unclaimed ones?"

The Matriarch tilted her head to one side and studied the Archmage as though he were a particularly revolting form of pestilence. "Are you all right, Archmage? You don't look all that well."

"Just answer the question, witch!" he roared.

Taken aback, she answered without thinking. "The morgue, of course, the city morgue where arrangements are made for a pauper's funeral."

"Thank you." His heels clicked together and he doffed his cap to her, before he strode away, his night-blue robe billowing out behind him like the avenging angel of darkness.

That night, as they did each night, Ares and Zelia set up the warded circle next to the border stone. They wove their magic so tight that they could not even view their hands once it passed beyond the boundary. The illusion would last until the morrow and they could only hope that the pretender would obey the ancient law and keep to his side of the frontier.

Then they moved onto the next stage of their nightly ritual, sliding through the mists of time to follow the elementals' progress. Again, they were intercepted by the Lady's second, Fante. Air interposed itself between her and the battling fairies.

"Lady, why do you return yet again? I would not have you hurt," Fante said. "If your mother . . ."

"My mother is not here now. Would you gainsay her only kin?" She raised a brow in enquiry.

More bluster than blow, the zephyr backed away. "As you wish," he said.

Ares unsheathed his great war-hammer, praying to Og that it be empowered with the god's lightning strike.

"Fire!" Zelia shouted above the din, and the rioting figures halted.

"What do you want, mortal?" A raging blaze crackled, placing emphasis on the final word as if to highlight her helplessness. It turned on Ares. "Put away your child's toy."

The hammer's wooden handle became hot to the touch and the adventurer dropped it.

"See, you have no power over us," it said.

"No, no power," Zelia said. "But once I would have called you friend."

"Foolish mortal, we are no friends of yours."

"Relations, then," she hastened to add.

"Bound only by the flimsiest of threads. A thread, I might remind you, that could be destroyed with a touch."

The air around them began to heat up.

"Have you no pity then for those weaker than yourself?" Zelia asked.

"Pity? For you and your kind? Ha! Only your royal connections save you and only your love for this half-elf at your side protects him. Leave us before we change our mind and decide that the thread that binds us is too confining."

Zelia lowered her head dejectedly.

Fante hissed, "I told you."

And the adventurer and maid were borne away in a swirling cyclone as air removed the fairy queen's child from danger's source.

Moments later, they found themselves again on the rock-studded Abdha Plain. A second flight of fairy descended, dropping Ares's hammer at his feet. He scooped it from the sand.

"My lady, I am sorry," Fante said as he genuflected and popped out of sight.

Ares replaced the war-hammer in its loop and tugged at Zelia's hair. "I think there is little we can do." He sat, pulling her down next to him. They leaned against one of the many boulders that dotted the salt flats of Abdha and it grunted. Ares looped an arm over her shoulder and the thought was gone. The maid sunk with a sigh into his embrace.

"Alone at last," he said, just as Nepharious Hex unfolded before them. "But not for long," Ares added, scowling at the jinn.

The genie had taken the time to dress and his

new costume, glittering under the three moons, would have been blinding in the full light of day. His silken pantaloons were spun with gold and his short waistcoat was studded with rubies and emeralds and trimmed with golden dinar. The clink of coins rivalled the sharp jangle of Zelia's bells as she jumped, startled, to her feet.

The jinn sat cross-legged in the air, carried by desert thermals. He dipped his head in an insolent bow. "You said something about a wish? How can this humble servant, lowliest of all Hexes, help you?"

Zelia gaped, and Ares seeing the maid non-plussed, intervened. "We travel to the oracle of Sala on the far side of Abdha. We would consult the goddess about the disturbance of cycles, the evidence of which is all around us. A disruption which has influenced you, great jinn—" he said, using flattery and personal motivation to power the spell "—as much as any mortal man.

"If any of the gods can assist us in our quest, then Sala can. So our first request is a simple one: Take us, all of us, the mounts, both horses and sand snails, the women, the camel-drivers, the goatherd." The adventurer listed each member of their group by name, for genies were always looking for ways to renege on their bargains. According to Zelia, it had something to do with the Jinn Code of Honour. "Take us to Sala," he said with a nod of satisfaction.

He pressed his mouth against Zelia's ear and said, "Let's see him wriggle out of this one."

Zelia struggled free of his grasp. "No!" she cried, but the warning died half-spoken.

It had been an unfortunate choice of words. As she opened her mouth to append Ares's request, they were transported away. Not to the oracle on the far side of Abdha. Nor to a temple nearer by, but to the Immortal Planes.

Ares tumbled, loose-jointedly at her feet, magicked into an enchanted slumber. Beyond him, Zelia could see the *terem* women as they sped about their assigned tasks fold into so many piles of black cloth. Only the elemental maid shielded by her blood stayed awake and upright, for the far rings of the immortal zones were more dangerous for the mortal than even the elemental planes. The genie, sitting cross-legged on his rag-rug, hovered above her head and watched her curiously.

The scene melted around them, as if they did not so much travel throughout the planes as the universes raced past them. One minute she stood upon blighted sands, with Ares curled at her feet, and the next they'd slipped into the ethereal plane, and she saw the rest of the cavalcade as so many floating corpses. And she hoped they, like her lover, were also fast asleep.

Zelia sensed the faint breath of air against her cheek and she thought she saw the broken fountain of air surrounded by earth elementals frozen in many different postures. Someone somewhere said: "WEEEEEE."

Then the next instant, she was submerged in a wet, green world, surrounded by surging surf and warbling water. Zelia was sure she was going to drown, but the gentle fingers of fluid buoyed her up to the surface. Zelia wondered helplessly if the others would survive the watery descent.

Before the thought could completely coalesce inside her brain, Zelia saw a salamander scampering across a sulphurous plain. Noticing her abrupt arrival, the creature halted to regard this strange vision from under a blazing crest. A tongue flickered out, twin spirals of flame lashed at her feet, licking at her toes. Zelia bent her knees to spring away and . . .

She leapt into the waiting arms of a wampyr. Night's creature gazed down on her hungrily, and she felt herself drawn into the baleful red eyes. Her throat tightened as ruby lips curved and elongated canines dimpled its chin, and it seemed she was being sucked into its soulless hold. Zelia collapsed in a maidenly swoon, only to revive in a realm that combined the worst elements of both darkness and fire. *Hades!*

The King of Kings blew upon the still-wet signature on the bottom of the contract. It had dried to a glistening red-brown and, under the demon's hot breath, the parchment began to curl. Satan fanned himself. Pun splayed limply at the base of the salamander throne.

The many archfiends and minions of Hades' court were positioned in a circle around the Pit of Death. Each held horns, of unicorn, of rune-osserous, to their lips. The broad end stuck inside the pool, and they spoke. "Bubble, bubble, burble, burp."

Every once in a while a bubble would burst and their words could be heard. "Libraries . . . paper . . . wood," they intoned in unison to unseen fire on earth's elemental plane.

There was an odd flicker of blue-white light – providing a sharp contrast to the backdrop of burnished oranges and dull black – as though something disturbed the ripple of reality's curve.

The King of Kings stiffened. The many glittering eyes surveyed his dark domain. A maiden of sky-blue skin and indigo hair sprawled at his feet.

And he was up with a flash, prodding the exhausted Pun with a gnarled toe.

"Get her!" the Devil roared. Pun scampered to the woman to get a closer look, reached out with his ivory staff . . . and she was gone.

Somewhere a voice bellowed: "Get her!"

And an imp in a funny cap poked at her with a human thigh bone. Zelia levered herself from the blistering ground and pushed her hair from her eyes. She shied away from a nightmare face that stood above the imp, melting and sloughing its skin even as she watched.

The legions of demons and fiends closed in around Zelia.

Blinding radiance bleached the darkness, as angels lifted her from the demons' grasp and she was borne aloft in a flurry of feathery wings. The Dream Fields appeared to be a place of blue skies and fluffy light clouds. Cherubim sang sweet melodies, enticing her to stay, and she would have succumbed except the scene changed around her again.

Each world they passed swam before her eyes as if they were alive with many writhing forms. Too small to be seen or even distinguished from their environment. Each member of the sleeping group acquired a shimmering aura as though something hovered above their nodding head. The jinn must have felt this too, for when she looked at him, he was swatting at the air.

The ground beneath her became more solid, more dense, weightier even than earth itself. Gathering her courage, Zelia lifted her head to view the weirdest place yet. Strange, because it looked so commonplace, almost like home. First it was crowded, not with people, angel, folk, fay or foul, but with buildings. All different kinds of structures, from crude huts to grand temples. Or what would have been grand temples if they hadn't been so jumbled. There was a tabernacle tilted atop a cloister, a shrine sprouting on its roof. Untidy churches heaped topsy-turvy upon rambling basilicas. Buildings as far as the eye could see.

The snoring sheik and the sleeping *terem* women were splayed across what appeared to be a cobbled street. Ares lay wrapped round her feet. Not a creature stirred and Zelia was just about to conclude that the eighth plane, home of the gods, was uninhabited, when she heard a bong and a clang.

A frying-pan came bouncing out of the nearest onion-topped basilica. The dwelling was a modest affair made of pink sandstone with tastefully curved pillars, a miniature version of Sala's temple on earth. The pan, however, was gargantuan, and Zelia belly-flopped onto the cobbles to get out of its way as it ricocheted off pebbled street and shrine wall.

Something dark streaked past her, and she realized she viewed the hooded form of a serpent, retreating into the safety of shadows.

Apsu or Sala. She didn't know which.

"And ssstay out!" A voice thundered from inside the temple and a head that was neither green, red, purple, nor blue, but all those colours combined, protruded from the portal. The flat snake-eyes spun wildly until they lighted upon the maid of blue. The goddess reared regally.

"Who are you to arrive on my doorstep unannounced?" The massive head swung and glared at the jinn. "*You* should know better." Nepharious did a pretty good imitation of a turtle, withdrawing his head between his shoulders until it disappeared beneath the spangled waistcoat.

The huge snake slithered further out the door onto the small veranda, coil upon coil of her. And Zelia expediently decided it might be better to stay upon her hands and knees. The snake glided silently closer to the sleeping mortals. Her great forked tongue flicking out to touch and feel each of them in turn as though considering them for dinner.

Zelia swung on the hapless jinn. "We meant the oracle, the oracle, you fool. You've brought us to the real thing."

"I always think it's better to go to the source, don't you?" Nepharious peered at her from between two buttons, fixing her with a sly grin.

Before the maid had a chance to reply, Sala spoke. The sibilant syllables bounced off the many dwellings of the gods, past and present. "Well, what bringss you here, mortal? You did not come to witnesss my domesstic ssssuffering, did you?"

"If you forgive me, great and merciful Sala, air, water and fire have escaped into the mortal plane. They disturb your sacred cycles."

"CCCCCycless. CCCCCycless! Disssturbed the cccyclesss, you sssay. Don't I know it! I haven't had a decccent night'ss ssleep for many rotationsss. Asss if I didn't have enough on my plate what with my clutch and all, and that ssskulking creep Apssu sslinking about alwaysss looking for a quick bite. Look at me." The healer faced the glittering serpent and examined her closely. "I've got ccccirclesss under my eyes!"

Zelia gulped. "You do look a bit peaked, so if you could just help us, well, I'm sure we'll all sleep much better for it."

"A little elemental blood hass made you foolhardy, mortal. I am not here at your beck and call. You and your wedding ssstarted it. You finissh it. I've got problemss of my own. If you'd have ssseen what I have to put up with."

Zelia recoiled, but the goddess caught her gaze and held it with her spinning eyes, deluging her with images of families lost, children dying stillborn. The healer in her whimpered and wept, and Zelia was lost within an eternity of suffering cycles. Seeing genuine grief, the serpent softened.

The world spun crazily, and the maid deflated like an empty cloak. Contrite, Sala transformed into her mortal shape and knelt beside the woman of blue.

"Your tearsss have touched my heart," the goddess said. Zelia raised her head to see a face, not quite human, covered in iridescent scales and framed by spirals of living snakes. Lizards adorned the goddess's wrists and ankles, just as the healing bells of Brigitta graced Zelia's.

Sala regarded her, and the series of membranous lids unfolded from curiously flat eyes until their full goddess potential was revealed. The woman caressed the healer's forehead with a green finger. "Now, child, finish what you have ssstarted."

The maiden fainted, a serpentine voice worming its way inside her skull. "Remember, you have all the toolsssss you need."

The still-blackened lady flopped leadenly into a patch of weeds next to the road. She was tired, so tired. By this time, Astra – and her many parallel selves – had covered the four corners of Daklha, flitting to and fro and darting in and out of planes, getting lost along the way. Her dread was such that she often found herself gliding between times so that sometimes she arrived at the gates of Al Khali weeks ago to find herself planning Zelia's wedding. Or to the same place during the more recent battle between the sheik and his followers. But always, she'd discovered that she had just missed her daughter and her fay cousins.

Bewilderment and her own flighty temperament often succeeded in driving the purpose of her quest from her mind, until she arrived in mortal present where the tiny queen could see the aftermath of the elementals' progress across mortal lands.

The guardians of earth's gates had died in their thousands. Their shrill screeches echoed eerily across the southern continent while the wooden vessels that housed their tender spirits were consumed by Brimstone's flames. Their seeds, the creatures' fragile link to immortality, were turned loose in so thick a cloud that the black haze threatened to blot out even the sun. It was this dust that darkened her visage now.

The airy elemental made an apathetic swipe at the dirt and sneezed.

In Abdha, the hardest hit, the once-parched soil bloomed with the foul, bulbous plants of the Miasmic Swamp. So depressing a sight was this, that the Lady Astra had escaped to the oasis state of Hamadan. Thinking herself safe and these irrigated lands still untouched, the elemental fluffed the leaf, punched a small dent for her head, curled into a ball and slept.

CHAPTER 11

Acting on some compulsion they did not completely understand, fire halted in the midst of battle. Stunned water and astonished air likewise stopped, exhorting their flaming cousins to battle. Fire took no notice, instead it dithered, collecting in little leaping pyres of confusion. Inside each flaming head, lovely voices like the thick belch of hot magma whispered of dusty libraries with vast tomes and city offices replete with records of birth and death. Dragon-tonnes of paperwork and invoices.

Sparkling droplets gathered on glimmering lips, and off rushed the many manifestations of fire – the tapering flames, the cheery blazes, the wildfires and the infernos – forgetting the brawl already in progress. They spun and turned, heading for the human cities, ready to gorge and grow fat on the promised documents and certificates of civilization.

Three bewildered flames separated from the rest. They longed to follow their brethren, but another voice – quiet, more insistent, more urgent and more persuasive even than paper's allure – beseeched them to remember all those who tarried in Brimstone's plane. Such a feast should be shared, it said, and surely, there would be enough for all.

Without the warmth and protection of their comrades, the three decided that the earthen plane was a cold and dreary place. And pictures appeared in their crazed brains. Images of warmth. Of sulphurous rock and glowing caves. Brimstone. Home! They needed no further enticement. Slipping between time, they emerged, tumbling, cascading, spilling into the ruddy corridors of the fourth plane.

"My, isn't it nice to be back!" said an infant inferno.

"Yes," said a pyre, "there's no place like home."

A third, who fancied himself to be a holocaust but was really nothing more than a smoking blaze, glanced around them. "Now, where's our fearless leader, Teknix, got to?"

The three fairies went off in search of their warlord.

Everywhere they went in Brimstone they stopped to regale their fellow flames with tales of earthly pleasure, drawing tantalizing pictures in the elemental mind. Impassioned conflagration and fervent fires congregated around them, slavering, as the three told their peers of earthbound treasures of paper and wood, until it seemed all of Brimstone trailed along behind.

Joi II rattled its many spines, reaching jubilantly for the desert sun. A second generation seraphim, the creature contained within its genetic make-up the memories of the parent plant, up to, and including, the point of death; for it was only in the final moment of extinction that the seeds of the parent were cast off. Thus, no memory was ever lost and the fledging knew its purpose from its inception. Joi recalled in infinite detail the great meeting that had changed its life and the life of its ancestors for all eternity. It knew of the great accord and understood its intent.

As yet, Joi II was still weak, a mere sprog, and it quaked within its spiky shell for, connected to its brother bushes, it could hear their wails and their cries as they died. Some of the voices were faint as other second-generation plants expired even before they had been able to grasp the earth with tender roots.

The tiny seraphim clanked and shook, knowing it would be a while before it had the strength to accomplish the task assigned to it. Given time it would grow, and even at this early stage of its development, the tiny shrub appreciated the irony of its situation that it, time's guardian, needed the protection only time could give. Eventually, Joi would be as strong as its parent, perhaps stronger, and rooted to the earthen plane it had no other choice but to linger here. So Joi extended shivering branches to the sun, collecting its warmth and turning the luminary's rays into nourishment, and it waited for its "time" to come.

Fire faltered, ignoring the conflict around them, and reversed direction, while their cousins looked on, sore amazed. They rolled off in a glinting river of yellow and orange, swinging around baffled water and befuddled air. Fante Zephyr darted above the tumult of fairies, one of the few still unhurt and unharmed, for the lady's second-in-command had not lowered himself to participate in combat, holding himself aloof and aloft. He stayed, trying his best to protect the helpless human population. As a self-proclaimed impartial observer, Fante took note of all that occurred in order to report what he had seen to his lady. Assuming she ever appeared.

As fire streamed away, the small wind was torn between following flame's path and assisting wounded water and injured air. His tiny person mirrored the internal division, for Fante was rent in two. A diaphanous head and translucent torso leaned towards exiting fire, and a second, joined to the other at the waist, canted back towards the maimed elementals. Water puddled at the fountainous feet of Aqua Prima, fluid's sovereign. She clucked and tisked with soft, squishy noises over water's fallen.

His gaze trailed after fire. Fante took advantage of this moment, exhorting his fay cousins to follow fire. The fairy folk, renowned for their wars and their rades, listened gladly. In a wet whirlwind, they gave chase.

The glass globe exploded in a million shards that caught and reflected the light of Brimstone's realm. In any other plane, the pieces would have showered down with a tinkling patter, but in fire's plane, they were immediately vaporized and descended as glittering molten droplets. The ink-black globules contained therein collected themselves, separating quickly from the shards before they turned to fluid. The spinning ball of black tar hovered for a minute above the liquified remains of the globe that had been its cage – unaware of the elemental behind it and unmindful of the dragon that had attempted to catch the ball before it fell.

In Satan's dark realm, the black spots had been just so much malice floating about. Disassociated from the rest, they were without purpose. Occasionally, one bit would meet up with another and, attracted, the two would bond. But once the pieces had been gathered, the process quickened. Trapped within their glass prison, malevolence met malice, corruption met perversity, and perversity, depravity. And knew themselves to be one and the same. So spite palled around with bitterness, and the once-isolated bits were isolated no more. Like met like and each recognized the other as part of a whole. Consciousness, of a sort, was born, and with it a wicked, wily intelligence, for the slime realized that the miscellany of drifting bits were part and only part of itself. A portion was missing still.

On unspoken command, a single jet speck disentangled itself from the swirling glop. With a burble of protest, it sunk into the shimmering fluid to watch and wait here at Hades' gate. The liquid glass darkened from orange-red to deeper vermilion. Then the remaining particles, both the black and the tenuous speckles of white, turned and fled, away from the court of the Demon King, away from Hades' gate. Freed, they scurried off to find any of their fellows which may have got lost here in Brimstone.

So intent was born . . .

Pyro Teknix stalked through the corridors of Brimstone, or more appropriately he was towed by his pet dragon that even now eagerly strained at the lead. As General Conflagration, he was penultimate leader of his people – the Supreme Holocaust usually being too lofty to condescend to deal with the day-to-day issues of the plane or do anything so mundane as rule. Brimstone's monarch scorned the little people, the blazes, the camp-fires, the flickering flames. Occasionally, Lord Holocaust would mingle with the bigger infernos but he would stoop no lower than that. This left the decisions and the real work to his assistant, Pyro.

For his part, the fiery elemental took his command seriously. He'd only just been promoted from Major Conflagration to General and still felt the need to prove his worth. As a young spark, Pyro had majored in ancient law, and the lawmaker in him quailed at flame's flagrant disregard for the old covenant. And he wondered why this crisis should come upon him so soon in his tenure.

Yet his brethren had been provoked by air, hadn't they? As fire had throughout the mortal turns. Despite himself, Pyro yearned to join his brothers on earth. He resisted, adhering to tradition, and he held those elementals who had not already escaped to the mortal plane with will-power alone.

Pyro marched along rigidly, his arm jerked out before him. The conflagration tugged back at the lead. "Heel!"

His dragon cringed, tucked its prickly tail between its legs and waddled compliantly behind its master. The dragon belched. A fire ball warmed Pyro's back. The beast halted to sniff a burning bush, and the general at the other end of the lead stopped also.

Just then, something came hurtling through Hades' gate. The dragon, dragging the reluctant elemental behind him, capered after what appeared to be a transparent ball. Pyro fell to his knees as the glass globe shattered. A boiling blackness seethed around him, darkening his already bleak mood, and for a moment or two he lost consciousness. Then it was gone.

The dragon licked at Pyro's cheek with a fiery tongue. Releasing the beast, the conflagration rose on wobbly legs. He bent over the pool of molten glass and stared from it to the flaming gate of Hades and then to the large Boulder of

Brim that marked the boundary between one plane and the next. His eyes followed the trajectory and he spied the salamander throne.

"Hmmm," he said.

A finger flicked at the puddle, and a stream of black slime oozed up his arm. Fascinated, the elemental scrutinized it, never before having seen its like, and in his official capacity of General Conflagration, he decided he should study it more closely. The tarry substance wrapped itself around the flaming arm slithering its way upwards until it had completely encased his shoulder and his chest. For a brief flicker, the elemental felt suddenly afraid. Then pitch-black hooded the sparkling crown, dimming it. The fear was lost while black thoughts of death and destruction insinuated themselves in Pyro's already overheated brain.

Poised atop the border stone that marked the Shamirian boundary, the new pretender, Dand Y Kazzam gawked at the many bodies that littered the desert floor. At first glance, they looked dead, for they didn't appear to be breathing. Only if he looked closely could he see that the sheik's colour was good and, intermittently, a chest would rise or fall to indicate that the slumbering calvalcade still lived.

Of all the members, only the witch stood

upright, exposing a fearful countenance to the light of the sun. Although her eyes were wide open, it was obvious that she viewed different vistas than the one he saw and reacted in an infinitely slow dance. A hand arced inexorably in a warding-off gesture and the pretender repressed the urge to recoil. The fingers plaited – ever so slowly – in the flap-wing dove of Brigitta. Expressions crawled across her features, surprise, fear and perplexity.

Around the prone group, the desert writhed with the many snaking vines of Apsu's Coat. They twisted gleefully around sleeping bodies of the sheik and his followers, sensing moisture in the still forms. Even now one wrapped itself around Zelia's ankle and tried to pull her down. An oily grin spread across the pretender's face as the tendrils embraced his enemies in a stranglehold.

The pretender raised his hand to signal attack. The eldest spun eyes wide with astonishment. According to ancient law, Dand Y Kazzam's reign was secured the minute the sheik had passed the boundary into Abdha. Dand had no need to fear his predecessor or his sorceress daughter. It would be unsporting to attack now, not to mention illegal.

Yet the usurper had learned a long time ago that the best enemy was a dead enemy – which was, forsooth, no enemy at all.

So his hand remained poised. One of the elders clutched his fist and pointed. A seething tempest approached. Rain lashed, winds blew, and all was coloured crimson, as if the blazing sun burned on the far side of the storm. It swerved, surrounding the sheik and sky-blue witch. A portion detached itself and headed straight for the usurper.

His fellow tribesmen dropped to their knees and prayed to the nameless one for deliverance. Dand Y Kazzam snorted, hiked up his belt, hunched his shoulders and pressed forward into the storm. Much to his amazement, he rebounded, or was gently repelled, from the maelstrom. The pretender put out his hand to touch the tumult, and something slapped it away. The usurper ducked his head and prepared to ram his way into the gale and was buffeted back for his trouble. He was stopped dead in his tracks to stare at this tempest which wouldn't let him enter, much less pass, while mocking voices sneered at him from within the swirling mists. The men exchanged worried glances. Their hands went instinctively to dagger and blade.

The witch woman was powerful, indeed, if she could call up a squall to shield herself and her father. Not about to be deterred by such wizardry, the usurper hacked and slashed at the gyrating barrier, but his weapons were lifted from his hands and tossed casually away, and bubbling laughter reverberated inside his head.

The pretender blinked. Somewhere within the reeling cloud he saw the terrified eyes of his mirror image. Time seemed to turn in on itself, like a serpent swallowing its tail, and he was everywhere and nowhere at once. And when he thought he could stand it no more – he had to laugh, shout, scream, cry, something, anything – the surging mass backed away.

The clansmen stood in silence. There was the soft, ping, ping, ping of water running off their soaked cloaks to the growing puddles at their feet. The usurper clasped the Chictaw wing, talisman of luck for those who wore it – besides, perchance, the reptile itself. The colours had run. It was a fake, and Dand tore it from the thong that hung around his neck, cursing the vendor who had sold it to him.

There was a shout of alarm, and, gesticulating wildly, the eldest waved at the sky.

The usurper looked up from the bleached wing to glance timidly at the heavens. A swirling column of flame had swept around the sleeping cavalcade and was bearing straight for them. Without so much as a by-your-leave, Dand Y Kazzam turned and ran, back towards the invisible fairy spires of the Al Khali that floated somewhere in the haze above the desert heat, abandoning the rest of the tribe to face fire's wrath alone.

With water and air at his heels, Fante pursued fleeing fire. The desert draught, air's mirror image on earth, whispered urgently.

"Come," it said. "The child is in need."

Soliciting help from blustering gale, he exhorted his fay cousins to hurry. Arriving only moments before fire, they fluttered around Zelia, her betrothed, her father and his sleeping women. Beyond a large craggy rock, another group of robed Shamir fell to their knees, beseeching the Nameless One for aid.

Fante snorted. They could not wait until some unnamed god betook it upon himself to answer their call. Air must act now or watch the queen's daughter and her beloved die.

With a single word, "protect", Fante and his airy cousins formed a ring around the helpless mortals, both those that slumbered and those that quivered awake. This was no time to differentiate among the combatants.

They blustered, they blew, they whipped and they twirled in a frenzied fairy dance. While the waking tribesmen fought to be free of the fairy ring. Fante drew back, and fire, determined to reach the promised city with all possible speed, veered from their course to follow the pretender's trail to Al Khali.

The zephyr sagged to land in a flurry of wings upon the border stone. The fairy wind rose from his perch and surveyed the humans, both those who were sleeping and those who were not. They were safe for now, and he turned his back on them to regard the fairy corps.

The murmur of waves and the mutter of wind whirred around him. Their cries of pain resounded throughout the salt plain and Fante shuddered. Being immortal, elementals could not die, but they could be damaged, even stripped of their element right down to their elemental core, which was the fairy equivalent to the human soul. So fire lost its glitter, water evaporated, and air dissipated; but none could be killed. It was a basic tenet of elemental law. So war, as it was fought on the other elemental planes, became a game. Not so now.

To Fante's shrewd eye, it seemed that their sojourn on the mortal plane had changed them and some of earth's element had rubbed off. As though, by campaigning so long in the mortal realm, water and air had become compressed, almost as dense as earth itself, thereby incorporating something of human mortality in the process. For far more had been injured in the continuing contest than in any battle ever held in the other elemental planes. And Fante feared that many of the fallen would never rise again.

Suddenly, Aqua's syrupy voice rose above that of the general clamour and din of fairy folk. "I bid retreat. We must treat our wounded and assess our losses . . . at home."

Horrified, Fante dropped his self-imposed impartiality. For the distressed zephyr realized that there was a larger issue here than fire's breaking of elemental law.

The seraphim, known to man as Martyr's Bush. If fire were left unchecked on Earth's plane . . . He shuddered at the thought. He could not let it happen. The zephyr swept down to grovel at Aqua's feet.

"My lady," he said. "You cannot leave earth's realm unguarded."

"Cannot?" she roared. "Who are you to tell me that I cannot?" Her two eyes, literally limpid pools, hardened with suspicion. "If I remember correctly, this is all air's fault." Fante stiffened, his outline becoming sharp and clear, but he did not rise to the challenge.

"And I notice, your Lady Queen is absent," Aqua added. "Was it not she who declared war?"

"Aye, water's most lustrous queen, you speak true. Have patience. Surely she must arrive soon."

Aqua sniffed with a sound like bubbles blown underwater. "Air! Such flighty creatures." She signalled to her lieutenants.

"But the seraphim," Fante interjected, reminding her of time's guardians.

"That is an earth matter, and none of our own. I'm beginning to think that there's good reason why we were instructed to avoid this plane."

"I beg to disagree. Only water has the skill, the talent," he said using fay flattery and appealing to her pride, "to cancel fire. Earth cannot dampen it, and air inflames it. Therefore, only water can defend the seraphim." Pleased with his rhetoric, he continued, picking up steam. "Only water can initiate the cycle that nourishes the seedlings and coaxes them from their shell.

"And what do you expect us to do? Pool around fledgling bushes in case, *in case,* fire decides to return? You know as well as I do that the seraphim are desert plants and would drown under our fluid refuge. Meanwhile, my people are in agony. Just listen to them," she gushed emotionally. And Fante knew the watery queen would soon start weeping herself.

The transparent figure deflated, and he gave up. With the burbling of liquid trumpets, Aqua Prima exited with as much pomp as she could muster. The effect slightly spoiled by the caterwauling of water's wounded. Fante felt ill as their anguished cries died into sodden nothingness. Now only air stood between fire and earth's ultimate destruction. He zipped in agitation to and fro above the sleeping figures. He had to find his lady fast!

The demonlord laughed behind his fair face. He was in fine fettle. Fire on earth streamed towards the cities. Even as he watched, the remaining fiery elementals on Brimstone's plane were being persuaded by his three messengers to renew the attack. While water had turned its back on flighty air, and earth, as always, had got lost in the shuffle.

In a sudden flush of enthusiasm, the great trickster created a brand new game. Chortling happily to himself, the archfiend snipped a length of spider's web with his razor-sharp talons and used it to tie Pun's wrist.

The court jester tried to smile back, but couldn't find it in himself to do so.

Satan hefted poor Pun, arms and ankles bound, so that the terrified jester was suspended above the Pit of Death. Mirrored in the pond, the imp observed the tumult below him, feeling no small amount of pity for the besieged mortals.

"You see," the Prince of Darkness gloated smugly. "It's the art of manipulation. That's what it is. I give a little twirl." The demonlord extended its gnarled forefinger in the air. The curved claw touched the crimson palm. He circled both finger and curled talon. It caught on one of the strands, and Pun's hand waggled limply. "And they fight."

"I speak," the archfiend continued, pointing at the pit, "and they obey."

Satan plucked at one of the strings, and Pun's arm rose in a clumsy wave. "I pull . . ." The King of Kings seized several of the cords and helpless Pun jumped about awkwardly, arms and legs getting tangled with the string. "And you dance."

CHAPTER 12

The sombre jewels that had once been Queb darted through Brimstone's realm, looking for pieces of himself. This essence of pure human malignancy throbbed and vibrated. So dark and deep that even the fiery breath of Brimstone could not lighten it. The reverse was true. The glittering golds, the ruddy oranges dimmed to a dun colour with Queb's passing. The substance so foul that Brimstone's dragons raced to get out of the way.

The crystalline shards of rancour poked into every pit, peeked into each crevasse and peeped inside the many cracks. Working as a unit, they hoisted burning rocks with a purpose which was not yet a thought. They crept into caves, oozed into nooks, and slithered into elemental dens.

Soon the roiling mass had located other bits of itself, a burning passion, a sizzling lust, and so this thing that had once been Queb was reconnected with the darker side of love. Next to a pit of molten magma was a quivering flash of red-hot rage. In the following ravine, boiling emotion, and later broiling fervour. And everywhere it went, everything it touched it infected with a bit of its own malice, madness and evil.

Pyro Teknix lurched drunkenly down Brimstone's halls as he followed malice's path. It fanned the flames of his righteous wrath, igniting his hatred at the mortal race and kindling his indignation. The conflagration descended deeper into the caverns, and he absorbed more of the fragmented spite that Queb had left behind. The contact changed him, muddied him, and his flame was no longer orange-red, but burnished brown. Darkness had insulated itself inside his fevered brain.

As if propelled, the fiery leader moved deeper into Brimstone's realms, tracing darkness's path to its source. Until he had descended deeper than any fire elemental had ever gone before. Past the dens of the flaming salamanders.

Past the lairs of free dragons and their cousins the fire lizards. To the uncharted range of Brimstone's sulphurous heart where water's gate opened its ugly maw to reveal the hated blue-green world. Suspended in the liquid, dolphins rollicked, porpoises played and colourful fish swam among rocky shoals. So hostile was fire to water that the gate between the two worlds was buried deep where there was little likelihood of the cultures colliding.

But Pyro ignored the crashing waves, engrossed as he was with the spinning grains of black, red and white that hovered before the entrance. He quivered excitedly before the umbra. With a cry of joy and delight, the elemental raced towards whirling globules, until he stood in the centre of the cloud. In the twinkling of a fiery eye, the particles adhered themselves to the fiery form, without so much as a sizzle. Pyro's spark diminished and his ardour cooled, until it was almost blue-black, while the particles sunk deeper into the flaming flesh. The great coil of darkness pierced the central solid core that ignited this creature of elemental flame, and, for Pyro Teknix, the light of law and reason went out.

He woke slowly, as if from a dream. The sea world of water thrashed and boiled as warbling water sprites cascaded into the third plane from air's far gate. Pyro inched cautiously forward, goaded by the malice that had made its home within his blistering brain. So close that he could have reached out and touched water, and at last he could hear what the vile fluid muffled. These cries weren't trills of effervescent exuberance. They were shrieks of agony. Water had come home to lick its wounds. The fiery lips twisted into a feral smirk. The exhilaration of immediate conquest gleamed in his blazing eyes. For if water had abandoned earth, then the mortal plane was left unguarded, except by puling air, and victory was assured.

Throwing his head back, the conflagration shrieked a great war cry. Powered by Queb's evil and lust, his screech carried far, shivering through the canyons and corridors of Brimstone, reaching into the many dens and lairs. Then he was off, rocketing up the halls in the wake of his cry. Away from the water's gate and his hated cousins. Bringing with him the bits and pieces that were Queb.

Up. Up. Up. Towards the surface where the route to earth lay open.

"To battle! To battle," Pyro shrieked.

Gathering all to him, he exploded from the depths. His people came flocking, trailing after him as he careered past. The infernos, the blazes, the holocausts, the pyres. As General

Conflagration, they were his to command. They slipped from sulphurous rock, gushed from glowing magma and erupted from laval flows. The salamander steeds slithered alongside the writhing elementals. Dragons caught the fever of their masters and bellowed their collective outrage. Fire lizards flitted above their flaming heads.

Fire would not be locked out of the Earth plane again!

The Lady Astra woke from her slumber. The elemental examined the veins in the leaf above her head. The sun beat down upon the short grasses, casting them into sharp relief, and she realized that the sun was too harsh to be air's elemental sun.

The Lady Astra climbed onto the leaf to warm herself, and for the first time she noticed her blackened body. Appalled, the fairy queen stared at her arms.

She looked almost solid! Like dim-witted earth. Consternation drove all other thoughts from her mind, and she dipped into a ready flower that still contained enough of the morning's dew for a bath.

Refreshed, the airy elemental crawled across a branching stalk and reclined, languidly. A frown creased her fay features as she examined the fertile flood plain. The lady cupped her chin in her hand and she thought and thought.

Daklha, Daklha, what had brought her here to the southern continent?

A faint blue finger tapped her temple. She was here for a reason, she knew it.

Astra got up on her hands and knees and peered between the blades of grass. Just as she was about to disappear into her home plane, Fante descended from on high to waver before her. And the search for her lost subjects came into sharp focus.

Fire rippled, poured and flowed through the gates of Al Khali, and the guard fled before its advance. This was not a military matter, they reasoned, but the responsibility of the fire brigade. The more duty-bound went to announce its arrival to the Emir, who had already vacated the city on an unannounced holiday at the first word of the flaming approach.

The brigade was out in force. Unfortunately, it consisted of one man and his donkey. With most of the houses made of mud-brick containing furnishings modelled out of sand, there was little here to burn, outside the government offices, and the unwieldy bureaucracy of the Emir had their own brigade. They needed it, for the administration of Shamir depended entirely on its paper and records for continuity. The government was intractable by necessity since rule had to survive the supervision of a series of frivolous sovereigns, who were selected at the annual horse race.

Overall, being Al Khali's sole fireman was a good job. There were nights off, and all the *kymus* he could drink was provided, because the fluid to extinguish fledgling fires had to come from somewhere. Furthermore, the employee received a fine, fancy uniform with all sorts of bangles and things.

Right now, though, the poor man had cause to rue his position as he hunched against a sun-baked wall, quaking before elemental wrath, his bangles clanking loudly. The donkey, at least, had had the good sense to leave the city along with the rest of the citizenhood; but the fireman was immured, fenced within a pen of flames.

One of the elementals darted forward and pinched the fireman.

"Fire brigade, huh? So all right, hot shot, fight fire." It capered around, brandishing blazing arms. "Wha'tza matta? Chicken?"

Around him, something that resembled money changed fiery hands as bets were placed.

"Come on. Come on." The elemental prodded the fireman.

A pyre strode up to the cavorting group.

"Let the mortal go," it said with a voice like an explosion. "You know we can't take prisoners. Besides, orders have come through from Brimstone. We are to return."

"What?" chorused the group. "And leave all this?"

The pyre smiled, a frightening thing to see. "Don't worry, we'll be back."

"Ah," said a blaze.

"Ah," said another, and they exchanged knowing glances.

Soon the full might of Brimstone would be clambering through time's door.

Miles away in Abdha, Zelia ceased her slow dance and folded upon the sandy plain. The rock which had once supported Ares had moved and stood many handspans distant. Splayed next to Ares, she was anything but still, for her eyes moved constantly as if she watched some sort of play projected upon her own lids. The maid and her sleeping companions were lost between planes – in a narrow strip that was none of the nine and a little bit of each. In this place, she was given a glimpse of the separate planes, as though looking through a window. On the fourth, she saw fire massing. Three renegade elementals mingled with their brothers who had stayed behind, inciting them to riot.

She spied Pyro Teknix who had grown huge, a coppery pillar the size of a holocaust. She heard his inflamed war-cry and she quailed. Her features reflected her fear as one of the many creeping vines of Apsu's Coat wrapped itself around her throat.

Vitreous Humour pivoted on his axis and inspected the empty glen. After having completed his spinning search, the sprite bounced over to his father.

"WEEEEEEE . . ." Ignacious intoned.

"Dad?"

". . . EEE . . ."

"Dad!"

"Wah. . . ?" With a speed that would have shocked any who might have been watching, Ignacious thought his reprimand at his son. *Quit interrupting, junior, this is important!*

"They're gone. Everyone's left," Vitreous said.

Too late. Ignacious had begun anew: "WWW-WWWWWW . . ."

Judging his father's mood, Vitreous decided not to press the issue. Although slow and cumbersome, his father was part-magma and, when pushed, could easily erupt like any molten volcano.

So the fluorite continued his fairy dance around the broken ring, awaiting word from his brother elementals.

Reason had long since vacated the mind of Philos the Benevolent. His eyes glinted maniacally, lighting the gloom. There was little enough sanity about, what with each minor curse turned into a ravening beast. Magic ran amuck across the northern continent so that even the peasants had power. Whims and fancies took material form, and everybody was king. Rationale had vacated earth to seek a more agreeable abode on another plane.

"It figures it would be a slow day at the morgue," he grumbled. "Nary a corpse in sight."

The Archmage shuffled down the corridor, talking to himself and dragging the body of Mad Thomas behind him. For a fleeting moment, Philos wondered why they had called the man mad. Thomas had seemed a most reasonable fellow when they spoke. A trifle loath to participate in Philos's experiment, perhaps, but who could blame him for that?

Still, with a little persuasion and the help of a well-aimed blow, Thomas had reluctantly provided the cadaver the Archmage needed for his second experiment. His first, Ampitere, had failed to bear fruit and he now lay in a pile of loose flesh and bones in Philos's secret laboratory.

The wizard couldn't forget about the intestines. This time, Philos would get it right. He was pretty sure that he knew what had gone wrong. *Entrails, too many blasted entrails!* And the Archmage wondered if his predecessor hadn't put a trifle too many in the recipe as a blind, as sorcerers often do. The Archmage just couldn't believe that the human abdominal cavity was meant to hold that many. He would have asked a healer, but Philos had the feeling that the Matriarch probably wouldn't approve of his activities; she had been touchy enough about the pig.

The Archmage rounded a bend in the labyrinthine tunnel system below the college and stopped. With a surreptitious peek over his shoulder, he stepped through the door into his laboratory. Philos slogged through Ampitere's sad remains and dumped Thomas on the table and then began to hack away at the body.

When Zelia next pushed her hair from her eyes, she was spread out upon the Daklhan sands. Creeping vines of Apsu's Coat had twined itself about herself and her companions. The dazed maiden wondered how they had come to the Miasmic Swamp in the far north of Abdha where the plant grew in profusion. As she watched in horrified fascination, the many vines sent experimental tendrils across the still-slumbering forms to see if they could get access to the rich liquid that pulsed within the human veins.

Nepharious crouched before her. "I wondered when you'd wake up."

"You! You!" The healer attempted to spring to her feet, but the vines kept her pinioned. She whispered a spell and the bindings dissolved. A slender thread sent a shoot across Ares's neck, and Zelia pulled Ares's dagger from the sheath and sliced through the strand.

"Why don't you use magic?" the jinn suggested.

"And exhaust my powers? No. Why don't you use your magic?"

"I would," he said craftily, "if you wished it."

But she wasn't paying attention. "How did we get here?" she asked.

"Where?"

"The Miasmic Swamp."

"You are where I found you on the Abdhan Plain," the jinn informed her.

The maiden ceased sawing at serpentine boughs and looked around them. "In the southeast? But the plants are native to the Miasmic Swamp."

"You've been asleep for a while. I don't know how long." He shook the hourglass that was attached to his wrist. "I've never been very good at this time thing. It's such a mortal preoccupation."

"Asleep?" She shook her head, bemused.

Nepharious eyed her, floating several handspans off the ground.

"Sala!" The healer pointed at him. "You took us there! To the eighth plane."

"As you wished," he said mildly.

"Right," she said, grimly recalling Ares's poorly-worded command.

"And what of all this?" she asked as she bent to the task of freeing Ares from the squirming vines.

"A lot has happened while you snoozed. The elements have passed you," and the jinn plucked at his waistcoat which now was a flagrant purple lined with eye-splitting yellow fur, "and I. I had to go and change again." Nepharious gestured around them. "Between rain and air blowing through, Apsu's spores have thrived."

The last of the vines fell away from Ares. Zelia prodded his shoulder, and he snorted.

"Ares," she said, and he swatted at her hand.

In desperation, Zelia yanked hard on the silver hair as a snaking tendril wrapped itself around his wrist.

"By all the gods!" the blue maid said as she struggled to pull his limp body onto a rock where it would be away from Apsu's deadly embrace. A wish for help fluttered on the edge of her consciousness and the genie, who had shed his body for the more awe-inspiring aspect of a floating head, zoomed in on her. The healer pushed the thought away and let Ares slide back to the ground, eye cast upon her relatives which even now disappeared under quivering leaves.

Forgetting whom she addressed, Zelia said: "Get them up!"

The genie gave her a sidelong look. "Is that a wish?"

"Wish?" She shook her head in exasperation, fished Ares's sword from his belt of scalps and stomped off. "Never mind. I'll do it myself."

Ares groaned and stared at Zelia through a curtain of white hair as she slashed at the vines. He smacked his lips and wiped his mouth with the back of his hand. "Gawd, who's turned trolls loose in my mouth."

"Ares. You're awake!" Zelia said, her voice sharp with frustration. "Can you lend a hand?"

His head turned creakily on his neck and he gaped at her.

"The jinn took your request literally," she said, "taking us to visit the goddess herself, rather than her oracle, and it would appear that we have slept overlong."

Ares's head wagged from side to side. "How long?"

"Long enough for all this to grow?" She indicated the vines.

"Wonderful, a fellow takes forty winks and the entire world goes to Hades in a handbasket. Just wake me up when this is all over. I was having a really great dream about a lady elf, as cute as a snow bunny. I'll just go back to that if you don't mind."

The adventurer lolled on the ground.

"Beloved," Zelia crooned.

The adventurer recognized the suddenly dulcet tones as a warning. The word "beloved" was tinged with sarcasm. If he didn't get a move on soon, she'd probably drag him bodily from his place. He opened a wary eye and found himself level with Zelia's booted toe. It went up and down less than a handspan from his face.

Ares sat up. "Not a good idea, huh? Mind you, I wasn't having lascivious thoughts about this particular lady elf. It was my mother."

"If you are all through playing around," she growled.

"My, my, haven't we woken up on the wrong side of the blanket today." He lurched to his feet. "What happened with Sala?"

Zelia grimaced. "She, uh, has her own problems. She seems to believe we have brought this upon ourselves and won't help. Although she did say something that was strange as I left."

"What was that?"

" 'You have all the tools you need.' "

"Any clue as to what the tools might be?"

"Nope," Zelia said.

"Wonderful!"

The Lady Astra took the shortest route, " 'tween planes". The next thing she knew she was fluttering through a slithering sea of vines. Her daughter hacked at a lashing branch that had a stranglehold on her sleeping father. Seeing Zelia's need, the elemental turned herself into a cutting draught, releasing the tendrils that tied him.

As the binding vines fell away, Zelia glanced above her head to see her mother bolting from the blue. In her wake came Fante Zephyr and many of the lost elementals. They descended in a flicker of silken wings, pinching and tickling the sleeping *terem* women, though none dared approach the sheik.

Mother and daughter moved away from the group to talk in muted whispers as the elementals fanned the sleepers, keeping the vines from nodded head or slowly-rising breast. Freed from this task, the adventurer went to join Zelia and her mother.

The jinn shook his head in disgust and summoned his carpet. Obviously no more wishes were forthcoming, and he decided that it was a good time to quit this place. Air elementals gave him wind. Of course, this was their gift to humanity – the gentle breezes that stirred the grasses, the gusts that powered the ships – but generally speaking, the fay folk left the genie feeling ruffled and out of sorts. The rug caught a handy air current, and Nepharious took himself away. He'd had enough of fairies to last him several mortal lifetimes.

"Zelia, ah, Zelia." Ares elbowed his partner.

"What?" Zelia asked, swinging on him.

The adventurer gave a swift sweeping motion that encompassed the surrounding desert before reaching to grasp his hammer.

Her irritation disappeared in an instant, and her jaw unhinged as the dark-robed shades of the rival Kazzam clan materialized from behind the many rocks that studded the plain.

Zelia stiffened, the words of a spell springing to her lips. The aura of magic enveloped her and she appeared to grow in height and size. Ares's cat-like pupils contracted as the sorcerous power radiated outwards. The members of the opposing clan cringed away, knowing her skills too well.

A few feet away, the sheik grunted and jolted upright, awakened by his own snores.

"Zelia? Ares?" He blinked. "Astra?" The sheik lumbered to his feet, brushing sand and bits of vine from his flowing burnous. "Wha—"

Zelia signalled him to silence and then raised her head to the heavens, grabbing the fairy queen by a fluttering wing. "Mother, take the others away."

Astra bristled, clenched Zelia's forefinger and pulled.

"Mother, please," she said as the groggy sheik took his place by his daughter's side, a ghostly double following in his wake.

"Oh," Astra said. Then with a feeble bluster, she gathered her people to her and they quit the field.

"Ahem," said one man, who was braver than the others. He advanced to stand before them. The sheik pulled his scimitar from his belt and waved it menacingly.

The man fell to his knees. "Oh, lord and master, we come before you to be absolved of our sins. We were wrong. We ask that you take us back. Heal this rift that has formed between us," he said, bowing so low that his forehead touched the ground at the sheik's feet.

Zelia's father seized the healer's arm and thrust her forward. "Do you swear fealty to my chosen heir?"

"Yes, m'lord," the other man said.

"All of you," the sheik added.

"Yes," chorused the group.

"Do you pledge to her as you would pledge to me?"

"Yes, my lord," they said.

"Then swear by the nameless one and kiss the hem of her, ah, er, skirt," the sheik stuttered, glancing down at the short jerkin that she wore, "as you would mine."

"Father, this really isn't necessary," Zelia hissed out of the side of her mouth.

"Silence," he replied. "This must be done."

One by one, the dutiful tribe approached. Some touched the hem of her jerkin to their lips. Others cowered at her feet, kissing the toe of her heavy boots. When the last man had made his obeisance, she stepped forward.

"There is one other to whom you owe fealty. One more wronged and more worthy of your oath than I." Zelia stepped aside to reveal the little prince, and the gathering tribe gasped, for they believed that the youth was dead.

A murmur drifted about the throng. "Magic, sorcery," they said and many held out their hands in a gesture to ward off the evil eye. Behind her, Ares sniggered. Zelia glared at him.

"Yes, magic – stronger than any of you have known – has brought him back from the Dream

Fields and decreed that he, not I, shall lead you unto the next generation."

Ares glanced quickly at the sheik who accepted this announcement with a nod of his head, unperturbed, as though he had been expecting it.

The men of the tribe rose with a cheer.

"Good," she said, turning to her father. "We have plans to make, you and I."

And they retreated from the group. Ares lingered next to father and daughter, watching as the tribe repeated the ritual with the son.

"Thank you, daughter, you are wise beyond your years," said the sheik, surveying the scene before him.

"It is better this way, although I acknowledge the honour you have done me. Someday perhaps, the people here will respect the silent strength of women, but that time is not now."

The sheik agreed. "Do you understand why I made them pledge to you first?"

"Yes, father, I do," she said.

"If there is to be peace, they must obey me in all things."

"Aye, father, as it should be." And with that, she curtsied, touching fingers to forehead, lips and heart, silently renewing her fealty before the tribe.

The newly-reunited clan was again sundered as the sheik sent his men to find the *terem* mounts that had wandered off during their enchanted sleep. The recently reawakened women left without a word to cook the evening meal.

And Astra – held in abeyance until the mortals had departed – hovered above Zelia's head, buzzing angrily. In her excitement, her words got garbled, so that they sounded like a rapier breeze clattering through autumn's dry leaves. Ares glanced from Zelia to her mother. The lady wavered expansively, so expansively in fact that she risked getting lost in the first stray zephyr that happened her way.

"I don't understand," he said.

Zelia listened intently for a second and translated. "Something about the Martyr's Bush."

"Martyr's Bush? What Martyr's Bush?"

"Small spiny plants that dot the desert," Zelia explained. "You've seen them. They grow the thickest around the portals of power."

Ares thought for a bit. It wasn't difficult to remember his first trips through the Daklhan portals. Having taken place during the fight with Queb, the stone circles were seared upon his memory. But plants, besides the treacherous vines, he could not call to mind. The adventurer shook his head. "I'm sorry. I can't say I remember them. I had other things on my mind at the time."

The blue maid nodded as the fairy queen darted in between the couple and billowed largely.

"Calm down, mother, I can't understand what you are trying to say."

The Lady Astra ruffled with a feeble breeze.

"They're what!" Zelia almost shouted, and Astra hid behind the adventurer's head.

Ares flinched, extracting the Lady Astra from a tangle of hair. "This doesn't sound good."

The Lady droned something unintelligible.

"My mother has informed me that the Martyr's Bush isn't a plant at all. It's a type of earth elemental or it was once."

"A shrub, an elemental?" Ares squawked.

Blue hair cascaded under the Shamirian sun and her bells clamoured as Zelia shook her head. The Lady Astra alighted upon her shoulder and whispered in a sky-blue ear.

"An accord? What accord?"

Ares's brain was filled with flickering images, which came in a confusing jumble. Mixed amongst thronging elementals, he saw images of the many gods and creatures of dark night. His eyes grew round as he turned to Zelia.

"What's all this?" he asked.

"I'm not really sure, but if I understand her correctly, many turns ago, Earth's plane was like all the elemental planes, timeless. Then man came, and he could not survive in such an unfriendly environment. So an agreement was struck and the portals of power set up to keep time contained within this plane. The Martyr's Bush are another result of the meeting, for it had been earth's elders who pleaded for humanity, and the gods demanded sacrifice for giving their aid in erecting the stone circles."

"That explains the name," Ares said. "But what does that have to do with us?"

"It would appear that the Martyr's Bush are the guardians of time's gates. Without them, the time will seep out, and the world as we know it will cease to exist." Zelia's head bent to listen to her mother. She lifted it, stared into Ares's eyes and shuddered. "She says that almost all the adult population has been destroyed. While many of the young seedlings have already taken root, their grip on the earth is not strong. Thanks to the hastened cycles, many of those have died prematurely, but already some of their seeds have flown, and, given time, perhaps they will thrive."

"Given time . . ." Ares murmured and their eyes locked as the full import of Astra's message came home to them.

The lady zipped around Zelia's head, trilling softly.

"However, another influx of fire would exterminate them completely."

The adventurer groaned.

"It gets worse. She sent her aide, Fante, to follow fire. Someone, or something, has called them home to Brimstone."

"Well, that's a relief," Ares said.

"No, it's not. Fante has just returned from the fiery plane and says something has stirred them. They plan to return and fight for earth's domination."

"You mean they're coming back?" he yelped.

"Yes, coming back in force." The blue maid grabbed Ares's hand. "We cannot step aside and let fire burn itself out a second time. The

Martyr's Bush will not stand up against a second purge. We must stop fire somehow."

"How? By fighting it?" Ares asked.

"If we have to," Zelia said.

"With what? Fire?" he quipped.

"If need be."

"And this small band is going to engage fire in battle."

"I believe more will be coming. She says the tribes are on the move."

"Great, so we've got a bunch of humans, all of whom can be roasted alive." Ares paced back and forth. "What are our other assets? Astra, how many elementals do we have at our disposal?"

Ephemeral wings lifted in a foggy shrug.

"Just a portion of my mother's people have been found. We think that some of them returned to the second plane, but we're not sure. Water has vanished completely except for a few trickles here and there. I gather most of our fluid friends have found Daklha an uninviting environment."

"A second influx of fire may mean another incursion of water, which for the Martyr's Bush, a desert plant, would be no good thing." Zelia glanced worriedly at her mother. "Although air, we can control."

"This is getting better all the time," Ares said. "Pray continue."

"The physical devastation is only part of the problem. The bigger problem is that the doors to the planes remain propped open. If there is another invasion, it's most likely they will never be closed again. Man cannot survive in a timeless state. The Earth plane as we know it will cease to exist, and man will cease to exist with it."

"I get the point. We have no choice. We must face fire even if we are fried in the process." Ares hefted his war-hammer, feeling its heavy weight. Still, it seemed a fragile weapon with which to confront fire. "We really have to stop getting involved in these family squabbles, Zelia, they seem to be hazardous to our health."

Zelia laughed mirthlessly.

"So now what?" Ares asked.

"We gather the tribes," said the sheik, speaking for the first time.

"And the air elementals," Zelia added, turning to Astra. "Mother?"

The elemental twittered nervously.

"Yes, mother, I know you spent many rotations looking for them. They are your subjects, and many have joined you here. So call the rest of them to you."

Finding her voice, the Lady Astra's surprised *"oh"* became audible. "I hadn't thought of that," she rattled, flustered.

"Can you do it?"

"Of course, I can do it," Astra huffed. "Just give me a few moments."

"Perhaps, mother, if you are going to try, you should move a little further afield. You know the doppler effect gets amplified the more elementals you gather. We have to keep mortal and elemental separate." Zelia pointed at a rippling band of cloud which, if Ares squinted, disintegrated into a cycle of spinning fay figures.

The adventurer stopped his pacing. "There's something else you haven't told me – where, just where, are we going to find this newest incursion of fire?"

Zelia winced and looked down at her feet.

"Don't tell me, let me guess," the snow elf said. "The Miasmic Swamp."

She nodded. "That appears to be fire's best access to the southern continent. My mother has a particular fondness for the Shamirian circle, and I think she'd blow them into so many guttering tapers if they trespassed there, so-o-o the Miasmic Swamp it is."

Ares shook his head. "I was afraid you were going to say that."

The tribe changed course, slightly, to head directly towards the Swamp. Vines of Apsu's Coat stretched as far as the eye could see. The plants draped torpidly over rain-washed gullies like serpents made fat and sluggish after feeding. Dotted here and there across the desert, almost hidden under Apsu's bloated belly, were the withered shells of Martyr's Bush. Next to the dead parent plant, a tiny woody replica. A ghostly reminder of their quest.

Each day, the caravan picked up other groups as pathetic as their own, for Abdha had been hardest hit of all Daklha. Its people wandered about lost, as if they didn't recognize their own lands. Each had dark hollows carved under haunted eyes. And it seemed as if the entire continent were on the move, led by instinct towards Sala's great temple.

From further south came the Quattarean – recognizable by the many rings and spangles that adorned wrists, ankles, arms, ears, fingers, toes, noses and even lips. Likewise, the Shamir ranged far from their tribal lands, driving gaunt beasts in search of water and fodder. They came in twos and threes. On foot, or horseback. The snails, unable to tolerate water, had died and their empty shells were scattered everywhere. Women followed, mobile columns of cloth that dragged, or carried, sick – and sometimes dead – children. The young supported old, and vice versa.

Zelia abandoned her Tocinian leathers for the robes of her craft, and each day she plied her trade, healing hurts great and small. To some, she gave sweet forgetfulness so they would overlook their trials. To others, she gave the strength to endure their long trek. With the badly wounded, the maid of blue called upon Ares's power to augment their own.

The sparkling cloth of crystal acted as a focal point for stragglers, its blinding brilliance calling all to them from near and far. Even the sight of a white-haired man and sky-blue maid brought comfort as their assembly grew.

Ares sat in the saddle looking back the way they'd come. The column stretched out of sight. *By the gods, did they have that many people?*

Air escorted them at a respectful distance, apparent in the band of dust that flanked either side of the cavalcade.

There was a loud explosion and a thunderclap signalling the jinn's approach. The adventurer's ears popped as Nepharious Hex – head only – appeared before them. The frightened mounts reared.

Without thinking, Zelia snapped irritably. "I wish you would st—"

The jinn leaned forward eagerly and Zelia clamped down hard on her reckless tongue. Ares glanced at her and gave her a weary grin.

Then he completed the thought, if not the

sentence, for her. "Can't you make a little less spectacular entrance?"

"I am a Hex!" His voice boomed, and Nepharious puffed up with pride. "I come from a long and vaunted line, I'll have you know. The Hex family is one of the oldest, and we don't settle for second best! Less spectacular entrance, indeed!"

Ares leaned over the pommel, cupped his hand over his mouth and said in a forced whisper that the jinn was bound to hear. "Someone told me that jinns are really the descendants of fire elementals."

A body materialized below the floating head, and Nepharious pulled himself up to full height, towering high above the mounted duo. "Jinns are no such thing. They are not the misbegotten children of elementals like trolls, or . . . or . . . elves." He spat the word at Ares. "I don't have the dubious ancestry of some I know." And the jinn eyed Zelia's blue skin and Ares's snow-white hair and tapered ears meaningfully.

"If you are no relation to the fire elementals, then why do you live in lamps?" Ares teased the irate jinn.

Nepharious didn't deign to dignify the adventurer's comment with a reply. Instead he continued. "We have strict rules about marriage and children. Jinn blood is the only truly pure bloodline on all the mortal plane. There are only eleven accepted family names registered on the rolls. Marriages are carefully arranged between families. We do *not* mingle with mortals, and we do not profane our blood with theirs. Surely, you've heard of the Genie Pool?"

"Sounds like inbreeding if you ask me," Ares muttered, and Zelia chortled.

"I don't have to stay here and be insulted," Nepharious sputtered. The jinn expanded until he was taller than the highest minaret of Al Khali and glowered down at them. Then he popped out with a sudden swoosh as air filled in the vacuum the genie had left in his wake.

"Good. Go!" Ares shouted at the rippling trail. Then he turned to Zelia. "The jinn almost got you there."

"You're right," Zelia said. "I must remember to guard my tongue, and you . . . you really shouldn't goad him like that. You're asking for trouble."

"Just our luck to get stuck with a temperamental jinn," Ares grumbled.

"They're all like that. An irascible bunch, the lot of them. In fact, our friend Nepharious is quite good-natured for a jinn."

Ares snorted derisively.

"I mean it. Most jinns would be doing some

kind of mischief, just to keep in practice. If nothing else, they'd be terrorizing maidens and tripping goatherds just to let off a little steam at the frustration of being bound by our command."

Ares looked thoughtful for a moment. "I thought I'd noticed one of the goatherds falling down a lot."

As he said this, a herdsman tumbled gracelessly to land, spread-eagled, upon the ground. He got up, coughing, and Zelia moaned.

"See what I mean," said Ares.

"I don't suppose you've noticed any frightened virgins lately?"

Ares's gaze fell on the cloaked figure that was Lady Hadidge. From here she looked like a column of charcoal. As if she overheard their conversation, she turned. Only her eyes were visible through the cloth.

"I can't say that I have," he said, indicating the many *terem* women. "But how would you tell?"

Zelia scanned the horde of cloaked and swathed women and said: "You've got a point there."

Legs up. Legs down. The hapless imp moved jerkily as a courtier tweaked at one cord and then another. *Elbow up. Elbow down. Hands up. Hands down.*

And Pun hit himself in the face. The jester lifted his head to gaze bleary-eyed upon Satan as he stared into the Pit of Death. The Prince of Darkness had tired of his new game quickly. Now, if the rest of the court would do the same, maybe the poor imp could get some sleep.

When the Lady Astra had given him this assignment initially, Fante had been thrilled. This was *real* responsibility, far greater than any he had been given before. Fante swelled with importance and soared away to do her bidding. His mission: to find each rocky form that was making its ponderous progress across the salt flats of Abdha and urge them to hurry, for the battle of battles drew nigh.

Bending all the already-bent rules of time and space until they screamed, the zephyr had halved and then twinned himself – scattering to the four winds – until there was little left of himself – just to ensure that not a single earth elemental was omitted from his quest.

It had been an impossible task from the start, and now he wondered why she hadn't sent someone bigger than him. A bluster, a gale. Better still, a tornado or a cyclone. Someone earth would sit up and notice. Of all the boulders, the stones and the rocks he had talked to, Fante had seen the light of recognition shine only once in the hard, pebbly eyes.

And the fairy second wondered why he bothered. The mortals didn't even seem to be aware of earth's presence. Although Fante suspected that Ares and Zelia knew because they gave the many stones wide berth and insisted that they be treated with respect. Only the jinn – with a lot of time to dither and dally between wishes – truly noted their movement. But Nepharious didn't hang around much, as if he were embarrassed to be seen in the company of such rabble.

The spent zephyr flitted feebly before the slanting stone and shouted in its craggy ear with all the apparent disturbance of a lady's fan in a gale.

"Alarm! Alarm! Fire invades the mortal plane!" he shrieked in a breathy puff. "Hasten! Hasten! Two arms! Two arms!"

The zephyr darted and swooped, perplexed. He wasn't at all sure about the "two arms" part. Of course, they would bring two arms, what self-respecting elemental wouldn't? Not that arms really were all that necessary to the elemental form, which could attain any shape they chose – but certain elementary proprieties had to be observed, didn't they?

Still, that was what the lady had told him to say, and he repeated her words loyally. "Two arms! Two arms!"

The boulder sat implacably on the sand and, exhausted, Fante slumped onto its rocky shoulder to scream in the stone-deaf ear one more time.

"Two arms! Two arms!"

The creature squatted, rigidly unmoved. The airy elemental's heart sank, as did his fay form, which slid leadenly to the ground – a breathless breeze lying at granite feet.

It was the best he could do. This was the last one. They would make it to the conflict in time, or they would not. The exhausted second, Fante Zephyr, could do no more.

The growing caravan moved with astonishing speed, urged on by the adventurer and maid, and they reached their goal, the Miasmic Swamp, in a two scant rota, accumulating more people as they went.

The Kazzam clan grew as the other Shamirian tribes swore allegiance to the sheik, his son and his fay daughter – allegiance normally reserved for the Emir. But the Holiest of Holies and the Nameless One's representative on earth had absented himself. Perhaps finding refuge under the desk of one of his many palaces.

The snaking groves of Apsu's Coat thinned as they drew near the swamp which was their natural home. The stones of Miasma canted in an ominous circle, casting long misshapen shadows before them. After they had made their rounds of the sick and the ailing, Ares and Zelia escaped to sit next to one of the many boulders that now studded the Abdha desert.

Ares hefted the reassuring weight of his warhammer and sighed. What he wouldn't give for an adversary he could see, feel or touch. None of this nebulous stuff, like time or disease. He wanted to fight something tangible, not sickness, sorrow and death. Something *real*. Something he could sink his hammer into.

A cool blue hand caressed his cheek. "What's wrong?"

The adventurer turned to face his betrothed and tried to smile. "You know this hero bit isn't all that it's cracked up to be."

Zelia placed a sapphire blue head on his shoulder and said, "I know what you mean. Before we could go where we wanted, when we wanted to go. No one cared where we were and what we were doing. People seemed a lot happier if they *couldn't* find us."

"Yes, I miss the old wagon," Ares smiled, thinking of their travelling days.

"And Flighty," Zelia added.

Ares chuffed. "That stupid chicken! I'd rather see it stuffed and served up on a plate."

Zelia ignored him. "But now we've got

responsibilities. People count on us. Rely on us. We have all this," her arm swung wide to indicate the entire camp, "to take care of."

The silver-haired elf followed the slender arm. "I know, and we can't leave them," he said. "But I'd give my belt," he grabbed the grisly girdle of scalps around his waist, "to go back to being a paid mercenary – a little better than most, but just like everybody else, just some bloke trying to make a living."

"Yet all this has come to pass because of our wedding," Zelia reminded him.

"Yes, I know," he said, drawing her into an embrace. "And I'm sorry I missed that."

"Me too," she said.

"We're agreed then? When all of this is over, we're going to elope. Go some place where there're no wizards, or relatives, or conflict."

"Do you think we can find such a place?"

"No." He leered conspiratorially at her. "But we can have some fun trying."

Nearly all of Brimstone's creatures had gathered. The central cavern was filled to bursting, and fire in its many manifestations spilled out to the corridors that radiated off the chamber like spokes on a wheel. Magma and lava, which is the earth's fiery side, attended. And, wandering among the crowd, water's more volatile members, the geysers, were spouting off to any who would listen.

And still more came. The sleek salamanders and the lordly wyrmes. Periodically, a fire lizard would slither into the throng, its bright glow lost among the glittering flames. Never in what elementals called history had there been such a meeting. Never had there been a need.

Even the Fell King was present, or an image of him was. For such an auspicious occasion, the Devil wore his Tenday best, with scarletine skin, serpentine tail and heavy-duty horns, wreathed by a flaming crown. All that would commend himself to fire and its denizens. Floating somewhere behind him, an imp with a woebegone expression dangled on a complex series of strings. The Demon King nodded and smiled to each passing elemental in a friendly way, but a wide circle had opened around him and his throne of flaming salamanders. It was hard to tell, as the elementals glimpsed nervously in that direction, if the Demon King attended in person or if this was a projection. For the likeness looked a little vague and fuzzy around the edges, but no one was going to get any closer to find out.

Next to the King of Kings was the leaping figure of Pyro Teknix. He had worked himself into furore, growing from conflagration to holocaust and casting down their supreme leader. Now Pyro stood in his former lord and master's stead.

Rumour ran riot amongst the crowd and kindling, words passed from flaming ear to flickering lip. Words like: library, paper, timber.

Those who had been to earth spoke of paradise. "They have buildings made of wood, constructed for no other purpose than to keep documents. Records all written on bits of paper and stored. Invoices. Fancy certificates with golden seals."

"Desks and furniture all made of wood," said the blaze. "Books, lovely books, and the humans they all wear garments of cloth." A few of the listeners drooled, tiny sparkling orange-red pearls that collected on lip and chin.

"In the north it is said that they have trees," said the third wistfully.

The meeting broke down in the resulting tumult, and the Demon King beamed on. Occasionally, he would lift a finger and point at a particular group and they'd fall to fighting amongst themselves.

Oh my, Satan thought, *weren't things working out nicely?*

"Order! Order!" Pyro flared explosively. The archfiend nodded at him. "Our esteemed guest would like to speak."

The Prince of Darkness rose majestically and graced them with a regal sneer. Then the King opened his mouth to speak. A flickering tongue of flame rolled from his mouth.

"We are brothers under the tongue, you and I," he said. "Made of the same stuff. Your desires and my desires are one. And the grievous insult we have suffered is the same, for have we not been banned from the mortal plane? And why? To protect man because he is too puny and weak to withstand our dazzling light. You have been wronged more than I, for have not the angels and their brother daemons stolen your secret so that fire's reflection on Earth has become man's slave?"

The many flickering tapers and flames began to grumble among themselves. "Wronged, that's what it is . . . Wronged!"

"Have not the seraphim," the demonlord shrieked the word, "been created to guard earth's door? I'd say that mankind has a lot to answer for."

The rumble turned into a roar.

"Throughout man's mortal time, you have been held captive here, as if you were the criminals instead of the victims of the crime. Are you going to take this lying down?"

"NO!"

The Demon King raised his arms, and his

great black cape absorbed the blazing light of Brimstone and reflected it back at them so that it seemed he stood within a pyre. "And I say, no more! If man cannot stand our brilliance, then let him step aside! Is it not time to go back through the portal to partake in the feast you so richly deserve?"

The elementals erupted. Flames danced. Blazes glittered and pyres leapt. Sparks reddened and darted about while lava spewed and magma boiled. Satan sat and regarded them benignly, but beneath his cape he snapped taloned fingers. A fiend crawled on hands and knees to the salamander throne unobserved. The Demon King gave him the signal, and from far and wide the many legions of devils, demons and imps poured into Brimstone. To irritate. To ruffle and rile. Provoking here, fomenting there, and generally ensuring that their elemental friends remained inflamed.

Chapter 14

As soon as the camp was set up along the Miasmic Plain, the War Council was called. A single elected official represented each of the four nations of Daklha. The sheik stood for Shamir while Zelia represented the Healer craft, and Ares the North. Aided from afar by Zelia's mother, the couple passed from mortal to mortal, preparing them for direct contact with the fairy queen. Astra voted for the elements as the only elemental present – water having long since vacated the mortal realm while earth was conspicuously absent.

Ares and Zelia presented their plan to the group who listened, awed and subdued. The idea was a simple one: to create a human barrier between fire and the rest of the continent. According to Astra, there was an ancient injunction against hurting humans unnecessarily. No mortal was harmed unless *he* did something foolish, like playing with fire or defying the winds.

"We cannot fight them," Zelia insisted as the first notes of discord broke among the conference. "We must negotiate somehow."

"With that bunch of hotheads!" Astra made a rude noise.

"We'll stall then," Zelia said, "until they cool down."

Around lip rings and golden lip studs, the Quattarean representative mumbled something about cowardice and Zelia swung on him, the bells of her craft flashing in the sun. "You would go out there swinging swords that will melt in your hands, and adhere to your flesh?" the healer asked.

Then she continued as if she hadn't been interrupted. "Air can act as a buffer between flame and the human contingent, but we have to keep mortal and elementals separate until the very last minute."

"That's it. That's all of it," the Quattarean protested in a quiver of jangling jewellery. "We're just going to stand around in a circle. For how long?"

Zelia looked at Ares who stepped forward to confront the slaver. "As long as it takes. Battle is a last resort. The merely mortal could not possibly hope to defeat elemental fire."

"We could be old men with very long beards before that happens," the Quattarean countered.

Ares didn't argue, he couldn't. That was the major flaw in the plan: it depended on fire seeing reason . . . eventually.

"And if fire breaks through the ring?" The Abdhan representative spoke for the first time.

"Then we fight," Zelia said brusquely. "But first we negotiate: Ares, my mother, my father and I. If something goes wrong, the sheik will signal. The bugle will blow. Then we advance as one. This is important. We must act in concert."

The adventurer stalked nervously throughout the small band. He did not like this concept of not-fighting, but he couldn't think of a better plan. Ever a pragmatist, Ares saw no point initiating a battle they were bound to lose. Something else was bothering him about the strategy, but he couldn't figure out what.

Further doubts were cast aside as water sloshed over his boot, and the adventurer froze, stunned. His eyes darted to a pair of water elementals splashing smugly at his feet. He bolted backwards and almost lost his footing. "What the—"

The Lady Astra gave a cry of joy. The Hamadi grinned and even the Quattarean breathed a sigh of relief.

"This changes things considerably," the slaver said.

"Not all that much," Ares said considering the pair. "The plan remains the same. Although it's nice to know we have the additional protection of water to extinguish any mortal unlucky enough to blunder into fire's grasp."

The lady flapped noisily above her cousins, chittering constantly. Zelia hovered nearby, and Ares thought he detected words in the garbled speech.

"I think that's it," Ares said. "My bride and I have a few things to discuss with the new arrivals. And we could all use some sleep. We'll tell you if anything's changed."

The council broke up. Even Astra vanished, leaving Fante to see their fluid cousins settled.

"Well, will they help?" He thumbed at water that pooled under his feet.

"Of course, they'll help. The problem is how much. There aren't many of them. Mainly those who lost their watering holes to fire. Unfortunately, we have no one noble among the fluid detachment. No one to command."

"How many are there?"

"A few," Zelia hedged.

"Enough to create a moat between human and flame?"

" 'Fraid not." And Zelia winced at Ares. "It's not a very good plan, is it?"

"It does have a few holes in it. Even if we are successful and convince them to return to Brimstone's plane, what are we going to do then? Post a guard? We can't close the door behind them. You said that it would require all the elementals working with the gods to do that."

"I know, but that's the least of our worries. I don't think we're going to be able to persuade them."

The small woman strode back and forth across the sand and slammed her fist into her hand. "It can't be like this. We can't be this helpless. Sala said we have all the tools we need."

The healer paused, propped her chin between thumb and forefinger, and thought. Wild light glimmered in her eyes. "Wait a second, I've got an idea."

"Oh, oh," Ares said.

"We've got to find Nepharious. I'll explain as we go."

"Oh, no," Ares groaned. "I've got a bad feeling about this."

Some time later, they hauled the bleating jinn

into the smooth glassine circle of Abdha. Both adventurer and maid halted in horror, arrested by the change that time had wrought. The stones had toppled and they lay scattered across the field, like dead soldiers. The bowl itself was as smooth and as slick as ice, and black as the finest dragon ivory. Nothing would live here for a long, long time.

"It is time for the second wish," Zelia said.

The jinn floated indifferently above the black mirror and yawned. "It's about time."

Her mouth opened and then snapped shut. She looked desperately at Ares who nodded with comprehension. If their wish misfired, or was in some way misunderstood, they and their fragile army would perish tomorrow – or was it yesterday? The adventurer was starting to get muddled, with all this time mucking about loose.

"We've got to try," he said to her. "It's our only hope." He turned to the jinn. "We want you to bring my mother back to me."

Nepharious sat up, clapping his hands. The rug appeared.

Ares hurried on to explain. "No, wait a second. There's more. We'll take you, at least as far as the mists. You are a creature of magic; you should be able to get through." The adventurer glanced at Zelia for confirmation. She nodded.

"And then we must return to prepare for the battle."

Nepharious eyed him sceptically. "You sure you don't want me to stay for that?"

"Ah," Zelia coughed. "Quite sure."

"You are to deliver a message while you are there." Ares gazed over the jinn's head at Zelia who had sidled up next to the genie. They grabbed him before he could protest and took him through . . . screaming.

"AAAAARRRRGGGGGGG!" The genie's cry of protest echoed about the circle. The startled rug leapt after its master, following in the aftermath of power.

The Lady Astra slipped between the planes. Passing briefly through her own realm, she heard Ignacious's rumbled "WEEELLLLL". Vitreous bounced from end to end, trying to get his father's attention.

Air's queen hesitated in front of Water's gate, took a deep breath, and dived in. Immediately, she was immersed in a sea-green world of kelp forests, coral cliffs and barnacle abodes. She half-swam, half-flew through the fluid medium. Seals and porpoises eyed this fay intrusion curiously. And they nudged what appeared to be a bubble, hastening her towards the fairy court.

The palace of the Prima was a fantastic filigree of fan coral and mother of pearl, with turrets of shell and barnacle-covered towers. The Lady Astra halted, treading water to consider the castle. Prima had always been prone to ostentation. A creature of air, Astra hated all enclosures. She shrugged and let the current carry her through the door and into the throne room of the rival queen.

"Astra, what a pleasure to see you," Aqua gushed.

"It is not pleasure that brings me, as you know too well," Astra said, and her rustling voice was muted by water so that it sounded more like the babbling of a brook or the whisper of wind across ocean waves. "Even as we speak, mortals gird themselves for war. A war we have brought upon them."

"Not I, nor my kind, lady." Water's queen opened her emerald arms in an expansive gesture.

"Is it not the elements that have ravaged earth's fragile realm?"

"And since when has earth been fragile? You know that it would take a thousand of us an immortal eternity or two to wear down one such as Ignacious, or even to get him to move for that matter."

"And what of our vow to protect man?"

Aqua stiffened, if such a word can be applied to water. The temperature in the throne room dropped, and the two queens stared icily at each other. "Let me remind you. It is not water who is sworn to protect man, but air. Water stands between air and fire as you well know, and it's not a very comfortable position to be in, let me tell you."

The Lady Astra pulled herself to her full handspan of height. "Then you won't help," she said.

"If fire breaches mortals' portals again, then we will come." And with an aqueous duck of her watery head, Prima dismissed air's fairy queen.

Thesbos, the Mayor of Thessalia, trembled under his desk. Somewhere behind him a foot swung in a deadly arc to connect with his hindquarters, and Thessalia's mayor jumped, bumping his head on a drawer.

Swearing, Thesbos scrabbled around inside his hiding-place so that he peered outwards. Putting on his best gruff face, he peeped from underneath the desk and shouted: "Who dares disturb me?"

"I do, little man." Philos's commanding voice came from somewhere above his head. Thesbos sighed and scrambled to his feet, dusting off the medallion of his office and picking imaginary fluff from his surcotte.

"I was, uh, looking for a pencil," he said.

"Of course, you were," the Archmage purred. "May I, ah, help you?"

Philos nodded.

"Er, how?" Thesbos said.

"These are troubled times we live in," the Archmage said, scratching his chin and looking sage.

"Yes, indeed, they are," Thesbos agreed, mimicking the magician's movements. Following the wizardly example, he stroked his beard and put on his most learned expression, but he only succeeded in looking foolish.

The wizard blew out from puffed cheeks. " 'Tis evil sorcery floating about which we at the college are sworn to combat."

"Good. Glad to know you are on the ball. Now if you don't mind I was looking for my pencil." Thesbos made to duck under his desk again, but Philos caught him by the scruff of the neck.

"Unfortunately, we find ourselves a little short of supplies. Vital ingredients for spells, ingredients which I believe the city can provide."

"I'm sorry. We're a little short on eye of newt, lizard's tongues and whatnot."

"Silence!" the wizard roared, "Don't presume to know what I . . . we . . . require."

Thesbos gulped. His Adam's apple bobbed up and down in his throat.

"You have, I believe, a morgue," Philos said.

"A morgue? Of course, we have a morgue. What respectable city would be without one?"

"Would you happen to have a body?"

"A body?" Thesbos shuffled the papers on his desk. "Yes, I believe we have a body. A cutpurse was brought in just last night, and someone else, too."

"Good. Good."

"Would you be wanting them?" Thesbos asked. "The corpses, I mean."

"No, the corpses are already taken care of. What we seem to be lacking is viscera."

"Viscera?" Thesbos squeaked, his voice going up a notch.

"You know, intestines."

"Ah, intestines, right, of course, silly of me," Thesbos stammered. "Sure, sure, take all the intestines that you want. Take bladders, take kidneys. Make yourself at home. Our morgue is your morgue, as I always say."

The Archmage bowed slightly, swirled and swooped away. Thesbos watched him for a few moments wondering how the wizard did that – swoop, that is. Philos always seemed to swoop wherever he went.

Absent-mindedly, the mayor settled into his

chair just as a rampaging spell came screaming through the window. And Thesbos dived underneath the desk to look for his pencil, disregarding the full pencil-case he kept in his pocket.

The people stood in battle formation. The strategy could be summarized in a single word: survival. The air elementals were to buffer man from their fiery adversary. The human combatants had been instructed to avoid engagement at all costs. The goal was to keep fire confined within the stone circle until they could be coerced, or tricked, back into the portal between the worlds. The signal would only be given if negotiations failed. Then and only then, as a last resort, would the trumpeter bugle attack.

Ares looked out upon the bowl of smooth, black obsidian. He lifted a brow and peered over at the sheik who sat upon his grand destrier. The adventurer sighed. The Shamirian leader would not be dissuaded from taking his mount into battle. Ares doubted that the steed would be able to stay upright on the slick surface, and he wondered if the Shamir didn't know how to fight except on horseback.

All the tribes and all the countries were represented. The much-ringed Quattarean stood elbow to elbow with Hamadan farmer, on foot, for both groups were too practical to go into the fray mounted. The survivors of Abdha poked around amongst the straggling remains of vines, making non-skid boots out of the thick leaves of Apsu's Coat. Soon other members of their makeshift infantry got the idea and were foraging among the few withering vines to create shields and armour from the scaled bark.

Air swarmed, separated from the human contingent by a thin trickle of water. A hush blanketed the crowd. All noise ceased. Not a foot shuffled, not a nose sniffed, not a single horse blew through loose lips. The silence became a tangible thing that pulsed palpably around them as they waited.

Ares shifted restlessly. If something didn't happen soon they'd lose half their men. What sane man would remain given time to think?

Until now, his and Zelia's reputation had held the band together, carrying the others along. But unless fire arrived soon, their followers would give up and begin to slip away. Not to mention, the air squadron. The adventurer glanced above his head at the circling figures. It wouldn't take long before air elementals lost interest, or simply forgot what they were here for.

All their plans had hinged on fire's speedy

arrival. Indeed, the tribes had rushed here, afraid that they wouldn't be in time. But what if fire tarried on the fourth plane? Or, like their elemental cousins, air, lost interest? Ares didn't understand much about the strange shifts and eddies of time, but he knew enough to realize that time, or what they had that resembled it, worked differently on the other planes. Their wedding celebration had lasted only one day, or night, on air's elemental plane, yet enough time had passed on earth for the Kazzam tribe to make its way from the desert to Al Khali. Long enough, certainly, for a revolution to take place in the sheik's tents.

"Ah, Zelia?"

"Hmm-m?"

"What if they don't come?"

"They'll come."

"Yes, but when?"

She gaped at him, his concern and the reason behind it registering slowly. Just then, there was a small explosion within the great portal. Everyone tensed, leaning forward in anticipation.

A single cheery camp-fire, always a friend to man, popped out from the gate. The group gave a collective sigh and relaxed. It fumed and, seeing Ares and Zelia, it darted to stand before them. The blue maid reached out and smiled.

"Yes?" Zelia knelt next to the tiny blaze.

"They come, they come, and are they ma—" The fire sputtered, but before he had a chance to continue . . .

BOOM, BOOM, KABOOM!

The very air around them detonated, and fire came billowing outwards. The flowing robes of the desert people were lifted, buffeted about on a scalding, hot wind. A cascade of orange split the blue sky to flow like a waterfall or a river of a million tiny golden figures with gleaming red eyes. Flambeaux figures poured over the glassy black floor. Flame rippled, spinning and spilling from some imperceptible trapdoor several handspans above the circle. Sparks flew from flaming brows. Embers arched, igniting cloth, and men began beating at their flaming burnouses.

The mounted tribes shrieked their eerie war-cry – a high-pitched squeal that made Ares's throat and head ache. The wall of men reeled. Zelia scanned the lurching line and frowned. The sheik put up a restraining hand, and the many tribes fell back a pace.

Cautiously, the sheik steered his mount forward. Its hooves hit the black mirror, and the poor animal did a graceless gambolling prance, all thrashing knees and flailing hooves. Its legs skidded out from under the beast, and the stallion went down. SLAM! The sheik slipped from the destrier's back and examined the splayed limbs, fuming. Seeing his distress, the ever-vigilant Lady Hadidge motioned to the *terem* women. The wives and concubines flowed around the beast, half-lifting and half-sliding the animal back to the sand. The sheik stalked after them, the conference forgotten.

Ares chuckled. "We warned him," he said. "Well, it looks like it's up to us." The half-elf extended his hand to Zelia. "My lady, shall we go parley?"

"Yes," she said. "Mother, can you call fire to order?"

"They are not mine to command," Astra admonished.

"Just do the best you can, mother," Zelia said.

Meanwhile, Nepharious was having troubles of his own, navigating the cloud of confusion the elf folk had placed around their settlements. Like their remote ancestors, the fairies, elves could manipulate time's eddies. They used this in the cloud they erected around their cities, and now that time was shifting about all over the place, it seemed the elfin cities had emulated it, slithering hither, thither and yon.

The jinn was lost. Well not lost, really, he knew exactly where he was. He was wallowing in the same blasted fog the couple had dumped him in, and Nepharious cursed the blue one's name. No, he wasn't lost. He just couldn't quite figure out how to get to where he was going from here. Of course, that was the purpose of the Cloud of Confusion – to befuddle and bemuse, and it seemed to be working quite well.

Disgruntled, the genie magicked up another fur to wrap around himself. *Hades, it was cold!* Who in their right minds would live in a place like this? And he wished himself away. The carpet hesitated indecisively. Nepharious barked a command at the balking rug as he called up another thick duvet. The additional weight of the wrap caused the rag-rug to sag, and the irritated genie, needing some place to vent his vexation, struck out at it.

It was just a small lightning bolt, but it was enough. The rug bucked in a sudden thermal and Nepharious grabbed onto its edge and yelled. Then the struggling carpet dipped into an air pocket. In his terror, Nepharious got a little rough as he tried to pull it out of a dive and they carpet-wheeled, end over end, before plummeting through the mists towards the rocky Szatmarian coastline, somewhere below. His howl of rage and complaint struck the ice flow and bounced back at him mockingly. Spinning, spinning, spinning, they penetrated the cover of cloud and the white ground rose up to greet them . . .

The representative of fire crackled belligerently. Pyro Teknix expanded hotly as he recited a list of wrongs dating from time's inception. From the daemon's theft to man's disrespect. Pyro flared, repealing the ancient agreement that banned fire elementals' access to the earthen plane. The creature blundered about the glass circle, flaming exterior rippling redly.

The Lady Astra wondered what had so inflamed the stodgy, old fairy. As a conflagration, he was more stable than most, but right now Pyro was babbling as much as any silly, watery brook. Looming large and loud, he recited chapter and verse of the elemental code. Air's queen grew bored. Her daughter Zelia feigned interest, but Astra could hear the echo of her daughter's thoughts, and she knew that as long as Pyro talked, Zelia would listen. Her daughter feared battle more than any other thing, even if it meant having to listen to this old poop for an eternity.

Astra's attention drifted, and the fay elemental body followed, wafting about on a self-made breeze. On the far side of the circle, the sheik ran his hands down the stallion's fetlocks, checking for broken bones. His touch was tender, and the Lady Astra remembered his gentle caress from an earlier date.

"And furthermore," Pyro sputtered.

The blustering old fool! the Lady thought and dismissed the conference from her mind. Her gaze trained on the sheik's long fingers as they kneaded the animal's flank. He had been checking his destrier in this way when she'd first met him so many rotations ago. Satisfied that the animal was unharmed, the sheik rose and mounted. Memories of yesterday got tangled with today. Lost in love's recall, times merged. The Lady could not let him escape from her advances. She glided down upon the sheik.

The one they called General Conflagration swelled to vermilion. The sheik mounted his steed and listened, oblivious to her approach. She zipped around his head. He shook it. She droned excitedly, and he raised his hand. The signalman perked up, standing at attention, eyes riveted to the sheik. His ears pricked, trying to catch some of the distant conversation.

The Lady Astra buzzed, excitedly. The hand inched higher, poised and ready to strike at the insectile whine.

The signal!

Seeing this, the trumpeter lifted his bugle and blew!

The blast sent Astra somersaulting across the

circle towards her daughter and blew sense into her foggy brain. Zelia's lover spun, gesticulating denial, and the lady knew she had to act. Astra called her people to her. They descended in a flutter of wings to carry the silver-haired elf and swearing blue maid aloft and out of harm's way.

The cry sounded and, shocked, the sheik stood up in his saddle. He'd seen aught to indicate the parley had ended. He stared at his daughter and her lover, so close to the tall column of flame, and was suddenly aware of the danger and all their carefully laid plans flew from his mind.

The sheik stabbed at the golden glow of flame with his scimitar. On cue, the horsemen careened forward.

Thousands of them!

CHAPTER 15

The many fine steeds hit the glassy surface like oil on water. Stallions glided every which way, careering into each other with a great flailing of legs. Hooves slipped, this way and that, and the many proud beasts performed a comical dance. The infantry, more cautious and much more vulnerable, kept to their places outside the circle of battered stones.

Suspended above them, Zelia swore harder while Ares simply closed his eyes. The presence of elementals and man within the close quarters performed its strange magic, and suddenly the number of skittering destriers and helpless riders doubled, as time bent out of true.

The couple were borne to the side of the field. Men, now twinned, advanced cautiously, trying to avoid the flying hooves and the shimmering flame. The successful flourished fiery brands, for fire was loath to fight its reflection on earth. The infantry, clothed in armour of Apsu's Coat and shod with its leaves, drove the elementals relentlessly before them. The glimmering line gave.

Suddenly, water came tumbling out of the portal to engage fire in battle. It gushed all about friend and foe alike, extinguishing the blazing brands and damping already sodden spirits. With its arrival, men and horses doubled yet again. Then fire rushed in and a boiling fog enveloped the battle line. Men and fine steeds screamed in agony as many were scalded and burned.

Maddened by pain, they cut and hacked at anything that was close to them. As often as not, stabbing younger, or older, versions of themselves, and many a fine man was lost. The more astute warrior recoiled rather than skewering a vision of himself. Those caught in a battle frenzy were not so discerning.

Zelia saw no less than four sheiks caught in the fray. Ares plucked at her sleeve and pointed at the circle. At least one version of the sheik and their many massed followers still stood outside of the circle.

As one, the couple turned to observe the centre of the maelstrom, wondering if somewhere at its heart two ghostly images of themselves were being broiled alive. Ares glanced nervously at his hands half expecting them to burst into flame.

Air eddied about them, diving into the tumult, and the number of figures multiplied not once but twice. Then, as if something had tipped the scales, the sheik at the sidelines raised his hand; the trumpeter lifted his horn to his lips and blew. The waiting horses plunged ahead, skating into the existing mêlée and got lost among the others.

One of the sheik's horses went down and he went down with it. Zelia gave a sharp cry and dashed into the battle, Ares on her heels. They were in the thick of it. Ares crouched, his war-hammer ready. A blade caught the dim light of the sun in steaming mists, and Ares deflected a blow that would have decapitated Zelia as she drove through the press of waggling bodies. She shrieked at the people to stop, but no one could hear her above the din. The bowl reverberated with the clash of arms and the thud of colliding bodies.

Someone, Ares didn't know who, cried retreat, and the air thick with smoke and steam freshened slightly. The trumpeter removed his instrument, grinned and winked at Ares as some *doppelgänger* trumpeted assault. The situation went from bad to worse. Some men ran in rout only to be met by a charge of themselves from several minutes ago. The battle erupted again around them as frightened men, trying to leave the field, fought with versions of themselves just as eager to get in there. Ares grabbed Zelia, pulling her aside.

"This is madness," he bellowed into her ear to make himself heard.

"But my father . . ."

The adventurer shook his head. "He's a grown man; he can take care of himself."

"But . . ."

"Take it from me. Fighting's my trade and I can tell a losing battle when I see one."

"But . . ."

Then her father erupted from the crowd, and Ares succeeded in dragging Zelia from the battlefield. The sheik came storming down on them, his burnous flapping wildly.

"What happened?" he demanded furiously. "Why'd you give the signal to attack?"

"I was about to ask you the same thing," she retorted.

"I didn't," he argued. "All I did was raise my hand to brush this gnat away . . ." His voice dwindled. Both whirled to face the Lady Astra.

"Mother!"

The fairy, deciding that now would be a good time to lead her subjects in their assault, grinned sheepishly and disappeared. A hot blast swept the field, and air herded man away from their elemental cousins. With a rapier wind, they sliced through clashing elements to thrash at fire here and buffet at water there. Blowing and squalling among their fay cousins, they separated fire from water, as a flail winnows the purple Lavantian wheat from chaff.

And the elements did what elements will do. Fire expanded and water spewed in rocketing spirals. But they backed away, just a bit, to eye their opponents.

The calm before the storm.

The trumpet sounded, and men attacked again, instinctively, slashing at anything that moved. Time unravelled a bit more. Horses slipped in and out of the waving hoes of the Hamadi farmer and the swaying sword of the Shamir. Elementals oscillated, vibrating at ever faster speeds, until they could not be distinguished from the elements they represented.

The Lady Astra again tried to orchestrate an attack.

"Are you going to return to the battle?" Zelia turned to her father.

The sheik grunted, "Uh, I think I'll sit this

one out," he said, adding, "there's already enough of me out there."

"Aren't you afraid that one of you will get killed?" Ares asked.

"I don't think so or I wouldn't be here now. I'd already be dead," the sheik said.

The adventurer considered this for a moment, all very confused by what was happening around them. It appeared if a person killed a younger version of himself – say a version of five minutes ago – all images died simultaneously. However, if the killer were the younger of the two, then the slayer had shortened his lifespan considerably, but was permitted enough of a respite to rue the deed.

Or was it the other way round?

The adventurer threw up his hands unable to work it out while the sheik settled in a cloud of white cloth at his daughter's feet.

"We've got to do something." Zelia swung on her partner. "It can't go on like this."

People were falling upon their swords, perhaps preferring the short cut of suicide to possibly killing a ghostly double of themselves in the turmoil. The more muddled were falling on things like camel droppings – realizing belatedly that, however distasteful, dung wasn't fatal.

The adventurer towed his betrothed away

from the chaos as the Lady Astra successfully implemented another brief respite in the battle.

Ares counted: "One, two, three."

A horn blew. Blades flashed.

The snow elf rolled his eyes to the heavens. "Look, Sala said that we've got all the tools. So let's review our options. Are we using every tool at our disposal?"

Zelia folded her arms across her chest and regarded the chaos, chewing her lip. "Well, we've got every friendly elemental, every able-bodied native and every implement on Daklha that even slightly resembles a weapon out there on the field, and it just keeps happening over and over and over again." Her eyes strayed to the battle. "I wonder how many times a man can die."

The clarion cry of horns echoed around them, and horse, man and elemental clashed again.

"What about magic?" Ares asked.

"It's all around us. You see it." She pointed at his curious cat-like eyes. "I haven't seen your pupils for days."

"It's around us, but are we *using* it?" He prodded.

Zelia stared at him, a dawning light in her eyes. "No, it's just bouncing around out there."

Her jaw drooped, and her head pivoted on her neck. She gazed out over the field at the bubbling fountain of water, leaping fire and whipping air, which Astra had managed to cleave again into separate factions. There were now no less than twenty versions of the sheik sliding around on his stallion, another had joined her father on the sand, and she noted another had emerged from the conflict and was already sprinting across the obsidian mirror.

"We can't harness that!" Zelia said.

"We've got to try."

"Where's that idiot jinn?" Zelia fumed.

"Did you hear me?" Ares stepped in front of her. "We've got to try."

"We could be burned up in the aftermath of power."

Ares gestured nonchalantly at the pyre of flames. "Power or elemental fire, take your choice."

Joi II quailed, a quiver of delicate but still undeveloped quills. A fiery column hovered on the horizon, battling with water and air. Occasionally the pyre would move, advancing slightly and the little bush quaked in its roots. Then the flaming approach would halt, and the fire would back away.

The tiny seraphim remained unnoticed in the commotion. The creature remembered its death and its purpose, for it possessed the recollection of how things were done, if not – at this stage in its development – the capacity to actually do it.

Flame fountained in a spinning spiral, and Joi saw its imminent destruction. The already-weakened gates started to crumble, and the creature reached deep inside trying to find the strength to alert its fledging brothers of the renewed breech. Within the fragile shell, earth's eldest – and youngest – tried to discover the means to accelerate the growth cycle enough to propagate more seeds as Joi II prepared to die.

Zelia and Ares joined hands, their powers merged, and when they opened their eyes again it was to observe the world with a unified mind. They searched the heavens for the ley, but they hadn't reckoned on the distortion caused by the presence of so many elementals. The lines snaked and twisted, corkscrewing round and round. The momentum of their motion grew ever more frenetic the closer the lines got to the conflict until, at its centre, they had tied themselves in a single knot.

The combined spirit, which was neither Ares nor Zelia but both of them, leapt. Ephemeral feet touched the whipping path of the grid. It coiled beneath them and they clung to the squirming lines. Then they moved further from the maelstrom. The ley smoothed and the couple raced away, a beam of light zipping through a single shimmering strand. As they neared the northern continent, again the strands dipped and lurched drunkenly as if the magical disturbance in the far circle of Abdha found its reflection in Eubonia. Eventually they had to drag themselves along the ley, and their earth-bound bodies, lying outside the stone circle, went through the same creeping mime.

Below them, elemental magic had run amuck. Every cottage had been turned to a castle, each more fantastical than the previous. Man's wishes had attained substance, and the earth groaned under the load. Spells flew to and fro, free.

Attracted to their sorcery, the enchantments chased after the couple, and they had to dodge and dart almost losing their tenuous grip on the ley.

Power coursed through the grid, rocketing along the strand from some unknown source, carrying them with it. Down, down, down, to the Isle of Knowledge, spiralling down into Thessalia, rocketing through the streets, and their dream bodies passed through ghostly pedestrians and even ghostlier incantations. Drawn to the Wizards' College, and down to the labyrinth below . . .

The Archmage raced back from the morgue. His

hood was drawn low so that it covered his features. The treasured intestines, kindly donated by a cutpurse that had no need for them, were clenched against his breast. His cloak was stained but he took no notice as he rushed through the forgotten corridors to his secret laboratory.

He dropped the sack on the floor and bent over the cadaver to examine the cavity, which was already filled with the normal complement of human viscera. The mage then extracted a handful from the bag and shoved them into the gap. Philos stepped back to inspect his work, turning his head this way and that.

Pulling up his sleeve, he felt around in the sack. Finally, his hand found purchase, and he yanked a handful from the bag and thrust them into the bulging abdomen.

"There," Philos mumbled. "That ought to be enough."

The wizard tried to rearrange them in a more orderly pattern and was just about to extricate his hands from the cadaver when Mad Thomas opened his eyes and stared at him. The Archmage froze. He recognized that look.

The body spoke with the voice of the fairy spawn, Zelia. "We need your magic," it said.

"No!" He roared. Power and latent enchantment that had been loitering about the laboratory waiting for the fun to begin surged through him into the cadaver. Both Philos's and Thomas's corpse lit up like Brimstone's fire. The Archmage did a jittering jig, his feet dancing across the floor and out from underneath him, while his body stayed upright.

His "no" rebounded off the walls and reeled off down the hallway. The aura dimmed; and the wizard collapsed, arm sealed inside the now-closed abdominal cavity. Mad Thomas sat up and brushed the remains of the Archmage aside.

The arms fell away, bloodless stumps, for the late Philos, the not-so Benevolent, had been sucked dry. The soulless homonucleus stood and shambled over into a corner to wait. Philos rose too, his eyes dead and blank, and lumbered to the opposite corner, for in death the Archmage had been successful as he had never been in life.

The homonucleus lived!

Zelia and Ares were ejected from the body of Mad Thomas forcefully and thrust back across space and time to the Miasmic Swamp. Sheiks sat in a ring around them. The couple peered owlishly at the throng and then fell into each other's arms. For the umpteenth time opponents parted, horns blared and the battle was joined anew.

* * *

In planes beyond planes, deep within her temple perched precariously atop a shrine to some long-forgotten god, Sala performed the promenade of cycles – the dance from which her symbol came. The dance by which the seasons changed.

She spun round and round and round again, tail caught in her mouth. Her eyes glinted harshly. The goddess rotated again. Sala swore around her tail. Somewhere there was the distant din of horns and she revolved yet another time.

All in all, being the goddess of cycles wasn't difficult. All she had to do, every hundred mortal rotations or so, was grab her own tail and make a complete circle to hurry the seasons along their path a bit. In exchange, she got plenty of admirers, obeisances and sacrifices. Generally speaking, it was an easy job with plenty of time to attend to her clutch.

At least, until someone had started mucking about with time's cycles. Since then the rite had become a daily affair, but even that hadn't been too bad. Then it came once an hour. Difficult at best, when she had an egg to guard and a hungry husband prowling about, but as goddess of cycles, Sala was philosophical. She knew that when things got out of kilter, it took a while to set things to right again. Such was the cycle of things. As a goddess you had to accept a certain amount of wobbliness now and then. It was a good time to show off your power if you were prone to that sort of thing. She wasn't, not like her husband, who travelled mortal lands daily to leave his imprint on the sands and take a quick bite out of the mortal sun, just so people remembered he was around.

Through the thousands of turns, Sala learned to be patient when dealing with the foibles of man. But this was the living end. She heard horns. Her mouth closed around her tail, and she spun again. The din increased and her pace increased likewise until she was a running blue, red, purple and green ring, and her eyes glittered no more. The basilisk pupils crossed dizzily.

There was a resounding crack, and the goddess wailed around her tail. The egg's thick yoke, the partially-formed snake already visible in its contents, spilled across the temple floor.

"That's it," she mumbled around her tail. "Enough is enough." And the goddess rolled out of the temple and spiralled off into the immortal sky.

The ice roof of the palace shattered in a shimmer of crystalline shards. Silenea Nivea whirled in time to see a bundle of rug, fur and curly-toed shoes drop like a leaden weight to the ground. It rolled and a few more things became apparent. The demon, whatever it was, could swear in any number of different languages, and its skin was as red and fiery as its temper.

The snow elf took an involuntary step backwards as arms emerged from the tangled knot and tore at pelt and hide, trying to get at the rug which, with amazing foresight, had slithered off into a corner.

"When I get my hands on you . . ." The turban-wrapped head of a jinn appeared. He struggled to his feet and kicked at the rug. The genie's foot tangled with the many furs while the carpet scooted to the opposite side of the room.

The lady with snow-white hair threw back her head and laughed, and her voice was like the tinkling of cool chimes. He turned on her with a curse forming on his lips.

"May I help you?" Silenea asked mildly.

"Oh," he said. "I didn't know that anybody else was here. You wouldn't happen to know Silenea Nivea, mother of Ares the Adventurer?"

The woman smiled. "I am she. I am his mother."

"Your son has sent me to find you, madam. He requires your assistance." The jinn bowed with a flourish and then hastened to explain her son's need.

While Silenea went to collect the requested wizard, Nepharious plucked a crystal ball from his voluminous pantaloons and gazed worriedly into it. The battle went ill, as clash and reclash left a few more men dead. The jinn cheered as blow met blow.

"Yay! Hurrah! Look out! Watch out behind you!" he hollered at the mute ball.

Flakes of snow blurred the image. The genie shook it, and the snow flurried about.

"Mr Jinn, we are ready?"

Nepharious turned to gaze upon the elfin wizard. The sorcerer was slender. Spindly. His beard venerable. His robes, like Silenea's, were snow-white without a bit of gold embroidery or glittering amulet. The jinn frowned, the sorcerer had none of the flash and pizzazz of his mortal counterpart. He looked fragile, as if he could be blown over by the very first breeze.

He would have to do, the jinn decided, one eye on the glass orb. *Time grew short*.

Nepharious ushered mother and mage onto his little square of abused blanket that he called a rug. If he survived this thing, he was going to ask his father for a proper carpet. A racy little number, maybe with a stripe or two.

Perhaps the rug read his thoughts, for it rose sedately from the floor and drifted, awaiting instructions. Nepharious paused, pondering his route. He did not wish to get lost in the magical mists. He didn't stop to think that his companions could perhaps guide him. With a sly eye on the warrior's mother, the jinn snapped his fingers. He'd give them the ride of their lives. He'd take the short cut between planes.

The cowering carpet picked up a whisper of the genie's wish and darted off, steered by his unspoken command, almost . . .

Silenea was enveloped by cold, cold the like of which she had never experienced before. It felt as if all warmth and feeling were being leeched from her body until she was numb.

And dark. So dark Silenea could not have seen a hand in front of her face, and when she looked down, she could not see her feet. So black that even her elfin nightsight couldn't pierce the gloom. The only thing that let her know she still existed was the feel of the knobbly, knotted rug beneath her.

Somewhere – that sounded far, far away but was in truth quite close – someone wailed. The magical rug trembled, and the next thing Silenea knew they were flitting through air's devastated stone circle. In this light she could see the mage who clenched her arm in a vice-like grip.

"WWEEEELLLLLLL . . ." someone said, with a voice like the grinding of glacier wall against granite.

The wizard gave her a baffled look, which she returned with a wry smile, noticing that tiny specks of something seemed to dance before her eyes. Then they were whisked away. Swiftly, magician, jinn and elf-woman were propelled into a wet, green world, where her clothes adhered to her body, and she felt she was being dragged down by their weight. Silenea held her breath until it felt like her lungs were on fire. When next she inhaled, they filled with the harsh stench of sulphur. Silenea wheezed and coughed.

Again darkness shrouded her sight, and they were in a fell, black place where a were-rabbit bared bloody fangs at them threateningly. Before she had a chance to recoil, the group was transported again . . . to Hades. An imp, wearing huge ears, a ridiculous belled cap and holding a bone, frolicked on the end of a string. It waved jerkily at them as they passed. Then daemons, cherubim and angels flew beside them, stroking white harps and singing sweet, sweet music.

Repeatedly, the elf-woman was struck by a

series of bizarre sensations, as if in each place she went something, or somethings, were cleaving to her flesh. When she looked at the magician, who still held her hand in a white-knuckled clutch, Silenea thought she saw twinkling mites, like midge-flies or small gnats, swarming around his head. For unbeknownst to them, everywhere they went they picked up the many pieces of Queb from the planes.

Meanwhile, the jinn beside her cursed the carpet roundly. "I said between the planes! *Between*, you idiot, not through!"

There was a glimpse of a street filled to overflowing with disorderly disarray of temples, and then the priestess of the snow elves was enveloped in something cold, soft, sticky and sugary. *Ice cream?* This was baked away in less time than it took to think about it when they arrived to stand, blinking, under the hot southron sun.

The bond with the college broken, Ares and Zelia rose shakily to their feet. The Grand Inquisitor shimmered into view. The long-range vision was as flimsy as gossamer, it wavered and waved in the eddying currents of elemental magic. His touch was gentle. He gave them a small charge of power that revived them, and they knew that the wizards were theirs to command. At that moment a horse came skating across the jet-black glass and went crashing through the phantom inquisitor. He vanished, the line severed.

A blinding flash ripped across the sky. All combatants halted simultaneously, mid-caper, swing or grope. The jinn, Ares's mother and a startled elfin mage loomed overhead. The magician's conical cap had slipped over his eyes, and he clung for dear life to Silenea Nivea's sleeve.

The rug swept down to the ground and skidded out from under the stumbling mage. Ares and Zelia helped him to his feet, straightened his cap. Microscopic flecks arced around the head of elfin woman, snow-white wizard and spitting jinn. Then they were gone. Lost among the turmoil.

Four heads bowed together, for only a moment, as they consulted. The mage nodded, then pointed towards the ongoing battle.

Mission completed, the jinn drew to the sidelines to heckle and harass the muddled warriors and their prancing steeds. A horse skidded from the tumult – the same one who had nearly pinned the couple not seconds before – and rammed the genie. Nepharious belly-flopped away, grabbed one of the sheik's scimitars, and proceeded to stab himself in the foot. The animal did a gambolling promenade, trying unsuccessfully to get its hooves underneath its torso, and toppled, flopping ungainly on top of the feckless jinn.

The mage raised his arms and began an incantation in the lilting elvish tongue. Silenea's voice joined the wizard's. Snow elves' sorcery is peculiar to their kind, just as human wizardry is different from, although dependent upon, fay magic. Zelia felt a mental nudge from Ares and dropped into a trance. They channelled their more mortal power to Silenea, enhancing the elfin power with their own.

The temperature started to drop, imperceptibly at first, and then like a snowball rolling down hill it gained in mass. Ice particles formed around them. The mortal combatants grew chilled. Many dropped their weapons and flapped their arms, beating their sides to keep warm. The crystals spread and mortal breath came out in billowing clouds as the elementals slowed, moving with drunken torpor.

Then the temperature plummeted, freezing water in the middle of a cavort. From somewhere across space, Ares/Zelia felt the tentative touch of the healers, followed by the wizards, and the couple added their magic into the spell. The frigid air turned icy. The clouds of mortal breath appeared as snowflakes, and the fire elementals were transformed into brittle, yellow shards. Something dark oozed from the frozen form of Pyro Teknix to slither under a fallen stone. The miscellany of red passions, black hates, along with a few shimmering bits of white love blended perfectly with blood-red sands and the scorched black stone. They met with their many brothers, already loose upon the field and slunk away.

An impasse had been reached, the battle a stalemate, neither won nor lost. Despite the cold, beads of sweat formed upon Zelia's brow. She was dimly aware as some of the mortals began to pick their sluggish way through the frozen elements. Others were still caught in the frenzy of battle, fighting themselves, while the more cautious – like the sheik – had collected the various images of themselves and huddled as far from the fracas as possible.

Nepharious freed himself from the horse and rose in a cloud of thunderbolts, preparing to fry the poor beast. But one of the many versions of the sheik stepped between the jinn and the floundering animal, and Nepharious had to be satisfied with mocking the paralysed elementals.

Of the elements, only air impervious to cold, flitted about freely, to tickle and pinch the frosty shells of their cousins. Frozen as they were, magic's creatures could be handled and returned safely to their home planes, but the sorcerers could not release their grip. It was taking all their strength to maintain this tenuous hold.

Already the wizards' energies began to wane, and the statues of fire and ice began to quicken.

Carrying the spark of human life, Queb like all men had many sides. Pieces of good glittered and gleamed with a pure-white lustre and mingled freely with rancour's jewels. Both lurked unseen inside Pyro's flaming body. Dark speckled with little pinpricks of light gazed through the fiery veil that separated it from the mortal combatants.

When the jinn had materialized, towing a woman with snow-white hair and a cringing wizard, the snake-like thread of black inside the flame froze. The mage flailed his arms, and this thing that once was the greatest sorcerer on the Earth plane saw the workings of magic.

Slumbering memory stirred, pricked with interest. When the temperature began to drop, Queb exited quickly before the fire elemental he inhabited broke into brittle splinters. So all that was once Queb – all that had been collected in Hades, gathered by Night and gleaned from Brimstone – escaped onto the Earth plane to meet other pieces of itself that lurked among the throng.

Curious, the not-quite-being shuffled around the contest, attracted by the human warmth as much as it was attracted to the smell of blood. Something about this place seemed familiar.

The tarry substance slid unnoticed onto the field, just another shade among the rest. Outside his fiery shell, the thing that was Queb recognized the lovely apparition with braids of silver. As the pieces of disassociated thought aligned themselves, something in the glinting speckles of good awoke. The string of parts gazed upon a once-beloved face and, in that instant, Queb realized for the first time that, long ago, he had been human.

A shadow fell across the heavens, blotting out the face of the sun. The bewildered tribesmen and the listless elementals glanced up to regard a giant serpent pivoting in the sky. The snaking body encircled the fragile earth, its tail clamped firmly in its mouth. It swore around its tail and then rolled with royal grandeur down from the heavens.

"Sala," Zelia breathed the goddess's name.

And time stood still. Arms poised in the middle of a killing stroke. Scimitars winked as wicked smiles in the harsh sun. Stallions were arrested mid-stumble, their bodies caught in the throes of a clumsy slide, legs askew. The goddess uncoiled, rising majestically until the great snake's head towered above the many combatants.

"You!" Sala turned on the jinn. "I might have expected to find you here. What have you been doing?"

Zelia moved to defend Nepharious. With a careless flip of her hair, the healer retorted, "Just what you told us to do, or, more precisely, didn't tell us."

The serpent reared until she balanced impossibly on the tip of her tail, glaring down at the blue maiden.

Ares moved between the two. "You only said we had all the tools." His arm swung in a wide arc, taking in the confusion of elemental statues. "And you see, we've given it everything we've got."

"Thisss iss the ressult?" the goddess screeched. "Thiss chaosss iss the best you can do? The progresssion of ccyclesss ssspeeded up ssso much that a battle isss ended before it hass begun, and then it iss begun again. I'm dizzy trying to keep up with it all."

Her voice took on a note of complaint, and she began shrinking to mortal size. The flattened head rounded. Nose, ears, and near mortal mouth appeared among the scales as the plates smoothed into shimmering green skin. Hard lumps of shoulders appeared beneath the head, and arms sprouted from the stumps, while soft bumps formed to make breasts. Soon the transformation was complete and there she sat, or coiled, with the torso of a woman atop a snaking tail.

The bewildered goddess turned sorrowing eyes upon Zelia. "And now I've lost my clutch."

Her expression changed, hardening. She closed her eyes with a series of membranous lids. A look of consternation flitted across her features, and the goddess's face split right down the middle, her skin peeling from her body. And Sala slipped from the dead flesh into a more awe-inspiring aspect. The hair on the goddess's head writhed. Ares stared and his jaw unhinged when the "hair" stared back at him with a hundred viperous eyes.

"What have you done with them?" Zelia asked, indicating the poised mortals and elementals.

"Nothing . . . yet," Sala said, and Zelia shivered.

Ares leaned casually against fallen stone. "Surely, you wouldn't hurt them?"

The squirming head of snakes turned to regard Ares. She scrutinized the elfin features. The lids flicked continually, as if each diaphanous lid was a lens that afforded a different perspective of the object viewed.

"You would be the betrothed?"

"I am." Ares bowed gallantly.

"You will treat your lady better than my hussband treatsss me? You will not eat your children?"

"Mortals do not eat their own, my lady," Ares said.

"A ssstrange people, humans," Sala noted. "They do not eat each other, but they would kill and disscard good fleshhhh."

"It's a little difficult to explain," Astra mumbled.

"Sssuch a wasste," she commented sadly.

The amazing metamorphosis continued. The tail cleaved in twain, forming legs, and the first bloom of hips appeared and the remaining scale turned to verdant skin.

"Well, it would appear that I musst do sssomething sssince you cannot," she said. "In my concccern over my clutch, it ssseemss I have been derelict in my dutiess. I sshhould have been more clear. The key, my dear, iss time."

"We do not hold time's key," Zelia said.

"Ah, but child, you do. Of all people, you, with your elemental blood, can command it. Are you sso new to your powerssss?" The woman caught Zelia's chin and looked deep into her eyes. "Yes, I can see that you are still uninitiated in time's cycles." Then she sighed. "Any who can passs freely between time'ss portalsss holds time'ss key. You jusst don't know how to ussse it yet." Sala continued, "Immortal time is a ccircle, not a line as humans view it." The goddess linked hands, making a circle with lithe, green arms. "And all you have o do to ussse it iss to turn it in upon itsself. Sssso."

The human visage vanished, and again the couple were confronted with the serpent biting ts tail, dancing widdershins around the group.

The frozen forms around them wavered, becoming fragile and gaunt. Ares shouted and Zelia gasped as the Quattarean, Hamadi, Shamirian and Abdhan, and the many fine teeds faded slowly away. The far camp likewise anished. Fire glimmered for a moment, even more brightly than before, and then it was gone. Water disappeared with a loud splash. Not even air remained. The glassy surface of scorched sand dissolved into many tiny particles. Immortal timelessness escaped with a whoosh and a roar as the stones groaned into a more upright position to lean listlessly against each other once more.

BOOM!

The earth beneath their feet trembled and shuddered, vibrating down to the roots of the mortal plane, as time's door slammed shut. Zelia reached for Ares. They drew together, staring at bloated vines that gulped greedily at runnels of rain. And the couple were soaked to the skin. The goddess reappeared in her mortal manifestation, holding off the rains with her hand.

"What have you done?" Zelia breathed the question softly.

"I have ssent them back to where they were before," Sala said.

"Before what?" Ares asked suspiciously.

"The rotation before your wedding to be preccisse," Sala said.

"You mean everything is as it was before?" asked Zelia.

"Not everything exactly. The one you call Benevolent is lossst to me. Although I don't know why you would want to call him that."

The adventurer looked at Zelia over Sala's emerald shoulder. "We don't call him that. I think he chose the name himself," Ares said.

Sala gave an unladylike snort. "Well, Sssatan has prior claim to hiss sssoul. The Archmage gave it willingly, and that cannot be undone. Even *I* cannot usssurp the Demon King'ss authority."

"If everything has been returned to the day before the wedding, then that means we're going to go through this all again." His voice rose an octave. "I mean, what's to prevent it from happening a second time?"

"You two are the pivotal point. Remember that you have free will, as all humans do." The goddess turned to Zelia. "You were right to concede to your mother'ss wishess, a dutiful daughter always should, but mortal and immortal planess were never meant to meet. The portals were clossed for a reassson.

"Today, your mother happily flitsss about her preparationsss. Even as we sspeak, the elementalss gather to casst the ssspell that will open the door. The choiccce is yourss," she said. "I don't know, but if I were you, I'd elope. Unlike your mortal brethren, the memory of thiss event already existss in your mother'ss mind. She knew it even before it sstarted. Remember for her all timess are one and life iss a cccircle. Ssshe will be disssappointed, but sshe will undersstand."

The body thinned, the curves again flattening

to straight lines. Her arms, which she held at her side, melded into her flank, and her legs fused. The great serpent bit her tail and then spoke around the rippling flesh.

"Choossse wisssely," she hissed at them, and then rolled back into the heavens. The rain closed in around them. She uncoiled and went streaking away, flickering her tail in farewell.

The adventurer watched her passing. "Interesting mode of transport," he said.

Deep in thought, Zelia said. "Huh?"

Delicate blue fingers ran through the unruly indigo mane. The maiden whirled with a harsh carillon of bells. She scanned the landscape, searching for the jinn. She spied him hiding under the rag-rug.

"Nepharious, we have one more wish for you, and then you are free. Go to my mother. Tell her . . . tell her that the wedding is off. Explain explain . . ." Her voice trailed away. "Oh, I don't know. Just tell her what happened, or wil happen if the ceremony goes on as planned."

"Is that even necessary?" Ares asked.

Zelia gave him a lopsided grin. "You know my mother. She has all the retentive power of a sieve. She may remember – someday. And she loves a do. You heard Sala, she already knew. I the preparations have progressed this far, she may decide to hold the party anyway. No, bette to spell it out for her. Have you got that, Nepharious?"

"Do I have to? I've already been through the nine planes twice already. My cousin Esmeralda's getting married. I've got a wedding to attend. I'd, er, like to catch a ride with my brother this time. Besides, your wishes are null and void. Remember, we've never met, have we? I don't even know you." He grinned at her, triumphant.

"Would you prefer if we were to meet again, you encased in a metal cage? No one has taken our memory away, and we may not look so kindly upon you a second time. So I'd hurry along if I were you," Zelia said.

The genie bowed, touching forelock, chin and chest. "Your wish is my command."

"Who knows, maybe this time you won't get lost," Ares said.

The jinn graced the adventurer with his most fearsome glower. "All right, if this is what you wish. You sure you don't want a castle or some jewels? I'm really good at them."

Two heads wagged in a mute negative.

"Oh well, suit yourselves." Reclining lazily on his carpet, Nepharious snarled a command and then gave them a jaunty wave as the rag-rug darted away. The couple watched him until he was no more than a speck upon the horizon.

"Wait a second, wasn't he supposed to turn left?" Zelia said.

"Don't worry about him. He'll get there – eventually," Ares said as he hewed at a tendril of Apsu's Coat that had twined itself around his calf.

She gave him a funny look. Rain poured down around them. It dripped in her face and slicked her hair to her neck.

"Where to now, my dear?" Ares extended his arm for her to take.

"Some place dry. Some place where there are no relations."

"Or magicians," Ares added.

"Or healers," said Zelia.

"Do they have such a place?"

"I don't think so," she sighed.

"Hmm-m-m." The adventurer pulled at his lip and gave another vine a healthy thwack. It retreated.

"How about away from here for starters?" Zelia said. "Out of the rain."

"Never let it be said that sorcery's heroes didn't have enough sense to get out of the rain."

"Sure." She gazed at him as he flicked water out of his eyes.

"All I said was: never let it be said," Ares quipped. "Not that either of us did have that much sense, mind you."

She harrumphed just as a loud wail echoed overhead. The maiden winced and glanced about them anxiously, expecting fire to erupt within the stone ring. Ares chortled and she glared at him. He thumbed above them, and Zelia looked up. A magnificent carpet, with sixteen horses woven into its fabric, scudded across the sky. Nepharious flapped behind, clinging to its fringe and screeching alarm, as the carpet veered wildly to avoid the Miasmic Swamp. Zelia grinned.

"I hear," Ares said, "that there's a farmer in the upper Uri valley with a wagon just looking for a couple of travelling mountebanks."

Zelia brightened. "Is it yellow?"

"Yes."

"With red trim and a green roof?"

"And purple runes written along the side," Ares said.

"Sounds perfectly ghastly," she said.

"I prefer to think of it as sufficiently garish to be wizardly. They are notorious for their bad taste."

The blue maiden nodded absent-mindedly. She missed the old travelling life she and Ares had had before all this hero-business had come up.

"Come along, my love." Ares enfolded her in a loving embrace.

"Can we pick up Flighty along the way?" Her voice echoed hollowly as they slipped between the planes.

"That idiot bird! Now what would you want that temperamental chicken for?"

They started to quarrel as their voices dwindled from within the circle, and the drumming rain rushed in to fill the silence left by their absence.

At least part of his son's assertion sank slowly through the stony scalp into the rocky brain, and Ignacious decided that maybe he had better hurry his speech along a bit. So the next word came tumbling out in lithologic leap.

"MAAYBEEEE . . ."

As the amazed Vitreous watched, earth elementals started to appear, moving backwards to seat themselves in a semicircle around their leader.

"WWWWWWWW . . ."

Water and fire rushed in, also backwards, and they began to fight. Astra materialized atop the cracked fountain and shouted, "!RAW SI SIHT" and lowered her fist to her side.

Vitreous continued rotating. Fire and water's fight turned into a quibble. Earth's prince whirled round and round, spinning like a top, trying to keep up with it all. Fire vanished, water vanished, only to reappear a few seconds later. The stones righted themselves and the cracks ran together. Trails of blackened grass shrank as though the circle were healing itself. The riot ran in reverse, fire becoming more and more subdued by the minute while air put humans down and they, landing mid-kick, danced away into the night. Reeling, Vitreous passed out, as the mortals backed out of the second plane with a polite greeting.

Sorrowing, the Prince of Darkness couldn't even be bothered to play with his new toy, and Philos hung as limp as a rag doll, except when the demonlord paused to twitch a cord or toss a malevolent thought in his direction.

Satan sank back into his salamander throne, and the creatures slithered to accommodate his shifting shape. The Demon King gazed dolefully at the boiling Pit of Death upon the rejuvenated Miasmic Swamp. At one time, he would have found pleasure in the writhing of poisonous weeds, but now he found the scene obnoxious.

It was as if it never had been. The Devil grimaced. *But then it hadn't been, for time had been turned in upon itself. Was human time such a fragile thing?*

A ghastly light gleamed in the baleful eye as the germ of an idea was planted and the seed took root. The visage looked a little less grim. Something in the pit stirred. The demonlord leaned forward as if electrified. Apsu bolted from the horizon and gobbled the sun, and the circle of Miasma and the desert beyond was blanketed in darkness.

The eye flashed, and the demon inhaled sharply. The hideous leer threatened to swallow his entire face when the archfiend observed the inky-black bits, so dark that they rivalled mortal night, slinking about the water-logged circle of stones. He recognized corruption, spite, malevolence and greed. Glittering black diamonds. Added to that were tiny spheres of red that pulsated with a burnished sheen. Hate. Anger. Rage.

Queb!

Chuckling, Satan again leaned back against his throne, and the salamanders cuddled him. Inside the Pit of Death, the penumbra cowered. The demon turned to his imp and gave a flick of a gnarled hand in dismissal.

Pun swallowed hard. He couldn't believe his ears, and they happened to be just about the biggest two things on his body.

"Yes, sir, that would be lovely, sir." He paused,

listening. "No, of course not. I wouldn't be at all offended. One can plainly see he's more suited to the job." The imp glanced at the wizard who, at this moment, was dancing like a puppet on a string.

"I hear that Plague and Pestilence have an opening," the Prince of Darkness rumbled.

The imp perked up. "Really, sire, do you think they'd take me? I mean I don't have any experience."

"I'll put in a good word for you."

"Oh, thank you, thank you." The imp frowned. "But I don't really have the right qualifications for the job," Pun mused out loud.

"Qualifications?" Satan said, staring at the jester as if he had taken leave of his senses. "Where do you suppose Sick Humour comes from?"

Somewhere under the soft swish of rain, the fabled city of Alba-Khur'ki watched the action. When the last of the slimy black stream trickled away, it moved from its hiding-place. The city was truly wretched now. It had been trying to find a place to light for many rotations, but each time it did, someone would come and it was forced to move again to hover somewhere between here, there and everywhere. Its awnings fluttered as it gazed upon the empty circle with porticoed eyes. Seeing it was safe, the ghostly metropolis appeared – sort of – and scanned the empty horizon before it settled with a faint squelching noise next to the Miasmic Swamp, pleased at long last to rest its weary foundations.

Tired and just a trifle touchy after a hard day of reordering time and the universe, Sala streaked across the temple veranda. She stabbed her head inside the door. It rotated this way and that on her sinuous neck. She spied the broken egg. The remains of the fledging serpent were nowhere to be seen. Apsu the Devourer belched non-committally. She glared at him, and he slouched away, wondering where he might find a quick bite.

As though reading his thoughts, Sala gave him a sibilant snarl, and the much abused spouse decided that maybe he'd just slip out for a while until her mood improved. Besides, there wasn't any food in the house, not even an egg for a fry up.

The goddess nodded her satisfaction at his departure and curled protectively around the remains of a single, solitary egg. Her mind returned to contemplate the wisp of unadulterated evil that she had observed lurking under a rock. The red of desire, sin and rage revolved around globules of inky black and a few sparse sparkles of goodness. The immortal, knowing the essence of things, recognized it for what it was – the remains of the wizard Queb which had found its way back to the mortal plane, and she wondered idly if she should tell someone about it.

Sala grimaced, deciding against it. Who was she to dally in mortal affairs? She had done more than her share for today. It was for man to solve human dilemma now. She was tired. With a sputtering sigh, the goddess lowered her hooded head over the forlorn fragments of her egg and closed her eyes. 'Twas time to hibernate. The great serpent yawned. Her tongue snaked out and touched the tip of her nose. Sure that she could sleep for turns.

THE END

And the adventures of Zelia and Ares continue in The Return of the Wizard.

·Appendix·

The Renegades World and its People

The universe

History

The universe, not unlike our universe, was formed when a nebula exploded, scattering rubble out into the spinning void. Eventually, the continuous rotation caused the debris to contract. Unlike our world, though, this did not result in a nice tidy little universe with a sun and the revolving chunks of rocks which are our planets. Instead, aided by the magic inherent in the Renegades' cosmos, it became a whorl. The separate strands within this whorl evolved becoming the planes, as like gravitated towards like, met like, married like and created more of the same.

While we here have the ozone layer to protect us from continual bombardment of space, they have the outer ninth plane, which many believe is a single great being, that the inhabitants of Renegades world refer to as "the one that binds them all". Even human religions, with their multiple gods, goddesses and godlings, take this into account, each honouring an unnamed overlord which controls the others. The behaviour of the immortals – be it god, elemental, angel or imp – seems to confirm this assumption, since they avoid the ninth plane and treat it with a reverence that exceeds that expected by the gods. Not even Satan has the impertinence to thumb his nose(s) at the ninth plane.

Needless to say, this evolution of the planes took aeons. As the strands separated and changes occurred, differences developed and certain immortal toes were stepped on. So rules were imposed, and deals struck. The most important of these concerned man.

A latecomer to the scene, humanity was created when a now-defunct god became bored and moulded his own image and likeness out of clay. As something added to the universe and concocted by a god, humankind was not considered indigenous to the planes. And man, like the god's other creations, the animals and the trees, was mortal.

In sculpting man's form, the god gave humanity a bit of himself. He was so enamoured of his reproduction that the god decided to give humanity an earthly existence, and he breathed life into the species. In so doing, he imbued it with an immortal soul. It is the reclamation of this spirit over which the immortal and the divines constantly vie.

In the ensuing struggle over man's soul, it was soon decided that Satan – as the Great Trickster and a being totally without scruples – had an unfair advantage. The angels, the gods and even the elementals were all constrained by their own sort of morality. The Devil and his dark minions were not.

So the first pact originated, which limited the demonlord's influence on man. This agreement prohibited Satan from the Earth plane, denying him direct physical contact with the mortal inhabitants unless invited. The Prince of Darkness could, however, send his lackeys to solicit support for his dark works and, when need be, project his image from the immortal planes to the earthly one. Once the Devil was summoned, it was assumed that the individual's soul was already in jeopardy.

A direct outgrowth of the first accord was the second, which saw the erection of time's portals. For to be mortal is to know time with a distinct beginning, middle and an end. To view time as linear in a non-linear cosmos was a definite disadvantage. While the unstructured universe did not seem to faze animals, who had not been empowered with the god-like trait of reason, it confused man, who was forced to witness many versions of himself all at one time. The ability to view one's own demise had a similarly adverse affect on man, predisposing him to evil. For the Great Trickster could promise anything, including immortality but, amoral as he was, Satan was not required to fulfil his covenant.

The subsequent dissension caused by man almost brought about his ruin. The gods, tired of their creation, whom they felt did not show the proper respect, and the angels, weary of contention and miffed by man's apparent lack of gratitude, felt man should be destroyed. Only elemental earth, from whose breast man had sprung, saw potential in the species. However, the combined apathy on the part of air and water, and the more selfish motivation of the darker species, allowed man to continue on what has now become the mortal plane.

The hierarchy of immortals

Each plane is self-regulated, with a self-elected (or self-appointed) leader, and each group has specific rules and regulations. Often, though, certain groups will merge. Thus, there are the elemental codes which cover all the elements, and the Night plane swears fealty to the Demon King. Only the gods are an exception, since they can rarely agree on anything.

Still, this is not to say that the immortal planes are without structure, albeit a bewildering one. The planes, after a fashion, are divided into gradations of magic and power, starting at the centre with the weakest and going to the outer plane which is the strongest. The gravitational pull dragged elemental earth to the innermost strata. Contained therein, are the feeblest of all species – not only animals, but also man. Travelling outwards, through the planes, one can perceive the expansion of power. So sorcerous puissance increases the further from the centre one gets, and the creatures within that plane gain in strength and abilities over the one previous.

Elemental magic may seem awesome to the mortal eye. It is, in fact, puny in comparison to that of the gods, goddesses and godlings who inhabit the eighth plane. Thus, it took the combined strength of all the elementals (not to mention the permission of the gods) to crack time's gate for a day. But a single god – or in this case goddess, Sala – could, by giving a little twirl, turn time back in upon itself. Sala, however, has an advantage in that she is the goddess of cycles, claiming rulership over the daily rotations and the seasons.

The classification of magic and magical abilities of mortal and immortal is outlined below beginning with the weakest:

Mortal wizardry – dependent upon and resulting from elemental magic
Elemental magic
Necromancy – emanating from the Darklands
Divine sorcery – associated with the angels and the daemons and culminating in:
Godhood.

Man is not without power, though, within this structure, for it is man's belief in a particular god that gives it vigour and vitality. Thus, a god or goddess loses strength when man's faith wanes. As a result, new gods are born, and the old forgotten gods and goddesses retreat into early retirement, generally in a huff, and refusing to traffic with any plane beyond their own.

Time

Time is probably the biggest factor differentiating mortal from immortal. For all short-lived species, there must inevitably be birth (a beginning), life (a middle) and death (an end or conclusion). Each a natural outgrowth of the previous.

Not true with the immortal for whom the concept of linear time is truly incomprehensible. In the planes beyond the first, past, present and future do not form a straight line, with each contingent upon what transpired before and resulting in what we think of as cause and effect. Rather, past, present and future exist simultaneously and could be likened to separate threads or skeins which float about the place, detached and dissociated from each other. And all times become one, happening concurrently. This gives the immortals an omnipotence, and what appears to be, a prescience. So the oracles of the gods can view the future or explain the past if they so desire.

Elementals, the most likely of all the immortals to visit the mortal plane, carry a bit of this timelessness wherever they go. Their appearance on the mortal plane can be disorientating for a human since their physical presence distorts the mortal time-frame continuum of past, present and future.

The mortal view

As would be expected on a plane where time is seen as linear, man views the Renegades' universe laterally. Therefore, what we would call "parallel universes" are considered part and parcel of a single universe. We think in three-dimensions, including the sky above. The citizen of the mortal plane tends to reason sideways, which means that the heaven as seen in the Earth plane is only the mortal sky. The sky in the adjacent plane is different, although some of the constellations, which are in truth aerial gates, may be similar.

Because of this sidewise thinking, primitive man used to view the universe as flat. This hypothesis has largely been dismissed as folly. More modern theories have replaced it to allow for at least some vertical movement. The more popular include: the Concept of the Eternal Ice Cream Cone and the Onion Theory. The former likens the nine planes to an ice cream cone with the most compressed and most dense Earth pushed to the bottom, and the more expansive and broader planes piled on top of it. This concept has been discredited since most people would agree that ice cream is a poor medium for tying a universe together. Of the two, the Onion Theory is the more recent and widely accepted by the human scientific community as being true. It was formulated by Sir Ph'ig Nu'ton, noted physicist, after he was hit on the head by a flying pumpkin at a football match.[1] This caused

1. In Renegades World, pumpkins, melons and other such vegetable matter are used instead of balls. This is supposed to add zest to the game.

a pretty nasty concussion – whereupon he decided that the universe resembled an onion (Sir Ph'ig wasn't very good at botany) which could be peeled layer by layer to reveal the next layer, or plane.

An inter-planar perspective

Unfortunately, nothing in the Renegades' universe is quite so simple or straightforward, and neither of the two human theories are completely accurate. A better comparison might be the rings of a tree, with its convolutions and folds which pierce the trunk at irregular intervals where weaknesses in the wood are exhibited.

The truth is, the human mind cannot truly comprehend what they call planes, and "planes" – implying something flat – is a poor choice of words, but the best that mortal language has to offer at this time.

In keeping with the Renegades World's preoccupation with food, probably the most accurate description of the universe would be a spaghetti bowl with its many noodles that twist and twine about each other. With the exception of the earth plane and the outer plane, the many planes overlap and intersect here and there. Thus, each plane has "gates" to every other plane where the two planes touch. So water has direct "gates" to air, fire, night and Hades, and even to the far outer plane. Again "gates" would not be the best choice of words since the elementals and immortals can travel anywhere and anywhen they please (unless bound by some interplanar accord which prohibits access). Windows would be a better term, but "gate" is the word that is used by the citizens, and so it is used here.

In almost all these things, earth and the outer planes are the exceptions. Earth, at the core, acts as the anchor which keeps the other planes rooted. While the outer plane contains them. Only on earth is the phrase "gate" truly appropriate, but here, the inhabitants talk in terms of portals or doors. The innermost plane is stolid and unmoving while the other planes tend to slither about a bit. The outer plane, slightly more flexible than earth, expands and contracts as needed to accommodate the fluctuating universe – containing it in a single, if not a tidy, package.

The planes

There are a total of nine planes. The first four belong to the elements: earth, air, water and fire. The next two are called the Planes of Death, and the last three are known collectively as the Planes of Immortality.

The inner plane belongs to the earth

THE ELEMENTAL PLANES	Earth Air Water
THE PLANES OF DEATH	Fire, or Brimstone Night, or Darklands Hades
THE IMMORTAL PLANES	The Dream Fields The Home of Gods Outer Plane (unnamed)

elementals, unobtrusive creatures who prefer to blend into the background. They became so enamoured of the earth that they actually became a part of the plane over which they ruled. True earth elementals are difficult to come by on earth, and, if seen, are rarely recognized by the mortal inhabitants. They are by nature inflexible, with a memory as long and as old as the earth itself, and the only elementals to have some concept of time. The second plane belongs to air. It acts as a buffer between the Earth and Water planes. Thus, air elementals have inadvertently become protectors of humankind, guarding them against waters' deluge. The next plane is water's realm. It too acts as a buffer, between air and the following plane belonging to fire. These two elements are prone to disputes. Air loves to whip fire into a frenzy while fire leaps into the heavens, invading their air space. The fourth and final of the elemental planes belongs to fire. It is called the Brimstone realm by mortal man. Here are found dragons, salamanders and other of flame's creatures.

The next two are the Planes of Death (although the Brimstone realm is sometimes lumped into this category). The first (or the fifth depending on the way you choose to count the planes) is the Plane of Night. It is a place of fell magic where wampyrs and werebeasts in all forms reside. It is home to incubi and succubi. This is a plane of lost souls and, according to the wizards, it is reputed to be the place where witches come after death. The sixth plane is Hades, equivalent to our hell. It is the dominion of devils, demons, imps and fiends, and the place where sinners – heretics and suchlike – go after death.

The final three are the Planes of Immortality, although again, this is not a completely accurate description since elementals are also immortal. The seventh plane is Day's domain, the nearest equivalent to our heaven. It is often referred to as the Dream Fields. This is where the good come to live out eternity. It is a place of daemons and angels. The eighth is the Home of Gods. Here all the gods, godlings, and goddesses – past and present – are said to abide.

Therefore, it is quite crowded.

In the final plane dwell being(s) so different, so incomprehensible to mortal mind that it(they) has(have) no name. Pure ethereal beings, or being. There is some debate as to whether or not there are more than one of these creatures. Some scientists, usually Ice Creamists, contend that the final plane is in fact one rather large (kind of cold and very fluffy) being. All agree that it(they) is(are) thing(s) of spirit. This plane, also called the Nether World, is the final ring that holds all the others together.

Since the accord, the planes intersect with mortal lands at sacred portals. Such places are usually marked by giant circles of stones, similar to Stonehenge. It is believed that those constellations, common to all planes, are celestial doorways, just as the stone circles are portals upon the land masses.

The luminaries (the sun and the five moons)

Legends about the luminaries vary. On the northern continent it is believed that the moons are the five daughters of Brigitta. Exact duplicates of herself which were cast off during the rape by the war god, Og, from which the godling, Ares, sprung. According to this tradition, the sister moons quarrel constantly, arguing over their husband, the sun, and this is why they seldom appear in the sky all at one time. The southern continent has no analogous myth about the moons. The sun, however, is another matter. They postulate that Apsu eats the sun every day, causing the night to fall – hence his name "devourer". His consort, Sala, the goddess of cycles, returns the sun to the sky by squeezing her husband until he vomits it forth. And so the day begins anew.

The gods

Each country has a god, goddess or multiple godlings. Sometimes neighbouring countries share deities, and each profession claims a patron. Gods and their related hierarchies come and go, gaining in importance or sinking into oblivion as societies change and evolve. This has resulted in enough gods and goddesses to fill not only a volume, but a library.[2]

The gods reside in the eighth plane. Needless to say, this plane is congested. The gods are peevish at the best of times, and people go to great lengths to appease them. In truth, though, the many gods and goddesses are usually too

2. The library is located appropriately enough on Godliness Boulevard in Thessalia, which not surprisingly runs parallel to Cleanliness Avenue, the road of washerwomen.

caught up with their own internal disputes – usually involving real estate – to interfere with man. However, it is better *not* to draw a particular god's attention, especially by mucking about in what they would consider their particular area of expertise.

A further consequence of this continuous evolution of the gods/goddesses is that Renegades World can boast some pretty bizarre divinities. One former god, god of bureaucrats, was worshipped with enormous quantities of red tape. Under the unlikely title of Xdizqtojaljluhtkdlfaut – bureaucrats preferring not to be understood – this god reputedly had the head of a stoat, the body of a gerbil, the wings of a dodo, the legs of a chicken and the brain of a pea. Others were worse, a horrific miscellany of churning parts. As man has become more sophisticated, his gods have become more tidy.

The current gods are common to all species. For example, man and elves alike honour Brigitta, but the ways of worship differ between the two. Elves, with their prolonged lives and isolated from human contagion, venerate her in her manifestation as the goddess of fertility. Man, subject to infirmity and disease, focus upon her curative powers.

While there are additional deities revered in

the outlying regions. Often these are the offspring of other gods – such as Ares, son of Og and Brigitta. They are referred to as godlings. Where magic is strong, especially near the stone circles, elementals are held sacred. Often deities vie for supremacy and "religious conflict" is common.

Current gods/goddesses include:

GOD GODDESS	SYMBOL	DOMINION	COUNTRIES OF WORSHIP	PATRON
Og	Hammer	War & Iron	Norvon Szatmar	Berserkers, adventurers & mercenaries
Ullr	The bear	Perseverance & strength	Uri	Nobility
Fennec	The fox	Craft, cunning & deceit	Firth	Merchants & thieves
Brigitta*	The dove Sheaf of wheat	Peace, healing & fecundity	Shalop Lavanthia	Healers' craft
Apsu the Devourer	Serpent	Evil & indigestion	Quattara & Abdha	Slavers, assassins, userers, insurance salesmen & used dung-camel dealers
Sala (wife of Apsu)	Snake eating its tail	Neutrality Cycles	Abdha Hamadan	Farmers
Ramman	Formless		Shamir Hamadan	Herdsmen
*Mother of the moons				

Generally speaking, the fairy folk are made up of the element they represent. Thus, true elementals, or fairy folk, usually remain in their corresponding planes, with a few notable exceptions. Some elementals may have an affinity for another element. For example, magma with its molten and explosive qualities resides not only on earth, but also in Hades and Brimstone. Geysers also fall into this category.

All elementals have the ability to travel between planes, within certain proscribed limitations already noted. They can appear anywhere and anywhen they chose and are not restricted to the use of portals, which exist more to contain time within its continuum than as entry points to the Earth plane.

Elementals could best be described as two-dimensional (or that would be the nearest human equivalent), although "undimensional" would be the more appropriate term. It is this quality that disturbs the normal mortal time frame. Elementals would most likely appear flat to a human, if they choose to appear at all. The fairy folk can, if they so desire, become three-dimensional, blowing up like a balloon, but it requires the expenditure of a great deal of energy. Furthermore, in attaining mass – or in this case volume – they tend to lose substance. Due to its unique qualities, it is only on the Earth plane that can they attain true mass, having three dimensions and, if they remain there for a long period of time, become quite solid. This, though, is a matter of personal choice. Usually they don't, considering the whole procedure much too bothersome just so they can appear more "normal" to mortals.

As a group, elementals are little understood. In modern times, they tend to avoid contact with man. Mixing with elementals can be hazardous to human health, and those they touch – assuming the hapless human survives – remain forever changed, making them "different" from the rest of mankind.

Earth

The first plane, earth, being the most dense, is the most hospitable to man. Earth, both the plane and the elementals, is unique in a number of aspects. First and foremost, it is anchored and it is solid. Furthermore, the earthy folk appear to have abandoned their own plane. Perhaps, this is because they are staid and stolid creatures who maintain a policy of non-interference with the mortal inhabitants, or more plausibly because rock-like earth moves so slowly that it cannot be distinguished from their environment.

Yet the mortal plane is peopled with earth's descendants, the brownie, the pixie, the sylph. Of all the elements, earth was the most likely to intermarry, thus a large number of its offspring populate their world. The other elementals also have their descendants on earth, but they are far outnumbered by their earthly counterparts. All the elements who can claim direct lineage are known as "true bloods". This group includes the elves. Their progeny, however, have been irrevocably altered by their environment, contracting to become a separate race altogether which has much more affinity to man than to their elemental forebears.

Fire

Elemental fire appears as flame in almost human form, with two arms and two legs and a feverish brow. They expand and contract according to mood – becoming small and slightly bluish when they are content; and larger, and red-hot, when they are angry. Through no fault of their own, they burn anything they come into contact with, whether they want to or not. The immortals can regenerate, of course, but for man this is almost always fatal. Hence, fire is the only element who is not represented on earth. Only its reflection – lacking in will and intelligence and therefore, easily controlled by man – can be found upon the mortal plane.

Air

The air elementals are the intellectuals of the fairy folk. They represent pure thought; without, however, the weight of earth, such contemplation is sadly lacking in practical applications. Therefore, they are inclined to be flighty and have a poor memory. Besides earth, it has the most affinity to man, who, like itself, prizes and nurtures the ability to reason. Because of this proclivity, air was set up as the protectors of man and vicariously earth, in the same agreement that banned fire from the mortal plane. Like their cousins, water, air did not appear at the conference, getting stuck with the onerous duty. Still, fire has never quite forgiven air who now guard the external gates from the mortal plane.

Air elementals appear to man as ephemeral creatures – faint images or outlines of near-human shape who expand and contract on their own currents. The closest analogy being smoke upon the breeze.

Water

Water is more stable (and a lot wetter) than either fire or air. They are emotional creatures who get extremely bubbly and effervescent when they are happy and weepy when sad. Like their element, they are fluid beings, who can either take human-style shape or puddle, dribble and flow, as is their wish. They are usually green or blue, although a few may be black or brown, reflecting stagnant waters or a mortal mere.

Water has an antipathy for fire and so has become the final ring of defence for mortal man. A task again assigned in the Portals' Accord, which they did not attend.

Their descendants

True elementals, or fairy folk, should not be confused with elves or any of their other descendants on the mortal plane. In times past, earth's realm was open to all. When the immortals closed the doors between the planes, some elementals chose to remain behind.

Through the aeons that followed, their long-term descendants were irrevocably altered by their environment, achieving mortal mass and becoming mortal also, albeit long-lived. These are the trolls, the goblins, pixies and dwarves (earth elementals), and the many different kinds of elves (air, earth and water) and the jinn (fire). Some believe that the explosive (and usually red-haired) Firthian has also been touched by flame.

With few exceptions, dwarves, elves and suchlike keep to themselves. The little people, brownies and pixies, have their adoptive families. The trolls guard their individual bridges and consume human flesh. The different groups usually stay in their separate enclaves. Goblins and dwarves inhabit the mountainous region in the north. Goblins make occasional forays into human settlements to harvest the more tender women and children, who will be taken to live in their caves and kept like cattle awaiting slaughter. The elves maintain their cities: the sea elves along the Shalop coast; snow elves beyond the northern wastes; wood elves in the foothills east of the mountains. For most part, their presence is never felt. Their influence wanes and their homes are protected from human incursion by magic.

The jinn is unique to the southern continent of Daklha. Some say it is the fire's scion since it is only able to survive in the arid desert, and it lives, quite notably, in lamps. Totally irascible, it is a point of interest that none of the elementals, even the fire elementals, are willing to claim the jinn as one of their own.

The mortal plane

Stated succinctly, man's world could be compared with medieval Europe and the Middle

East. In the north, the system is feudal. A small, elite group of nobility govern a large peasant base and an even smaller merchant class, while guilds dominate all other aspects of human existence. The southern continent of Daklha is desert, and the society that has developed resembles that of "our" Arabia.

The position of women is poor. On both continents women are property, owned first by their fathers and then by their spouses. And there is a lively slave trade in little girls even outside the slaver state of Quattara. Independence is a trait which is frowned upon, and any woman who lives alone is immediately suspected of witchcraft. Polygamy is common on the southern continent of Daklha, where women are segregated into *terems*. In all countries, save Shalop, their legal rights are nil. They can neither own land nor inherit it.

(For more idea of the geography and habits of the peoples of the mortal plane see the Appendix to *Healer's Quest* and the map on page vi.)